A Child
OF THE
King

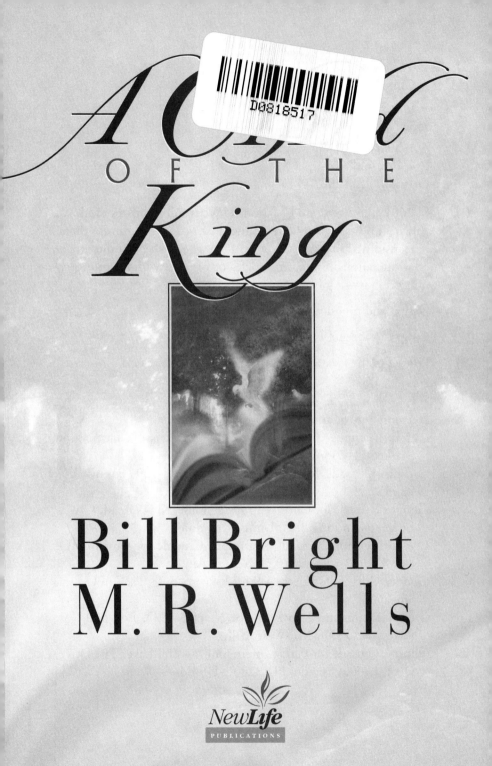

Bill Bright
M. R. Wells

NewLife
PUBLICATIONS

A Child of the King

Published by
New*Life* **Publications**
A ministry of Campus Crusade for Christ
P.O. Box 620877
Orlando, FL 32862-0877

Design and production by Genesis Group

Cover by Koechel-Peterson Design

Printed in the United States of America

For more information, write:
L.I.F.E., Campus Crusade for Christ—P.O. Box 40, Flemington Markets, 2129, Australia
Campus Crusade for Christ, Canada—Box 529, Sumas, WA 98295
Campus Crusade for Christ—Fairgate House, King's Road, Tyseley, Birmingham, B11 2AA, United Kingdom
Lay Institute for Evangelism, Campus Crusade for Christ—P.O. Box 8786, Auckland, 1035, New Zealand
Campus Crusade for Christ—9 Lock Road #3-03, PacCan Centre, Singapore
Great Commission Movement of Nigeria—P.O. Box 500, Jos, Plateau State, Nigeria, West Africa
Campus Crusade for Christ International—100 Lake Hart Drive, Dept. 3400, Orlando, FL 32832, USA

Contents

❦

Dedication   5

Acknowledgments   7

Prologue   9

1 Leaving Day   *11*

2 A Person of the Book   *18*

3 An Offer from a King   *30*

4 The Price of Adoption   *37*

5 The Appearance of the Dove   *46*

6 Fateful Choices   *57*

7 Beasts in the Shadows   *70*

8 Confrontation at the Bridge   *82*

9 Reflections on a Winged Horse   *89*

10 Alfric's Mission   *96*

11 In the Presence of the King   *104*

12 Lost and Found   *115*

13 The Crowns That Could Not Be Stolen   *121*

14 The Ring Does Its Work   *129*

15 Baubles, Bangles, and Quilts   *135*

16 A Jewel of No Price   *140*

17 First Fruits and Second Chances   *149*

18 Gwyneth Meets the Shepherd   *155*

19 The Gifts Unlike All Others   *167*

20 Salt and Light   *177*

21 The Meaning of Friendship   *183*

22 A Different Kind of Armor   *187*

23 Abaddon's Fury   *199*

24 The Truth About the Birthright   *207*

25 More Revelations   *214*

26 Love Fruit   *220*

27 Ragnar's Reward   *228*

28 A Hope and a Future   *241*

Epilogue   247

A Word from Bill Bright   249

Resources   253

Acknowledgments

WE ARE DEEPLY grateful to the countless people whose prayers and support encouraged us through the long months of crafting this novel. We owe special thanks to writers Helmut Teichert and Nancy Schraeder for sharing our vision and for offering invaluable ideas and suggestions throughout; to John Barber for his theological review; to Jan Dennis for his insightful critique that helped us focus and enrich the story; to Joette Whims for her astute editorial guidance; to Lynn Copeland of Genesis Group for the page design and layout; to Dave Koechel for the cover design; and to the staff of *NewLife* Publications for their tireless efforts on behalf of this project. Most of all, we thank and praise God without whom we could do nothing.

Prologue

~※~

A GNARLED HAND beckons the listeners close around the white-haired storyteller. Flames dance behind him as he begins to speak.

"When the nights grow dark and the stars grow bright and families tell stories by the fire, a few of the old ones recall an ancient legend. It's about an orphan lad whose deepest yearning was to have a father. It's the tale of his struggle with an evil prince and of his quest to know truth from lies and of his search for love—a love that never dies.

"Our story begins in the long-before times in the kingdom of Withershins. This land was so named because it had turned away from the sun. That suited its ruler, Prince Abaddon, well, because he hated the light. Indeed, he taught his subjects to believe that light was darkness. Only a few were no longer blinded to the truth. They were known as the *People of the Book*. And this is their story, too."

CHAPTER 1

Leaving Day

❧

JOTHAM COULD hardly believe the long-awaited day was finally upon him. In just a few hours, he would face his fellow orphans on the lawn of Flotsam Manor. Standing stiffly in a new suit of clothes in the fading autumn light, he would somehow endure a speech from Nabal, the orphanage's burly, pompous director. Those of his peers not lulled to slumber by the long-winded words would applaud politely. Then, with much fanfare, Nabal would present Jotham with his birthday gift from Prince Abaddon. Like all orphans reaching maturity, he would receive a small cloth purse with eighteen copper coins, one for each year of his life. The Leaving Day ceremony would end with Nabal crushing Jotham's knuckles in one final phony handshake. Then clutching a bundle of his few possessions, he would leave the orphanage for good and stride out through the weathered wooden gate to meet his future.

"So, Jotham," jeered a familiar voice, startling him from his reverie, "surely now that your Leaving Day has come, you will break your silence."

Jotham leaned back against the old oak he called his grandfather tree. For a moment he listened to the whispering creek trickling past him through the orphanage grounds.

At last, frowning slightly, he peered up at the smug-faced fellow before him. Though close in age, the two could not have been more different. Jotham was slight of build with sensitive, finely chiseled features. His unruly blond hair tumbled into liquid brown eyes that were haunting as if filled with tragic secrets. In contrast, his companion was stocky and brawny, his thick limbs bulging with muscles. His brown hair was greased back, his dark eyes glaring, his lips twisted in a perpetual sneer. He looked like he could have flattened Jotham with one swipe of his massive arm—and would gladly have done so. Yet Jotham did not flinch.

"Come to wish me luck, Ragnar?" he asked wryly.

"Why would a fellow with your talent need luck?" Ragnar taunted. "Hasn't Elwin claimed you're the finest apprentice woodcrafter he has ever taught? I'll wager he has written to all the best artisans, urging your employment."

"He has been very kind," murmured Jotham, his thoughts drifting to his teacher. Since age twelve when all orphans must choose a trade, he had trudged three miles each day to the nearby village of Brynmor to work in Elwin's shop. At first he had feared the tall, thin, stern-faced man with the frosty white hair and the temperament to match. Though Elwin's patience was as short as his fingers were long, his love of his craft was contagious. Soon Jotham's fertile imagination was seeing marvelous shapes in blank pieces of wood. As his nimble fingers had learned to free and perfect them, he had won Elwin's grudging approval, and finally his praise.

"So who will you work for?" Ragnar persisted.

"I haven't decided," Jotham answered. He did not tell Ragnar the reason. There hadn't been a single response to Elwin's letters. Elwin couldn't think why. Jotham could, and it worried him. Had someone discovered the secret he guarded, the long-ago secret his mother had told him on her deathbed, the one about his father?

Ragnar's words intruded once more, dripping scorn. "What's wrong, Jotham? Can't you choose between your many offers? Or are you holding out for something better? Perhaps you think the great Magnus himself will come knocking at your door! You think to win a post in Magnus' shop and move to our great capital of Acrasia, and one day fashion furniture for Prince Abaddon himself. Well, maybe you will indeed carve chair legs and footstools for our ruler. And when I am a general in his army, I will visit his palace and prop my feet up on your work."

Ragnar leaned close, his sour breath whipping over Jotham like a foul wind. "Then again, you may keep no post at all when others learn how strange you are. Always looking over your shoulder, thinking someone's watching you!"

Jotham felt his skin crawl, not because of Ragnar's words, but because at that very moment he indeed felt unseen eyes upon him. He sensed that they were peering from within a clump of nearby bushes. The thought of Ragnar's gleeful scorn held him back for the slightest instant. But this was his Leaving Day. Such taunts could touch him no longer.

With a suddenness that stunned even Ragnar, Jotham launched to his feet and lunged for the bushes, hands outstretched. His fingers closed on something soft and squirming. A guttural squeal pierced the air as he struggled to withdraw his arm. He was gripping the writhing form of a giant frog.

Ragnar doubled up, helpless with laughter. "Ah, there's your spy," he gasped. "Been taking notes on lily pads all these years. And now he's going to tell all."

Jotham hardly heard the words. He was staring at the frog's bulging eyes. Within them Jotham sensed a perverse intelligence, an evil so intense it made him shudder.

But before he could ponder this, a new voice interrupted. "Where have you been, Jotham, my lad? And what are you doing with that poor, harmless creature?"

"He doesn't think it's harmless, Nabal, sir. He thinks that frog's been stalking him," Ragnar chortled, turning to the orphanage director who had just walked up. Then he paused so that Nabal, as always, could sternly rebuke Jotham for his strange suspicions.

"One more proof of the lad's great imaginative genius," boomed Nabal, his beefy jowls shaking. Ragnar's jaw dropped. Jotham, also stunned by the unaccustomed kindness, unconsciously loosed his hold on the glaring frog. Wrenching free, it leaped out of Jotham's hand and vanished into the nearby vegetation.

Nabal, crooked teeth beaming, waved a parchment in Jotham's face. "This came for you by special messenger. I've read it twice already, and I still can't believe it!" Oblivious to having opened someone else's mail, Nabal unfurled the letter, cleared his throat, and read it aloud.

> Dear Jotham,
> I have learned from a trusted friend who has watched you closely that you show exceptional promise in our craft. He commends both your skill of hand and creativity of mind. At his urging, I am offering you a position in my shop. For your efforts, you shall receive normal journeyman's wages and your lodging. If you agree to these terms, my messenger shall arrange your transport to Acrasia to begin your employment. I look forward to your reply.
> Most cordially,
> Magnus, Master Woodcrafter

Jotham stared dumbstruck as Nabal babbled happily, "Such an honor! The most famous woodcrafter in all of Withershins! You're a credit to Flotsam Manor, and old Nabal, too. Imagine! Elwin recommending you to Magnus!"

"He...he didn't," stammered Jotham. "They don't even know each other."

"Don't be silly," scoffed Nabal. "Perhaps he told you that. But it had to be Elwin. Who else has been watching you work and knows your talents like he does?"

For a moment, Ragnar was speechless with envy. Then he found his voice. "I know, Jotham. It was the frog. And it's up to no good, that's for sure, so you'd best turn Magnus down."

"He'll do no such thing!" boomed Nabal, face and bald head flushing so red he looked for all the world like a giant tomato. "He'll seize his chance, he will! And you will seize a broom. Since you've time on your hands, you'll sweep Flotsam Manor spotless. Now, get to it."

Looking like he'd sucked on a sour grapefruit, Ragnar hurried off. Jotham barely noticed. His skin prickled anew. This strange turn of events was proof. Someone *had* been spying on him. But who? And why? Somehow Jotham doubted it was just to do him a favor. And what of the frog with the strange eyes?

"Come, my boy!" Jotham felt a fleshy arm flung around his shoulders. Nabal's voice boomed in his ear. "We must find the messenger and tell him you accept." Nabal steered him back toward Flotsam Manor, never noticing the troubled look on Jotham's face.

But if Nabal missed it, the towering figure in the black velvet robe did not. He appeared as if from nowhere. In his hand he held a giant frog. For a moment, he gazed after Jotham. Then he spoke to the creature. "Did you see the lad's expression, Elymas? He does not rejoice blindly in his good fortune. He senses something more at work. And he is right. He has more wits in his small toe than that fool Nabal has in his whole head. I shall yet gain in the son what I lost in his father."

The next voice, a guttural croaking growl, came from the frog. "You'll gain nothing but trouble, Your Highness. Mark my words! Jotham has shown no great love for you, Sire. And who knows what he was told."

The robed figure's eyes glinted with cruel cunning. "If anything was said, it was long ago. Memories and words can be twisted. In Magnus's shop, he shall meet only those who are loyal to me. And I bade Magnus to lodge him in the same rooming house as young Alfric, Lord Killian's son."

"A worthless fellow! What good can he do you?" growled the frog.

A faint smile played at the corners of the robed one's mouth. "Even those who are worthless have their uses, Elymas. Alfric's greatest ambition is to serve me. He shall influence Jotham. They are close in age, alone and friendless in a large city. Both need an ally. They will be friends, I think. And there are others I shall use to test the boy and shape him to my purpose."

"Then perhaps you will need my services no longer," the frog croaked softly.

The dark figure laughed mirthlessly. "Did you hope to be excused? Is that why you let him catch you?"

The frog's eyes bulged in terror. "I didn't..."

"And you won't again, will you?" The tone was deadly.

"No, Sire."

"Let's hope not, Elymas." The voice grew pleasant. "And your task shall have its benefits. You shall once more live at the palace."

⌦⫘⌫

SOME HOURS later under a glum September sky, Jotham's Leaving Day ceremony took place almost as he had envisioned. Nabal's speech was boring. Jotham's birthday purse had no more or fewer coins than expected. But instead of walking through the gate as he'd imagined, Jotham rode, his belongings tied behind him on the messenger's horse. They would spend the night in Brynmor where Jotham would share his news with Elwin. In the morning he would board a coach to Acrasia to begin his new life.

As Jotham turned for one last look at the dreary walls of Flotsam Manor, a sudden breeze ruffled the branches of the nearby trees. He fancied they were waving good-bye, tossing red and gold leaves after him in fond farewell. Jotham did not hear the dark words that floated behind the leaves, whispered on the wind. "Learn well, Jotham. For the moment, you will carve in wood, and Magnus will be your master. But some day you will carve my will on the hearts and souls of men. And you shall be great like your father... no, greater. For you shall not turn from me!"

CHAPTER 2

A Person of the Book

THE WINGED horse reared up at Jotham, nostrils flared, eyes flashing fire, as if straining to burst from its gleaming mahogany prison. Still, something was not quite right. Jotham closed his eyes, picturing the same horse in his mind. The veins on its head stood out more clearly than those on its carved image. Jotham bent to correct the problem, wood chips flying under his skilled hand. The fanciful horse was the focal point of the hope chest he had fashioned, and he wanted it perfect.

Around him, the other workbenches were silent, their occupants gone for the day. But Jotham could not stop creating at the stroke of a clock. Magnus, understanding this, had long since given him his own key to the shop. His employer's growing trust and their kindred artistic spirits had helped make the past six months some of the happiest of Jotham's life.

Now lost in the face he was carving, Jotham did not see the other face, the one pushed against the shop's window. But he felt the watching eyes. His skin prickled as it had in his days at Flotsam Manor. He jerked his head upward, saw the frowning gaze, and grinned with relief.

"Alfric!" Jotham sprang to unlock the door. His friend burst through in a shower of white. Though spring had officially started, stubborn winter had flung one last snowstorm in its wake. It had cooled the air, but not Alfric's impatience.

"Hurry Jotham, or we'll miss her!"

"Then go on without me," urged Jotham. "I must finish my work." He strode back to the chest.

Alfric followed. "Please, Jotham. I need you there!"

Shrugging, Jotham picked up his carving tool. "Then wait. I won't be long. And if we're too late, you can always ask Gwyneth another night."

Alfric looked alarmed. "No! I must ask her now before my courage fails!"

"You've spent long enough building it up," Jotham bantered, eyes twinkling. "I should think it would last one more day. And what if she says no?"

"Then I will be the most miserable man alive," groaned Alfric.

"No, I will," sighed Jotham, "because I will have to cheer you up. Though I must say, you'll be in good company. She has turned down many others."

"Small comfort," said Alfric ruefully. But he knew that Jotham was right. Gwyneth seemed an almost unreachable prize. All young men in Withershins desired her. Petite of frame, yet strong and athletic, this eighteen-year-old girl had a figure and face any artist would be pleased to paint or sculpt. Her rich auburn curls framed a creamy complexion adorned with luminous eyes, a small pert nose, and full, merry lips that parted often in laughter. Not only was she a great beauty, but she moved in the innermost circles of wealth and influence in the kingdom.

Jotham returned to his carving. He spoke without looking up, his voice full of mischief. "Take comfort in this, then. If she spurns you, at least she won't beat you at horseshoes as she once did."

Alfric's face reddened. "Why did I ever tell you that story? Forget it! It was long ago."

But how well he remembered. Suddenly, he was twelve again, tall and gawky, cringing under his father's disapproving glare. Before them towered the great doors of Abaddon's palace.

"Why I brought you on this trip I'll never know," his father barked. "You're sure to embarrass me. At least try not to fall on your face when you bow to the prince."

"Oh, don't bow! Don't go in at all," cried a high, lilting voice.

He turned to find a freckle-faced girl in reddish-brown pigtails grinning up at him. "Stay out here and play horseshoes with me!" she pleaded.

His father brightened. "Now there's an idea! Do that, Alfric! And see that you win!"

The girl tugged at his arm. "I'm Gwyneth. Come on."

For the next hour, the clank of horseshoes blended with her laughter as she beat him soundly. At last, his father returned with a tall imposing figure in a fancy uniform gleaming with medals. The girl ran to him and hugged him. "I won, Father! I'm a champion!"

"And I fear my son is not, General Bogdan," his own father had scowled.

"Don't be too hard on the lad. My Gwyneth beats all the boys, Lord Killian," the general beamed as Alfric stood shamefaced.

For weeks after, his father had taunted him, "You lose to everyone, even little girls like Gwyneth." Alfric hoped he'd never hear her name again.

That had been nine years ago, and Alfric was a gawky

boy no longer. At twenty-one, he was over six feet tall with a sturdy, muscular build. His piercing blue eyes were complimented by shocks of jet-black hair that set off a well-shaped face and a determined chin. To the casual observer, he displayed a confidence bordering on brashness.

But beneath that bold exterior still beat the hesitant heart of a boy all too often criticized and diminished. He'd had more problems with his father, many more. At last, he had moved to Acrasia to make his own way. One night he had gone to Cuthbert's Tavern, a popular gathering place. Gwyneth was there, and the instant he saw her, he was smitten. But she had shown no interest in him—at least at first.

"I used to wonder if she remembered... about the horseshoes, that is," Alfric mused to Jotham's bent head. "And if she thought me a hopeless failure, like my father does. And if that's why she wouldn't notice me. But you changed that, Jotham. That's why you must come tonight. You're my good luck charm."

Alfric leaned over Jotham's shoulder. "I don't see how you can make that horse much better. And time is fleeing..."

"Oh, all right," sighed Jotham, giving up. "I'm nearly done anyway." Moving swiftly, he replaced his tools and put out the shop's oil lamps. Then locking the door behind him, he followed Alfric out into the storm.

Before them veiled by the swirling snow lay the city of Acrasia. Like the rest of Withershins, most days in the capital were drab and gray. A thick mist hung over its sprawling expanse like a giant cloak of hopelessness. Not so the nights. When darkness fell, the city stretched like some enormous cat and sprang to life.

This late March night was no different. In the nearby district known as Gullet Grotto, lanterns blazed in the taverns. Steaks sizzled. Ale and wine flowed freely. Shouts and laughter mingled with the roar of conversation.

Alfric led Jotham toward the revelry, still reminiscing. "Yes, my luck with Gwyneth began with you. It all started the first night you met her. Remember?"

"That was the first time you took me to Cuthbert's," Jotham answered. The truth was, he'd met Gwyneth before this, but he kept it to himself.

"Yes, that's right," said Alfric. "You were speaking of your mother's death and how young you were. And how all you had left of her was a quilt she'd made. Gwyneth overheard and came and talked to us. She said she'd lost her mother at a young age too."

"But her mother hadn't died like mine," Jotham frowned. "She'd run off with a lover—which must have been far worse! I felt so bad for her!"

"Not as bad as she felt for you when she learned you had no father either," Alfric reminded him. "She thought you must feel quite alone. And you told her you had, until I'd befriended you. But now I'd become the family you never had."

Alfric's face grew dreamy. "And then she smiled at me..."

"And you've had me building you up to her ever since," Jotham laughed.

But Alfric didn't hear him. Suddenly the snow, and Jotham, and the fast approaching lantern lights of Cuthbert's all faded from his view. All he could see before him was Gwyneth, and that smile. Jotham's praise seemed to be working. More and more, she had sought them out. And now, tonight, he would take a new and daring step. He would ask her to join him for dinner...

"Alfric, look out!" Jotham's warning jolted Alfric out of his reverie just in time to avoid slamming into the tavern's signpost.

"See what happens when you walk around in a fog of love?" Jotham teased. "Good thing I was here or you would have banged your head and bled all over this nice white snow."

Alfric reddened. "So what? It will get all muddy and smudged soon enough anyway."

Jotham's face grew pensive. "I know. I wish it wouldn't!"

As he stared at the snow, a scene from his childhood flashed through his mind. He was standing before his mother, his new clothes all muddy and smudged. "Oh, Jotham, I told you not to play in those," she sighed. "Your naughtiness will be the death of me!"

Not long after that, she became ill. When she died, he went out and dropped icicle tears on the snow. How he wished he'd kept his clothes clean and wondered if that might have saved her.

Jotham felt a tug on his arm. "What's with you? Are you coming?"

Snapping back to the present, he followed Alfric through the tavern door. Instantly, they were caught up in a swirling sea of humanity. Though frequented by all ages, Cuthbert's was especially popular with the city's youthful elite. It was swarming with diners, crammed at wooden tables packed so closely together there was barely room to move between them. Suspended from the ceiling were giant kegs carved with the names of those who had "conquered the quart"—a local term designating winners of the nightly drinking contests. Buxom waitresses in full skirts and skimpy blouses squeezed among the patrons, balancing overloaded trays whose contents rattled and swayed.

Alfric quickly spied Gwyneth, who was surrounded as usual by a crowd of admirers vying for her attention. She had not seen them enter, and he thought that was just as well. He would first secure his favorite table, then watch and wait for just the right moment to approach her.

Jotham nudged him. "Looks like someone's in our spot."

Alfric followed Jotham's gaze and received a most unpleasant shock. His table was indeed taken. Its female occupant contrasted sharply with the youthful throng around her. She was somewhere in her mid-sixties, dressed in peasant garb. Though she was familiar to Alfric and probably most others in the room, no one sat with her. Alfric well knew the reason. The Widow Nessa belonged to the People of the Book.

Alfric turned accusingly to Jotham. "See what comes of taking so long? Now what do we do?"

Jotham gazed back, unruffled. "We could find another table."

Alfric scanned the room, scowling. "There are none."

"We could leave," suggested Jotham in a mild tone.

Alfric's scowl deepened. "No!"

Jotham studied his friend thoughtfully. "Then maybe we should join the good woman. I doubt she would mind. Perhaps she won't stay long. When she goes, we shall have the table to ourselves."

"And what will people think of us in the meantime?" Alfric demanded. "You know her kind are suspect. Besides, she'd probably quote us nonsense from that silly Book of hers!"

Jotham wasn't so sure it was nonsense. Years ago when first working for Elwin in Brynmor, he had served a customer named Yarin, who was especially gentle and kind. Much later, after Yarin had moved from the village, Jotham learned he was a Person of the Book.

"Have you ever wondered what this Book says?" Jotham asked Alfric. "I must confess, I have often wished to look inside."

"Have you, now!" exclaimed Alfric, getting an idea. "Then perhaps it is time to satisfy your curiosity."

Alfric turned and pushed through the crowd. Jotham followed, feeling strangely uneasy. The widow was reading her Book, but she looked up as the young men approached.

At first glance her face, though pleasant enough, seemed quite ordinary. Time had loosened and wrinkled her skin and furrowed her brow. Her hair was mostly gray mixed with a forgettable brown. Her nose was a little too large and her lips a bit thin. But the beauty of her soul and character shone through and transformed this simple canvas of a face. Jotham was drawn by it instantly, and smiled at the widow. Alfric gave her a withering stare.

The widow showed no reaction to Alfric's hostility. Instead, she smiled and held out her hand in greeting. "A good evening to you both."

Jotham clasped her hand, but Alfric kept his own arms stiffly at his sides. "It is not a good evening yet," he replied. "The weather is too cold and the tavern is too crowded. Nor did I wish to speak with you. But my friend Jotham is curious about your Book."

Alfric's words jolted the widow's heart. *No wonder I felt impressed this night to come here with my Book*, she thought, amazed. Normally, she did not frequent such places. But the inner guidance had been strong, and she had long ago learned to trust this still, small voice. Now at last she had this chance, a chance she had longed for these many years.

Striving to remain calm, she motioned to Alfric and Jotham. "By all means. Please sit down. We will read a portion together. You shall soon see its value."

Alfric snatched the Book instead. "I do already!" he gloated. Holding it up before Jotham, he flipped its pages roughly. "Normally, this Book is good only for kindling. But tonight, it shall buy us a table."

"Don't, Alfric!" gasped Jotham, horrified. "Give it back!"

"Gladly...for a price," Alfric answered, glancing slyly at the widow. "What do you say? The table for your Book! Will you trade?"

The widow jumped up in alarm. "Yes, of course. Just be careful, I beg you!"

Jotham reached for the Book. "Please, Alfric!"

But it was too late. Alfric turned one last page, accidentally ripping it loose.

Jotham gasped in dismay. The widow winced. Alfric stared for an instant, uncertain what to do. But he quickly recovered, shoving both the Book and the page in the Widow Nessa's face. "Here, take your precious Book!"

"So I shall," she said, clasping it to her. She gave Alfric and Jotham a long, searching look. "But I'll leave the page with you. Perchance one of you shall read it."

The widow hurried away. Jotham watched her go. When he turned back, Alfric had crumpled the page in his hand. "Read this? Never!" he sneered, tossing it across the floor. He took a seat, motioning Jotham to do likewise. "Come, sit down. And stop looking so troubled. All is well now."

Jotham sank reluctantly into a chair. Somehow he felt dirty and smudged, like the day he had muddied his clothes. "All is not well!" he frowned. "We had no right to treat the widow so!"

Alfric bridled. "Don't be silly! That's how the world works. The way to get what you want is to go and take it!"

Jotham frowned. "If that were true, I'd have a father. And I don't."

Alfric's face clouded. "Be glad! As I've often told you, you're better off without one! He could have been like mine. Good thing we don't speak anymore. Just thinking of him makes me lose my appetite!"

"Which would be a pity," soothed a new voice. "We've got fine kidney pie." A full-figured woman in a long, flowered skirt swished between them, placing two tall mugs of frosty ale on the table. "Your usual, lads. And what else will you have?"

"Nothing yet, Alcina," answered Alfric. "Someone else may join us."

Alcina chuckled knowingly. "Then I fear you'll lose your appetite for sure. But your guest may be hungry. And if you wish to impress her, I have a few suggestions."

As Alcina launched into the merits of goose-liver paté and rare prime rib, Jotham turned away, staring sadly, lost in his own thoughts. Then, without warning, his eyes met Gwyneth's.

From her look, Jotham felt sure she sensed his mood. She gave him a questioning smile, then beckoned with her finger.

Suddenly, Jotham knew that he shouldn't have come. He would not be a help to Alfric, but a hindrance. Turning back, he endured Alcina's praise of peach custard. Then he spoke. "I'm sorry. I'm not myself tonight, Alfric. All that talk of fathers, I guess. I'd best be going."

"No, you can't!" Alfric's tone was panicked.

Jotham insisted. "Really, it's better this way. I won't be good company. Why don't you go ask Gwyneth, and I'll edge toward the door. I won't leave until I see things are going well."

"But what about our table? We'll lose it," Alfric argued.

"Perhaps Alcina would like to rest her feet for a few moments. She can drink my ale." Jotham rose, handing her some coins to pay for the drink.

"A fine offer!" Alcina exclaimed, settling heavily into the chair.

Alfric hesitated. "All right, then. Wish me luck."

The pair clasped hands. Then Jotham turned and began to thread his way through the mass of humanity toward the exit. Suddenly, he heard a crackling sound. Glancing down, he saw something crumpled under his foot.

The Book page! thought Jotham. An irresistible impulse seized him. He must have it! But even as he bent to retrieve it, caution stayed him. Alfric must not see him do this. It would only cause problems between them.

Jotham glanced in Gwyneth's direction. Alfric had not yet reached her. Their eyes met once more, and again she beckoned him. Then Alfric stepped between them, blocking Jotham's view of her. Seeing Alfric's back turned to him, Jotham seized his chance, reached for the page, and slipped it into his pocket.

Across the room, Gwyneth turned her anxious gaze to Alfric. "I just caught a glimpse of Jotham. He seemed troubled. Is something wrong?"

Alfric chose his words carefully, wanting to be truthful without sounding like he'd failed Jotham. "It's just that, though we are close, every now and then he longs for the father he never had."

"Perhaps I could join you and help cheer him up," she offered.

Alfric's heart soared. This was the perfect opening! "I'm afraid he's just leaving. But your company would cheer me! Would you do me the honor of joining me for dinner?"

A look crossed Gwyneth's face that Alfric could not read. She paused for an instant, then rose and reached for her coat. "I was leaving myself," she told him. "I meant merely to stop for a moment or two on my way out. Perhaps another time I will accept your kind invitation."

Alfric helped her on with her wrap. Gwyneth smiled brightly. Then she was gone. He gazed after her, his heart leaping. She had not said yes. But she had not said no.

JOTHAM WATCHED his friends for a moment before slipping out the door. The storm had stopped. As he trudged down the street, Jotham turned for one last look at Cuthbert's and saw someone hurry outside. He wasn't quite sure who it was, but the form seemed familiar. Ducking around the side of a building, he watched as the figure craned its head, searching the night. At last it disappeared into a waiting coach. Moments later, the coach clattered past him. It belonged to Gwyneth.

So Gwyneth hadn't dined with Alfric after all! Jotham knew he should feel disappointed for his friend. Instead, he was strangely relieved—and he didn't like the feeling. He felt like a traitor to Alfric. Then again, didn't taking the Book page make him a traitor too?

Jotham wasn't sure. But he would read the page, regardless. Having made this decision, Jotham stepped from hiding and turned toward home.

CHAPTER 3

An Offer from a King

JOTHAM COULDN'T stop thinking of the Book page as he hurried through the frosted landscape. What a magnificent night! The storm had swept the sky clear, peeling back its perpetual wrapper of haze to reveal the glorious sparkle of seldom-seen stars. Jotham fancied they were trying to shine their light inside his pocket as if they too were curious to see this writing from the Book. Even the snow crunching under his feet urged him onward. "Crunch, crunch! Faster Jotham! Get home and read it! Quick!"

He hastened his pace, leaving the taverns behind as he traced his way back past the shops of Craftsman's Row. Most artisans, including Jotham, worked in this sector. They lived just beyond it in a rustic corner of Acrasia known as Odd End.

The place wasn't really odd at all, but rather quaint and charming. The homes, though small, were whimsically shaped, and no two were alike. Their gates bore large decorative signs with their owners' names. On their outer walls were murals of craftsmen at work painted by a local artist.

Sprinkled among these small family dwellings were larger rooming houses. Single people alone in the city, both artisans and others, favored such lodgings. The quarters were affordable, adequately furnished, and well kept.

Jotham lived in a small second-story addition to one of these rooming houses. His quarters had a separate outside entrance, and he liked the privacy. Swiftly climbing the snow-caked stairs, he thrust his key into the lock of a plain but sturdy wooden door. With a gentle creak of welcome, it yielded to his touch. Fingers fumbling slightly from cold and excitement, he lit an oil lamp, bathing the room in its soft, flickering glow.

At first glance, the room and its contents seemed unremarkable enough. The walls were made of rough lumber. The lone window was an interesting round shape, but rather small. The furnishings consisted only of a narrow bed pushed against one wall, a chest, a coat rack, a small table, and two chairs.

Yet a closer look revealed that what this furniture lacked in size and quantity, it made up for in design. Each piece was marvelously fashioned, its parts perfectly fitted together. Each was adorned with intricate and fanciful carvings. Of course, these were not the original furnishings. They were Jotham's own creations, made from scrap wood in his spare time. They were a silent showcase of his talent and promise.

The room had one other adornment—a finely stitched but faded quilt. Large daisies with laughing faces and intertwining stems frolicked merrily across its folds. His mother had made it for her marriage bed. The quilt was Jotham's last link with her—and with his father. He often imagined his parents lying beneath it. What dreams had they dreamed? What hopes had they shared with each other late at night? If only these silent threads could talk, what stories they might tell!

But this night, another story consumed him. Perching on the chair, he pulled the rumpled Book page from his pocket, smoothing its creases. As he did so, his heart sank. When he'd stepped on it in the tavern, his storm-dampened shoe must have smudged the page. The writing was blurred beyond recognition, except for a couple of lines at the very bottom.

Jotham hunched over the words, straining to read them. *"And this great King will be a father to those who have no father. He has offered to adopt those who come to him as his own. To become a child of the King you need only..."*

There the writing stopped.

I need only what? Jotham wondered. Then he caught himself. *How silly! This couldn't be real. It's only a story. But just imagine if it is real!* he thought wistfully.

Jotham stared at the page again, murmuring the words that stirred such longing in his heart. *"A father to those who have no father..."*

The present faded from Jotham's consciousness as a scene from his past played out on the stage of his mind. It was another snowy day in a long-ago winter when he was five. A marvelous sled glided past him, steered by two laughing children. At last it stopped short in a shower of snow.

As the children climbed off, Jotham ran up, eyes shining. "Oh please, can I try that? Can I ride your sled? Just for a moment?"

"No, I should say not!" sniffed one, a mean-faced boy. "Our father built it just for us. If you want a sled, why don't you go and ask *your* father?"

Tears stung Jotham's eyes. "I...I don't have one."

The boy's sister shrugged. "Then I guess you're out of luck."

Jotham's cheeks burned. A voice screamed inside him. *It's not fair! I don't have a sled, or a father! And they have both!* In a flash of anger, he jumped on their sled and pushed off.

For one glorious moment, he felt himself flying over the snow. Then he saw the huge tree trunk rushing to meet him. He tried to turn the sled, but it wouldn't obey. With a mighty smack, sled and tree collided, and the ride was over.

Amazingly, the sled escaped harm, but Jotham was covered with bruises. As he lay in the snow, sprawled and aching, the children ran up screaming. "Thief! Thief!" they cried, their pointing fingers wounding him worse than the tree had.

But the worst part of all was later when his mother asked him how he got hurt. He didn't want to tell her. But she got the truth out of him like she always did. He was sure he'd be punished. But he wasn't. She just held him and sobbed, and that pained him more.

As the scene faded, Jotham pondered the page before him. He wondered, *What would it be like to have a king for a father? Would that mean I would live in a palace and be rich and rule over people like Prince Abaddon does?*

Jotham wished he knew what profession his own father had followed. But his mother would never answer his childhood questions. She refused to speak of his father or even tell Jotham his name. It was only in the last moments of her life that she had pulled back the cloak of secrecy ever so slightly. He had been seven then.

In his mind's eye, the flickering lamp in his room melted into another lamp, flickering in the bedroom of a small country cottage. His mother had lain ill in that room for what seemed forever. But that day, Jotham felt a strange sense of dread. When his mother called for him, he fled to a kitchen cupboard.

How long he hid there, crouched and quaking, he didn't know. At last the cupboard door opened. Pots tumbled and clattered as strong, sturdy hands pulled him out. He looked up in terror at the grave face of the neighbor woman who'd been caring for them. "You must go to your mother, Jotham," she told him.

"No, please! If I don't, it won't happen!"

"What won't happen?"

"Something awful!"

The neighbor woman wrapped her arms around him. "You can't stop it, child. Be brave now."

Then she brought him to his mother, pale and wasted in her bed, and left them alone together. The strange smell of sickness smothered him as his mother drew him close. Her whisper was weak. "I won't be with you much longer. Always remember that I love you."

As she kissed him gently, Jotham's eyes blurred with tears. He clung to her, blinking them back, searching her face. "Did Papa love me?" he choked at last. "What happened to him, Mama? Did he get sick too? Or did he just go away and leave us?"

A look passed over his mother's face that Jotham had never seen before. When she spoke, her voice was taut. "He didn't want to go. Soldiers came and dragged him off in chains. They said he committed high crimes and treason against Prince Abaddon. You weren't born yet, Jotham. He never even saw you."

His eyes grew wide. "What did they do to him, Mama?"

Sadness washed over her face like a wave. "He was sent far away to a solitary prison deep in a desert wasteland. It's a place from which no one returns. He must be long dead now."

His mother's words pulsed with desperate urgency. "You must forget your father and never speak of this to anyone. No one must ever guess you are his son. Or they might think..."

As her sentence trailed off, new questions ripped from

Jotham's throat. "Think what? That I was like him? Was he really that bad, Mama?"

A sudden flush spread across her face, like one last blaze of flame from a fading fire. "Your father was a good man!" she gasped.

Jotham threw his arms around her. For an instant, she returned his embrace. Then she fell back on her pillow. She was gone.

The last moments with his mother faded from his mind. As if it understood his sorrow, the oil lamp flickered and went out, leaving Jotham in darkness. He didn't bother to relight it. Instead, he stared into the black, pondering the course his life had taken since his childhood.

Alone in the world at his mother's death, Jotham had been hustled off to Flotsam Manor. His mother's modest home and goods were sold to help pay for his care. He had been allowed to choose just one keepsake. He had picked the quilt.

His life could have been worse at the orphanage. His body was fed and clothed, even if his heart was not. Mindful of his mother's warning, he said nothing of his past to anyone. Still, he sensed that someone knew. Someone was lurking in the shadows. At odd moments, he felt eyes upon him. As time passed, he grew more wary. The other orphans noticed. They concluded he was strange and aloof and mostly shunned him.

But here in Acrasia, his life had changed. He had felt an instant kinship with Alfric, who had also suffered taunts and rejection. Yet Jotham had not told even Alfric the full story of his father. Some deep intuition still bade him heed his mother's caution.

And there was another reason. Alfric gave unquestioning loyalty to Prince Abaddon. Jotham knew he could not do so. His mother's dying words had raised disturbing doubts. If his father was a good man as his mother had insisted, could he have done anything so awful? Why had Abaddon been so harsh with him? Was he really a traitor? And if so, did he have good reason to be a traitor?

Jotham's thoughts turned to the People of the Book. Though many Acrasians considered them suspect, Jotham saw no cause to take offense at them. If they were all like the widow, they must be good people—and perhaps rather good storytellers.

Jotham reached through the darkness, fingering the tattered page before him. This offer from a king was really quite intriguing. Even if it was just a fairy tale, he'd like to hear more. And why shouldn't he? What harm could it do? Tomorrow, he would take the Book page back to the widow and ask her to tell him.

CHAPTER 4

The Price of Adoption

⌗

JOTHAM DID not have to work the next morning. It was Free Day in Acrasia. Once a week on this day, shops closed and the craftsmen were at leisure. For most, this meant sleeping an extra hour. The streets of Odd End were still fairly empty when Jotham set out for the Widow Nessa's cottage.

Almost everyone in Acrasia knew where the widow lived. This area, home to small farms and peasant dwellings, was called Farmers' Furrows. The road led Jotham outside the city proper and east through a more rural setting. It was quite a pleasant walk. Though the mist had returned, the weather had warmed and the snow was quickly melting. It soaked through the soil of the grassy fields, shook loose from tree branches, and dripped in dancing rivulets from the sloped roofs of the small neat peasant cottages that dotted the landscape. Passersby waved and smiled, and Jotham returned their greetings.

At last, Jotham reached the widow's gate. Perhaps he imagined it, but the fog seemed to lift a bit as he entered. High in a tree, a squirrel with a snow-tipped tail chattered down at him. Jotham fancied it was shouting a welcome. "Come in! It's a nice place! A nice place!"

The widow's humble home seemed no different than the others he had passed. Simple steppingstones led through a modest yard to her front door. Logs were stacked beside the entry. A nearby table crammed with pots and tools revealed the widow's interest in gardening.

Only the metal doorknocker seemed a bit curious. It was in the shape of a crooked shepherd's staff. Jotham reached for it, but was jolted by an unexpected voice behind him. "May I help you?"

Jotham spun around to find the widow herself coming toward him. She was dressed exactly as she had been the night before, except a bit mussed.

"I . . . I just . . ."

"Why, you're Jotham! The young man from the tavern!" The widow smiled, then pointed to herself with a laugh. "You must forgive my somewhat sorry appearance. When I reached home last night, I found a neighbor on my doorstep. He asked me to come quickly and attend his wife in childbirth. I'm pleased to say I helped her bring a fine baby boy into the world! But by the time I cleaned him up, I didn't look so fine myself!"

Jotham chuckled, put at ease by her gentle humor. The Widow Nessa had quite a reputation as a midwife. It made him curious about something. "When you help birth these babies," he asked, "do you see them again? Are you ever invited to their birthdays?"

The widow's face clouded. "Seldom," she sighed. "The People of the Book are not popular party guests." Her face cleared, and her eyes began to twinkle. "But I like to think I came to the birthday that mattered most!" Her eyes grew questioning. "And now, you must tell me why you've come."

Sudden guilt flushed Jotham's face. He held out the Book

page, feeling miserable. "I came to say I'm sorry for what happened last night. And I'm sorry your Book got damaged. I meant to save this page, but I ruined it instead. Alfric tossed it aside. I didn't see it. I stepped on it, and my shoe was wet and..."

"It's all right." The widow laid a gentle hand on Jotham's shoulder.

The grace and kindness in her manner gave him courage to continue. "Alfric said the Book was full of fairy tales, but I don't see what's wrong with that. I read just a bit where the ink wasn't blurred. It had something to do with an offer of adoption from a King. I must say it intrigued me since I never had a father myself. Do you know how it goes?"

The widow's eyes sparkled. "So you'd like to hear this story, would you?"

Jotham's own eyes lit up at her words. "Oh, please!"

"Come in then, and I shall tell it to you over tea." The widow opened the door, and Jotham followed her inside.

He felt as though he had stepped into another world. It wasn't the décor that was so different, it was the paintings on the walls. They made it seem as though a piece of a foreign land had been chipped off and dropped right into the middle of the widow's sitting room.

"Did you do these?" Jotham asked, gesturing toward the artwork.

The widow nodded, looking pleased. "Do you like them?"

Jotham moved closer, studying a watercolor of a tree bursting with strange-looking leaves and tantalizing fruit. "I like this one. What a marvelous tree! I've never seen anything like it. Where does it grow?"

"It grows in Dominus," she smiled.

"Dominus?"

Her smile widened. "The King's land."

Jotham shivered with delight. "Oh, I see. It's an imaginary tree. I like to imagine things too. But I carve them in wood."

He moved on to a painting of a gleaming golden palace set high on a hill with a river flowing down through its courtyards. "And is this where the King in your Book lives?"

"He is there, and everywhere," the widow said softly.

"This King must have amazing powers," gasped Jotham, tingling with excitement. "What does he look like? Have you drawn him too?"

She grew solemn. "He can't be looked upon, or drawn. But I have drawn his Son. Can you pick him out?"

Jotham searched the walls, pausing before a painting of a regal figure in a jeweled crown and flowing white robe. He stared at the portrait, transfixed. Never had he seen an expression of such sorrow mixed with such love—not even in his mother's dying eyes.

The widow's voice murmured in his ear. "Yes, that's him. Prince Morning Star."

Jotham's gaze remained riveted on the painting. "His face. It's . . . remarkable. I tried to carve a face once, a real person's face. My carving was just a poor copy. But you have imagined a face far surpassing any real one I have ever known."

He turned to the widow, looking wistful. "I wish this Morning Star was real! He would be well worth meeting if he were!"

"Come," she beckoned in reply. "You shall have your story now."

Taking Jotham's elbow, she steered him to an eating table in a cheery corner of her kitchen. In no time she had made a pot of tea and poured them each a cup. Taking a seat, she set the Book between them, opened it, and began to read.

Far back in the reaches of a time before time, in the very, very beginning, a King reigned who was greatest of all. None was holier, wiser, or mightier than he was. By his will, worlds were born. All he made was filled with goodness. Where he ruled, there was peace and beauty everywhere.

But danger loomed. Among the King's servants was one who grew jealous and prideful. He wished to reign in the King's place. He and those he persuaded to follow rose up in rebellion. They lost.

But though he and his followers were banished from the King's court, this dark prince did not give up. He prowled the shadows, seeking to deceive and destroy. At last, he stole a part of the King's domain. He tricked the people and turned their hearts from the King to serve him instead. They sold themselves, their descendants and their land into slavery to him and his ways. Their hearts and minds became darkened. They began to confuse good and evil. As time passed, they forgot the King. Many came to doubt his existence and to think the stories of him were but fairy tales.

Jotham's grip tightened on his teacup. Did this story have a deeper meaning?

The widow looked up. Their eyes met. "The story continues on the ruined page," she told him. "But I know it by heart. Would you like to hear more?"

He nodded wordlessly, and she began again. "But though they forgot the King, he did not forget them. He gave them a Book to remind them of who he was. It spoke of how much he loved them. It invited them to return to him. But they could not come to him on their own."

Jotham's heart beat faster. "Why not?"

The widow looked grave. "The dark prince held them fast, and they could not buy their freedom. They were only poor slaves. Still, there *was* a way."

"Someone bought them back?" cried Jotham.

The widow nodded. "Yes. The King sent his own first-born Son, Prince Morning Star, to rescue them. This King's Son lived among them, and taught them, and ransomed

41

them once for all time. And though their evil ruler strove to hold them captive still, some saw the truth and fled. They sought the King and found him—as will those who seek him now."

The widow smoothed the crumpled Book page, then read the words that had piqued Jotham's curiosity the night before.

> And this great King will be a father to those who have no father. He has offered to adopt those who come to him as his own. To become a child of the King you need only...

She turned to the next page of the Book, completing the sentence. "...go to the border, call for Prince Morning Star, and receive his gift."

The widow stopped reading and looked up at Jotham. He stared at her, amazed. "That makes no sense! To be free one must accept a gift? What gift?"

"He will tell you that himself," she said softly, "if you go."

Jotham's whole body quivered. "You don't mean to say the King and Prince Morning Star are real? But how do you know?"

The widow's face glowed. "I have met them. The King adopted *me!* All the People of the Book are his children. As for Prince Morning Star, my painting is but a poor copy and pale shadow of his surpassing glory."

Jotham's head swam. "Oh, if only it were true! But it can't be! Why would some distant King care that much about me?"

"Perhaps he is not as distant as you think," the widow murmured. "Indeed, the border is not far."

"And yet *so* far!" cried Jotham. "It's forbidden. Everybody knows that! Abaddon will let no one go there except the soldiers who guard it, and even they are terrified! I met one at Cuthbert's just after he returned. He said the road leads through a frightful wilderness. Strange apparitions rise up in the night. Eerie shrieks pierce the stillness. Even in the daytime, the air is alive with a constant rustling and crackling. It's as though wild beasts are lurking in the shadows, stalking, waiting to pounce."

"Abaddon and his forces are indeed like beasts," the widow scowled. "They will try every means to frighten and turn back would-be travelers. That is why I myself will go with you and guide you, if you are willing."

Jotham frowned at the widow. "If you were adopted, as you say, why are you still here? Why didn't you stay with the King?"

Jotham saw in the widow's eyes the same inexpressible look of love and sorrow she had captured in the painted image of Prince Morning Star. It was almost as if her face became his for an instant. "Wherever I am, I am with the King. I returned to tell others about him. But though I dwell here, I do not belong here. Nor would you if you came back."

Jotham winced, imagining what it would mean to "not belong." He would be an outcast, like all the People of the Book, like he had been at Flotsam Manor. Surely Magnus would no longer employ him. And Gwyneth would shun him. That would be painful. Their friendship, though casual, had been special. As for Alfric...

Jotham's face clouded. The widow saw. "What is it?" she probed gently.

"It's Alfric," sighed Jotham. "He's the closest friend I've ever had. I can't vanish without a word to him. But I couldn't tell him, could I? He'd only try to stop me!"

"Yes, I fear so," she replied. "But you could write a letter and leave it with me. Explain to him what you've done, and why. Once I have guided you safely to the King's land, I will see that he gets it. Perhaps it will soften his heart."

"Or break it further," Jotham murmured. "He's just had a great disappointment. If I leave now, he will feel completely abandoned. And he doesn't understand about fathers..."

Jotham's voice trailed off. *A father! Could I really have a father?* This thought seized him and pulled his heart toward the border. Just as quickly, his doubts pulled him back. He didn't think the widow was lying. Still, she might be deceived. But what if she wasn't, and this was all true? Yet what about Alfric? And back and forth and back...

"I...I don't know," Jotham groaned at last, torn and miserable. "My whole life I have longed for a father. And yet..." He swallowed hard. "If I did decide to go, when would we leave?"

The widow's voice was urgent. "The sooner the better! I shall wait at the western crossroads at sunset. Should you choose to make the journey, meet me there. Once night falls, we can start for the border." She gazed at him intently. "And keep your wits about you! The dark prince has his watchers everywhere!"

Jotham felt his skin prickle. The nearly forgotten image of a giant frog loomed in his memory. Jotham wondered what the widow would say if he told her about its strangely evil eyes. Somehow he doubted she'd make light of his suspicions as Ragnar had. Yet he did not want to tell her now.

Silently, he rose. Just as silently, she led him to the door.

As he hurried away, the widow gazed after him anxiously. *Jotham's heart seems drawn to the King,* she thought, *yet his bond with Alfric is strong. It might keep him from the crossroads or at least compel him to reveal his plans. Then, powerful forces will be set in motion to turn him from his purpose.*

But other forces will also be at work, she reminded herself. *Forces far more powerful than Jotham, Alfric, myself, or even Prince Abaddon. I can take comfort in that.*

Closing the door, she turned to gaze at another painting on the wall. On its canvas, a graceful white dove was poised in flight, surrounded by a golden light. Its delicate face radiated wisdom and peace. The widow smiled. A look of great peace washed over her face as well. "Yes, I can take comfort in that," she murmured. "Great comfort."

CHAPTER 5

The Appearance of the Dove

~※~

THE NEXT FEW hours of Jotham's life passed in a blur. He went first to Magnus's shop. Just in case he did go with the widow, he must finish the hope chest. He owed Magnus that much, and besides, the piece was for a special customer. Only when he'd perfected the last detail was Jotham satisfied. He polished the winged horse to such brightness that his own face gleamed back at him from its shining flank.

After putting away his tools, Jotham placed a note atop the chest, explaining he might need to leave on pressing personal business. If so, he did not know when or if he could return. The letter ended by thanking Magnus for his kindness. As he locked the shop, perhaps for the last time, Jotham felt such regret that he thought surely he could not go to the border after all.

But Jotham's mood changed as he wound his way through the stands of the colorful outdoor market that sprang up in the tavern district every Free Day afternoon. Peasant vendors purposely picked the time when the rest of Acrasia was at leisure, knowing well that more would come to browse and buy. The market was a jungle of wares from home gardens, kitchens, and workshops—everything from sausages and pies to painted flowerpots. Rosy-faced children shouted the merits of their parents' goods and wrapped purchases in coarse paper as their elders smiled in approval. Jotham bought provisions for his journey—a loaf of bread, a water flask, and a small torch for nighttime travel. He listened as one young boy told how he and his father had made the cheese they were selling. The father nodded proudly and gave his son a quick hug. For a moment, Jotham wished he could be that son. He swallowed the lump in his throat, purchased a large wedge of aged cheese, and turned his heart once more to the border and the King.

It was mid-afternoon when he climbed the steps to his upper room once more. Pulling out a small leather satchel, he packed it with the goods he had bought and a few items of spare clothing. As he did so, the struggle raged anew. Should he go or not? If he didn't make this trip, he'd never know if he might have gained a father. But if he went, he would lose the life he'd built here. He might even be killed.

Jotham set the satchel on his bed, staring sadly at the quilt that covered it. He must leave even this lone link with his parents behind. It was far too heavy and bulky to carry. Besides, it might get damaged or ruined on the journey. Maybe Alfric would keep it safe for him. He'd put that in the letter, too.

Drawing a deep breath, Jotham sat down to the task he had purposely left for last, his letter to Alfric. Not wanting to cause trouble for the widow, he said nothing of their time together. He wrote only of the Book page and the offer from the King and how it stirred his heart. As he tried to wrestle his deepest yearnings into words, he thought of Alfric's yearnings for Gwyneth—and of his own friendship with her. Ever since they'd first met at Magnus's shop, he'd felt empathy between them. How he wished he could bid her good-bye or write to her also. But he dared not. Didn't her father command Abaddon's armies? He remembered the widow's warning, *"The dark prince has his watchers everywhere."*

Jotham's skin prickled. Instinctively, his eyes darted to the window. Had he seen something? Or was it simply a figment of his fears? Jotham leaped to his feet. And then he heard something... a loud plop, followed by a low grunt.

Jotham felt his blood turn to ice. His heart hammered in his ears. Every nerve ending quivered. Whoever was lurking, he would catch! He sprang to the door and jerked it open.

"Jotham!"

The cry distracted him. Had he looked down, Jotham might have seen the loathsome creature that sprang past him over the threshold into the room. But all his attention was commanded by the frowning figure of Alfric bounding toward him up the stairs.

"Where were you?" Alfric demanded. "I looked everywhere for you! Don't you want to know what happened? Don't you care at all how it went with Gwyneth last night?"

Guilt flooded Jotham. "Yes... yes, Alfric. Of course I do!"

Alfric seized Jotham's arm and pulled him inside, closing the door behind them. He spun to face Jotham, looking as if he would burst. "I asked her to dinner. And she said she was leaving... but perhaps she'd dine with me another time. Jotham, I have a chance with her! I have a chance with her!"

Jotham stood speechless, but Alfric didn't seem to notice. He seized his friend's shoulders. "If only I had my birthright! It might help my cause! I must gain my inheritance. You must help me find a way."

Jotham's face blanched. "Surely, you don't wish your father dead!"

Alfric looked startled for a moment. Then he laughed bitterly. "Oh, it's not from my father! He won't leave me a thing.

He's made that quite clear. He will give it all to my small half-brother Bowen. My father chose him as heir in my place before the child could even wipe his own nose. No, this birthright comes from my mother...Jotham, are you listening?"

Jotham had been trying to concentrate, but his mind had wandered. Alfric had a chance with Gwyneth after all. If something developed between them, they might not even miss him.

"Jotham?"

"Sorry, go on."

Jotham tried to focus on Alfric again. But now the strange feeling had come back, that eerie sense of being watched. In spite of himself, his eyes wandered, searching.

Alfric continued, "As I was saying, the birthright's from my mother. It was passed down in her family. But at some point it was lost. She only learned of it shortly before I was born. She died soon after. In such cases, Prince Abaddon takes the birthright to hold in trust. Now that I'm of age, I can receive it. But there's a condition. First I must...Jotham, you haven't heard a word I've said!"

Jotham forced his eyes to meet Alfric's accusing stare. "No, really, I have."

"I doubt that," fumed Alfric. "All I've done is bore you. You've been looking everywhere but...What's that?"

He spotted the satchel. Alfric rummaged through its contents and fixed Jotham with a wounded frown. "Are you going somewhere? You might at least have told me."

Then he spied the letter. Before Jotham could stop him, he snatched it.

Alfric read in a moment what Jotham had labored so long to write. Anger flashed in his eyes like lightning. "Go to the border? How could you even consider such a thing? I told you the Book is nothing but lies and nonsense! Yet you spurn my counsel and risk untold dangers to chase a phony promise from some fictitious King. You must value my opinion very little, and value me less."

"I do value you," Jotham protested.

Alfric's eyes bored through him. "Then don't go!"

For one awful moment, Jotham's world stood still. He felt Alfric's pain. Alfric's father hadn't valued him. Now he thought Jotham didn't either. But was going to the border any proof of that? Surely people you value could be wrong, couldn't they?

The widow's voice echoed in Jotham's mind. *"They sought the King, and found him—as will those who seek him now."*

Jotham made his choice.

Alfric must have read it in his face. "Very well! If you don't value me, perhaps you'll value this!"

In one swift motion, Alfric seized the quilt and jerked it off the bed, sending Jotham's satchel flying.

In a rush of horror, Jotham knew just how the widow had felt at Cuthbert's. Images flashed before him: Alfric holding the Book high, the page tearing loose, Alfric crumpling it in his hand. Now, Alfric had his mother's quilt!

"Give it to me!"

As Jotham lunged forward, Alfric threw the quilt over him. A thick cotton darkness descended on Jotham. He flailed and kicked, his cries for help stifled in the quilt's muffling folds. Strong arms wrestled him to the ground. A heavy form settled on top of him. He felt hands seize his ankles, winding something tightly around them. The same hands reached under the quilt, forcing his arms behind him and binding his wrists as well.

Then for one terrifying instant, Jotham thought he felt something cold and reptilian brush against his cheek. The next moment, the quilt was thrown off and Alfric gagged him with a scarf. "That should keep you for now! I'll be back!"

Alfric seized Jotham's key off a wall hook and strode toward the door. Jotham heard it slam. The key clicked in the lock. Footsteps pounded down the stairs. Then there was silence.

Jotham was so stunned by what had just happened that at first he lay still, paralyzed by a storm of emotion. He was angry with Alfric, but angrier with himself. Hadn't he known Alfric might try to stop him? How could he have let this happen? What was it the widow had said? *"Keep your wits about you!"*

Jotham forced his mind to focus. He was bound with bed sheets. The knots were thicker than rope. He had an idea. Like a human tube, he rolled himself toward the wall. By leaning against it, he managed to slowly maneuver himself into a standing position. Reaching behind him, he felt for the key hook, slipped it into the bulge of a cloth knot, and tugged.

It took great patience, but at last Jotham felt his bonds begin to loosen. In his haste, Alfric hadn't tied the knots as well as he might. And Jotham was skillful with his hands. But time was short. Through his small round window, he could see the haze-shrouded sun dropping toward the horizon. It was setting. The Widow Nessa would be at the crossroads. How long would she wait?

At last Jotham managed to wriggle one hand free of its bindings. His spirits rose as he finished untying himself. But the locked door still stood between him and freedom.

He ran to the door and tried to force it open. It stood firm! Nothing Jotham did could budge it. There was no escape through the window, either. It was too small to squeeze through, and the ground was twenty feet below.

Jotham saw the daylight and his chances slipping away. He unlatched the window and peered out. The street looked deserted. Still, if he called, someone might hear. After what the widow had said, he hated to draw attention to himself. But he must risk it.

He opened his mouth to shout and felt something crawling up his leg. Jotham had been so intent on escaping he'd forgotten his eerie feelings. Now he realized their cause. Leering up at him was a giant frog. Jotham stared at its eyes and shuddered. That look! He'd seen it once before, in another frog, at Flotsam Manor.

The widow's voice echoed again. *"The dark prince has his watchers..."*

Jotham grabbed for the frog. It leaped aside. He heard a low growling croak. The frog was on the quilt. He dove for it and missed. As he jumped to his feet, it landed on his back. He clawed for it, but the frog clung to a spot between his shoulders that he could not reach. Jotham pressed himself against the wall, trying to rub it off. As he did, he glimpsed the lengthening twilight from the corner of his eye. He was losing precious time!

Just then, the frog let go. Jotham raced to the window, but the frog leaped ahead of him, bounding onto the sill. It crouched as if to spring right at his face. Jotham gagged in horror as his mind screamed a silent plea, *Someone, help!*

Suddenly, both he and the frog were bathed in a golden glow. Jotham had the impression of something diving downward from the sky. The frog let out a hideous guttural screech and fell backwards outside.

Suddenly, Jotham felt the brush of wings against his cheek as a soft, feathered form hurtled through the window past him into the room. He turned to behold a magnificent snow-white dove surrounded by the same soft golden glow like a halo. *It must be some strange trick of the deepening twilight,* Jotham told himself.

The bird hovered, wings beating, soft gentle eyes gazing into Jotham's own. Then it circled the room. Jotham thought it was looking for a way out. It must have become disoriented. He waved his arms, trying to guide it.

"Come on, little fellow! Go this way! The window is this way!"

Instead, the dove veered toward the door.

"No! Go back! You'll hurt yourself!"

Jotham sprang for the door. The bird flew straight toward him. In desperation, Jotham yanked the knob. A golden halo of light engulfed him—and the door swung open.

With a flutter of wings, the dove soared past him. Jotham stared after it, speechless. But the fading dusk jarred him into action. When the satchel had fallen from the bed, it had spilled its contents. Jotham swiftly repacked it. Then he turned his attention to the quilt. After what had happened, he couldn't entrust his treasure to Alfric. Luckily, there was someone else who might keep it safe for him. He knew just where to leave it so it would be found, and this place was on his way to the crossroads.

Folding the quilt, he seized his satchel, and hurried into the falling darkness.

THE WESTERN crossroads was so named because it was located just beyond the western boundary of the city. The Widow Nessa, living on the east side, had to cross Acrasia to reach it. This was not as far as one might think. The city was narrower east to west than it was north to south because it was located in an irregularly shaped valley rimmed by hills with mountains beyond. These formed a natural wall around the city—with one exception.

On the western side of Acrasia there was a gap between these mountains like the space between the thumb and forefinger of a hand. Here the main road branched from a central point, or crossroads, into many others flowing outward to the far reaches of the kingdom like so many tributaries of a river. Roads from outlying areas of Acrasia flowed into this central point as well. Here in the shadow of the nearby Fortress of Belial, the widow waited with a sinking heart.

She had arrived early for the rendezvous, her own provisions for the trip packed inside the carrying bag she normally took along on her midwife's duties. She'd been hopeful at first, but her fears grew with the lengthening shadows. Had Jotham decided not to come? Or worse, had he been found out and had some obstacle thrown in his path? Intuitively, the widow suspected the latter. But she was determined not to give up. If need be, she would stay all night on the slim chance that Jotham would appear.

The crossroads was a busy place in daylight. The clog of traffic was constant and colorfully varied. A stream of foot travelers, riders on horseback, wagons, peddlers' carts, and pack animals laden with wares flowed into and out of the city. Amid this hustle, a smaller road, not much bigger than a path, wound away from the others. It was largely untraveled except for occasional military use. This easily overlooked path was the road to the border.

If the path was hard to find in daylight, it was nearly impossible to see at night when the darkness blurred distinctive landmarks. Only someone who knew the way as well as the widow could be sure of choosing correctly. If Jotham managed to come after all and missed seeing her, he would not know which way to turn. Yet she dared not wait for him in the open. The People of the Book were forbidden outside the city limits after dark. She might be recognized since there was still a small trickle of passersby. If she were caught, the penalty would be severe.

The widow retreated to a grove of trees a few yards from the roadway. Settling herself on the ground behind a large fir tree, she peered into the blackness, pleading in her heart. *My*

Father and King, bring Jotham! Prince Morning Star, protect him!

For some indeterminate length of time, she persisted in her vigil. But the waiting and watching grew tiring, and at last she dozed. What seemed but moments later, she was startled awake by a hand shaking her shoulder.

Jotham! Her mind shouted the name even as she struggled back to consciousness. Luckily, her lips kept silent. She turned to find herself gazing into the frowning eyes of one of Prince Abaddon's soldiers.

The soldier's torch flickered in her face. "Aren't you the Widow Nessa?" he asked. "Why have you broken the law? You know the People of the Book are not allowed here at this hour!"

Cold fingers of fear grasped the widow's heart, but she struggled to keep her face and voice calm. "I did not intend to get caught here," she replied, telling part of the truth. "But I became tired and rested by this tree. A midwife doesn't always get a full night's sleep, you know."

The soldier's face softened. "I may know this better some three weeks hence. My wife will soon give birth. I had thought to ask you to attend her."

"Of course!" the widow smiled. "Pray, tell me her name."

"My wife is called Brie," said the soldier. "And I am Devlin." The soldier spoke more kindly to the widow now. "In gratitude for your consent, I will overlook what's happened here. This time, I will settle for escorting you home." His face grew stern. "But if it happens again, things will go far worse for you."

"I understand. Thank you," she murmured, relieved the matter would be dropped, yet dismayed that she must now abandon her post. Devlin led her to his horse, which stood munching the still-brown grass nearby. Having tied her bag behind the saddle, he mounted and pulled her up behind him. As they galloped back toward the city, she did not notice another shadowy form watching in despair from the cover of some bushes.

Hurrying toward their meeting place a few minutes earlier, Jotham had spotted the soldier. Slipping out of sight, he had watched the fellow check the area. Gripped by dismay, he had seen the soldier lead the widow out from behind the trees.

Alfric must have guessed the widow's involvement and reported her, Jotham reasoned. *Very likely I've just witnessed her arrest. But I can't risk returning to Acrasia. Yet I doubt I can reach the border alone. I'm not even sure which path of the crossroads leads there. What am I to do?*

Suddenly, a magnificent snow-white form fluttered out of the darkness. It circled low above him. Jotham caught his breath in amazement. It was a dove, and it looked just like the one that had flown in his window. Spreading its wings wide, it soared toward the crossroads and turned toward him, suspended in air. He fancied the bird was beckoning him! Some strange prompting bade him to follow. And having no better plan, he obeyed.

CHAPTER 6

Fateful Choices

⚜

ALFRIC HAD no clear plan when he burst seething from Jotham's room. At first, he strode the streets, blown by his emotions like debris tossed by a tornado. But as his passions began to cool, he realized he had made a terrible mistake.

"I can't hold Jotham prisoner forever," Alfric fretted to himself. "Nor do I wish to report him and get him in trouble. But he'll never listen to me now. Not after how I've treated him. And I can't say I blame him."

The dreaded voice of Alfric's father screamed inside his head. *So you flubbed it again, eh? Just like always! Can't you ever do anything right? You're hopeless!*

Alfric clutched at his head as if to squeeze the voice into silence. *No! I'm not hopeless!* He breathed deeply to calm himself. Surely there was someone who could reason with Jotham. What of Magnus? But no, telling him might cost Jotham his post. Who else?

Gwyneth! The name flashed like a beacon in Alfric's mind. Surely she would have some influence with Jotham! She would not be at Cuthbert's this early. But she might be at home. With new purpose, Alfric turned his steps northward and set off in haste.

THE AREA WHERE Gwyneth lived was officially named the Northern Heights. But the people of Withershins called it the Heights of Power. These six hills on the northern boundary of Acrasia were home to the leading luminaries in the realm—high-ranking army officers, chief advisors, and leading nobles. The elevation of their houses reflected their position in Abaddon's constellation of power. Rising stars moved upward. Fading stars moved down—or to the less prestigious Southern Heights across the city.

Abaddon's palace sat like a crown on top of the highest hill. Just below it was Bogdan's estate. Alfric had never been inside, but he had seen it from a distance. He earned his livelihood tutoring the children of Acrasia's elite. Many of his pupils lived on these heights, and one on this very hill, so he knew it well.

More important, Alfric thought to himself as he hurried on his way, *the soldiers patrolling the area know me. Still, will they let me pass all the way to Bogdan's gates? And if not, how will I get there?*

"Make way!"

Alfric jumped at the shrill command. Then he smiled. He knew that voice.

"Stand aside, I say!"

Instead, Alfric turned to confront the speaker, a scowling twelve-year-old boy. He was sitting beside a servant on a horse-drawn cart. His dark eyes blazed, his red hair flamed, and one arm stuck straight out, finger pointing imperiously. Alfric stared back, undaunted. "Take care how you talk to your teacher, Master Edan. I must soon give your father an account of your progress. And I fear I must tell him you are lagging in your manners... not to mention your studies!"

The boy's hand faltered. "No, don't! I... I didn't know who

it was."

Alfric looked at him sternly. "Then you shouldn't have spoken so. But I shall overlook it if you do me a small favor."

The boy's eyes narrowed. "What?"

"You must take me up the hill all the way to General Bogdan's grounds."

Edan's gaze grew calculating. "Then you must tell Father I'm doing quite well in my letters."

"I will tell him you're improving. And see that you do," retorted Alfric.

"Very well," the boy gave in grudgingly. "But you'll have to ride in back. And don't crush the eggs!"

Alfric clambered into the wagon, which was loaded with foodstuffs and other supplies, and squeezed himself down among the bundles. It was not the most comfortable ride. It seemed as if the packages around him and the road below were having a contest to see which could pummel him most. Once, trying to steady himself with his hand, he did crush an egg, mashing yolk and white together in a gooey ooze. Try as he might to wipe it off, a residue stuck to him with slimy determination.

Still, the trip was much quicker than it would have been on foot. *Almost too quick*, Alfric felt, having second thoughts. Was it wise to confide in Gwyneth, after all? What if she felt compelled to tell her father? The mighty Bogdan stood second in power only to Abaddon himself. His contempt for the People of the Book was well known. What would he do to Jotham if he found out?

And what will Bogdan think of me? Alfric wondered uneasily. *What will Gwyneth think? I have been like a brother to Jotham. Will she blame me for what's happened? Will telling her dash this new hope I have of winning her? Or will she be flattered that I seek her help? Besides, where else can I turn?*

Preoccupied with this inner wrestling, Alfric now lost

track of time and their progress. With a sudden jolt, he real-ized the cart had stopped. Bogdan's massive iron gates loomed before them, caught in the last fading rays of twilight.

Alfric jumped to the ground. "Thank you, Master Edan. You'd best be going. They'll be looking for you at home."

The servant lifted the horses' reins, but Edan stayed his hand. He eyed Alfric curiously. "Not so fast. First tell me your business here."

Alfric had expected the question. "I see that you have an inquiring mind," he replied. "But would you not rather ask how much I will shorten your next lesson in gratitude for your help?"

The boy's eyes gleamed. "How much, then? By half?"

"A fair bargain," said Alfric. "But it will be lengthened by each moment you tarry!"

Edan seized the reins from the startled servant and shouted to the horses. They sprang forward. For a moment, the cart lurched out of control. Alfric leaped aside as the servant grabbed the reins back, turned the horses' heads, and depart-ed in a clatter of flying hooves and dust.

Alfric strode up to the gates. A pair of sentries stood watch. "Is Gwyneth at home?" he demanded. "If so, I must see her!"

The guards eyed him scornfully. "You are not the first poor, drooling fool to say so," scoffed one.

"Nor the first to be turned away," sneered the other.

They drew their swords. Alfric stood his ground with a bravado born of desperation. "If you wish to avoid her dis-pleasure, you'd best take her my message. Tell her Alfric has come with grave news of her friend Jotham. He is in great peril and needs her assistance."

The sentries now seemed less sure of themselves. They whispered together, then turned to Alfric once more. "Very well," said one. "I'll inform her while my companion guards you."

The soldier who spoke slipped inside the gate past a life-size statue of Bogdan on horseback and vanished into the greenery beyond.

Alfric stared after him, his mind swept up for the moment by the grandeur before him. The magnificent grounds of Bogdan's estate bore powerful witness to his vast wealth and unparalleled prominence. Scattered among the towering trees and manicured shrubs were sculptures celebrating his prowess in battle. Choice horses were housed in his own private stables. The dwelling rising above this small empire was built of a rare peach marble. Its sweeping columns gave an appearance not only of elegance, but of enduring strength.

Alfric thought surely nothing could shake the foundation of such a splendid structure. Yet it seemed the People of the Book believed otherwise. They claimed Bogdan's home, Abaddon's palace, and indeed the whole Northern Heights, rested on unstable ground. According to their lore, one day a vast earthquake would shake these mighty hills and topple all that was built upon them. A great crater would open in the earth and suck everything into its yawning abyss, even Prince Abaddon himself.

Alfric's father had heard of this strange belief directly from a Person of the Book. He had told it to Alfric as proof of their delusions. Now Jotham had fallen prey to these delusions!

"Pardon, sir!"

The voice that intruded on Alfric's thoughts was breathless and panting. The soldier had returned, and his manner had changed completely. "Gwyneth bids me bring you at once. This way, please."

Alfric followed the soldier. The grounds passed by him in a blur. The soldier led Alfric up a short flight of broad peach-colored marble steps and through an ornately carved wooden door. Then he retreated, leaving Alfric alone in a vast entrance hall.

Alfric's eyes roved the room. He was awestruck. Never had he set foot in a hall like this! The floors were inlaid with marble. The walls were paneled with rare and exotic woods and hung with costly tapestries. Suspended from the ceiling was a crystal chandelier, the light from its host of candles dancing on its facets like an endless multitude of fireflies.

But what most captured his gaze was a large oval mirror. It was mounted on the wall directly opposite the door. On its dark wooden frame, above the glass, was carved a likeness of Gwyneth's face. Never had he seen any carving so lifelike! He drew closer until his own face was reflected below hers. For one glorious instant he stood completely still, drinking in the image.

"Alfric!"

He looked up to see Gwyneth rushing toward him down a sweeping flight of curving marble stairs. "What is it? What's happened to Jotham?" she demanded anxiously.

In his mental turmoil, Alfric had failed to plan what he would say. The story came out in a rush. But Gwyneth responded just as he had hoped.

"You have done well to come here. I will go with you at once and speak to Jotham myself. I shall soon persuade him of the utter folly of his quest! But we must keep this to ourselves. No one else must find out, least of all my father! His disdain for the Book and its followers knows no bounds. He'd renounce anyone who embraced it, even his closest friend." She did not add that her father had once done that very thing.

"Yes, of course! I'll tell no one!" Alfric's voice was emphatic.

Gwyneth snatched a bell from an entry table beneath the mirror and rang it. A servant appeared. "Call for the coach," she commanded. "And fetch my wrap."

Moments later they were speeding toward Odd End,

perched opposite each other on the red velvet coach seats. They said little, lost in their own thoughts. Alfric, dazed by the events of the past few hours, felt as though he was in a waking dream.

That dream became a waking nightmare when the coach arrived at Odd End. They found Jotham's door unlocked. The prisoner had vanished. Alfric felt like a fool in front of Gwyneth . . . a fool and a failure!

"He couldn't have escaped! I don't believe it!" Alfric kicked the discarded bed sheets in frustration. His eyes scanned the room. "His satchel is gone. He must have left for the border."

"We shouldn't assume so yet," Gwyneth frowned. "The hour is late. He doesn't know the way. Perhaps he's gone to someone for aid—a Person of the Book."

"He knows only one," said Alfric grimly. "The Widow Nessa."

"If he's with her, we will find him," cried Gwyneth. "To the coach!"

THE WIDOW was deep in the Book when the pounding invaded her consciousness. Who was beating on the door? It was not that long since Devlin had left her at her gate. Had the soldier returned . . . and if so, why? "All right! Patience! I'm coming!" She hurried to the door and flung it open.

Alfric towered above her like a raging volcano. "Where's Jotham? What have you done with him?"

His words stunned the widow. Then she felt a surge of joy. So she had been right. Jotham had been detained. But he must have managed to break free. Now she must delay his pursuers.

"Answer me!" Alfric's voice was strident now. "I warn you, don't try to hide him! I have powerful help!"

"Yes, I can see that." The widow turned to Gwyneth. "Greetings Gwyneth, daughter of Bogdan." Her gaze widened to include them both. "I fear I must disappoint you. I have not seen Jotham tonight," she said truthfully. "You must forgive me if I don't invite you in," the widow added shrewdly. "The hour is late and I am very tired."

Her words had just the effect she hoped on the two young people. Suspicions heightened, they demanded to search the widow's cottage. Feigning reluctance, she let them enter, knowing full well their fruitless efforts would buy Jotham precious time.

"It's no use. He's not here," Alfric groaned after they had scoured the place. "He has started for the border. We're too late!"

Gwyneth's eyes flashed. "No we're not. He's on foot and alone. He can still be caught."

She bolted out the door, Alfric at her heels. The widow stood watching as their coach melted into the darkness. Then she closed the door softly and moved to the painting of Prince Morning Star. The Prince's expression was a portrait of utmost humility, yet utmost majesty. Looking at it, the widow's own face filled with tenderness and hope.

"I feel in my heart that Jotham has indeed begun his journey," she murmured. "And he, too, has powerful help. That help will guide him on his way and hover closest when he feels most alone."

⌒═══╫═══⌒

NEVER HAD Jotham felt more alone than on this dark and misty road guided only by a sliver of moonlight and the small torch he had brought to light his path. The dove had vanished as suddenly as it appeared. He wondered now if he had been mistaken about the bird. Perhaps it had not meant to lead him after all. Suppose this road did not take him to the border?

Or suppose it did? Was there really a Prince Morning Star? If so, would he heed Jotham's call as the widow had promised? What would this Prince be like? What gift would he offer that Jotham must receive in order to be adopted? And if Jotham did not take the gift, what would happen to him then?

The questions chilled him. He shivered, though this night was not nearly as cold as the one before. The snow had all melted. But the dampness in the air seemed to increase as he trudged onward. So did the wind. He had more than one momentary fright as strange "somethings" brushed against his cheeks. But he soon saw that they were only stray leaves blown by the rising gusts. He felt like one of those stray leaves, cut loose from his past with no certain shelter from life's storms. In fact, one such storm might well be brewing, judging by the distant lightning flashes on the horizon.

"Snow one night, and a thunderstorm the next!" Jotham mused. "How odd!" Yet it was hardly surprising. The weather in Withershins was frequently strange and unpredictable. Jotham often wondered if nature itself had somehow gone awry. "And it is bound to be even worse on the queer path I now travel!" he shuddered.

THE WIND WHIPPED Gwyneth's hair back, slapping Alfric's face as he slipped inside Bogdan's stables behind her. Though the thunder was still faint to his ears, the horses' hearing was keener. They shifted nervously, tossing their heads. Undaunted, Gwyneth grabbed a saddle and entered a stall.

"Steady, Astra," she whispered, flinging the saddle on the back of a sleek chestnut mare with a white star emblazoned on her forehead.

"Which horse shall I take?" Alfric asked.

Gwyneth glanced back, scowling. "None. My coach will see you home. As I've told you, it's best that I go after Jotham alone. My mount is both swift and steady of temper. I shall soon overtake him and convince him to return with me."

Alfric bristled. "And have no one to protect you from the dangers of the road? I think *not!*"

"I am quite able to protect myself," Gwyneth flared. "And besides, you would only slow me down. No horse can keep up with mine except Titan." Gwyneth gestured to a black stallion in a nearby stall. "No one but my father can ride him, even in calm weather. You could never manage him!"

"You'll soon see what I can manage!" Alfric's words caught Gwyneth by surprise. Before she could stop him, he had thrown the stall open and leaped on the stallion's bare back. The animal plunged from the enclosure, bucking and rearing. To his credit, Alfric stayed on longer than Gwyneth expected. It took two full minutes for the twisting, churning horse to hurl him to the ground in a crescendo of kicks and whinnies.

The sound of hoofbeats thundered above the black steed's triumphant snorts. Bogdan burst through the stable doors astride a towering Palomino stallion. As Alfric scrambled to his feet, miraculously unharmed, Bogdan leaped down and seized him by the arm. Though thirty years Alfric's senior, he was fit and firm with a grip like iron.

"Who are you? What is the meaning of this?" Bogdan barked.

"Please, Father," gasped Gwyneth, "his name is Alfric and..."

"Alfric, son of Killian?" These words were spoken by a second rider who now galloped up to join Bogdan.

Though they'd never met, Alfric knew the face. Its image was everywhere. One glimpse sent him falling prostrate. "Yes,

Sire," he whispered.

"Rise!"

The quaking Alfric struggled to his feet beneath the burning gaze of Prince Abaddon himself.

Gwyneth, who saw the prince often, simply curtsied politely. While outwardly calm, her mind was racing. Her father would doubtless question why her horse was saddled. She would simply tell him . . .

"Young man, what is your business with my daughter?" Bogdan directed his question to Alfric.

Alfric responded before Gwyneth could stop him. "I meant no harm. I only sought her help."

"The matter must be dire to ride forth in this weather!" Bogdan's scowl encompassed them both now. "Nor shall Gwyneth engage in such folly, especially now that I am here to stop her. If need be, I shall handle this myself. What has happened?"

Gwyneth bit her lip. "The matter is private. I cannot say."

Abaddon dismounted and swept forward, eyes boring into Alfric's head. "Then perhaps you will tell us. Speak up! I command you!"

Alfric hesitated. He had given Gwyneth a promise of silence. Yet how could he refuse a direct order from his ruler? He swallowed hard. "A friend of ours has been deluded by the lies in the Book. He believes that he can be adopted by some King. We think he may have started for the border and we hoped we might still stop him."

Bogdan's face grew darker than the sky outside. "Why bother? The dangers of the road will soon finish this traitor. His death will be no great loss."

"Yes, it will!" Gwyneth's outburst took Bogdan by surprise. Her next words surprised him even more. "He has great talent. It was he who carved my likeness on the new mirror you like so well."

Alfric's jaw dropped. "You don't mean . . . the mirror in the entrance hall?" Gwyneth's carved face danced before his eyes. His mind reeled with shock. Why had Jotham never mentioned this?

Bogdan, too, was taken aback. "The one I commissioned from Magnus? You must be mistaken. He crafted it himself."

"Magnus meant to," said Gwyneth, "but when we spoke of it, Jotham stood nearby. I sought his ideas for the carving. And he asked, 'What does your father love best?' 'Me, of course,' I replied. By the next day, he had drawn my face. He thought Magnus might carve it, but I asked Jotham to try his own hand. You know the result."

All this time, Abaddon had listened intently, saying nothing. The others, focused elsewhere, did not catch the flicker that now crossed his face. It was a look of dark dismay mixed with utmost evil. It vanished in an instant, masked by a feigned concern. "This must be Jotham, the orphan lad!"

Bogdan's eyes widened in amazement. "You know of him, Your Highness?"

Abaddon nodded gravely. "I have sometimes followed his progress. He shows great promise. He would be a loss indeed. And I suspect he is more victim than traitor. Having no family, he would be ready prey for the false hopes of that accursed Book."

Bogdan's face softened. "If you wish me to go after him, Sire . . ."

The prince's answer surprised them all. "I will go myself," he told Bogdan. "Though your horses are swift, I have swifter means of travel. You must wait here with Gwyneth until my return."

Abaddon turned an approving gaze on Alfric. "And you must wait here with them," he said in a show of kindness. "You have proved yourself loyal and your judgment sound. I know that you seek to serve me and gain your birthright. We must talk of that, and of your future, when I return."

"Yes, Your Majesty," gasped Alfric, his heart leaping.

Abaddon turned abruptly and swept out through the stable door. The others did not see what happened next. A bolt of lightning flashed across the sky. For an instant, Abaddon stood framed in its jagged light. And then . . . he simply vanished.

CHAPTER 7

Beasts in the Shadows

‿⟊‿

JOTHAM PUSHED gamely onward against the now gale-force gusts. He had long since placed his torch back in his satchel. He dared not risk having it torn from his hand or soaked beyond use by the storm. He might have even greater need of it tomorrow. Based on what he'd heard, the distance from Acrasia to the border was at least a full day's journey. It would be night again before he reached Dominus...if he reached it at all.

Lightning flashed. Thunder pealed, as though the storm itself were roaring in cruel laughter at his plight. Unseen clouds cloaked the last small slice of moonlight from view. Total blackness descended along with a downpour of rain.

Above the sound of rushing water rose an eerie shrieking howl. Icy fingers of fear clutched at Jotham's throat. He fought to shake off the tightness. "It's just the wind," he tried to assure himself. Yet he had the uneasy feeling something else was out there. Jotham shivered despite the water flooding over him. If only he could see!

As if in response, another huge bolt of lightning crackled

across the sky. In its luridly grinning glare, a new horror was revealed. A vast formless monster roiled up from the bowels of the storm, looming in the darkness, threatening to engulf him.

The lightning faded in a clap of thunder. Blackness fell once more. Jotham shuddered. *Not* seeing the monster was worse! He wished to brace himself, to face it squarely, to die fighting it bravely—if die he must. But thus blinded, he was helpless prey. Even if he was on the road to the border, it would do him no good. Any instant the lurking beast would pounce and finish him!

Lightning slashed the night yet a third time. The beast was nearer now, sweeping toward him like a raging creature-tornado. As this latest flash faded, he imagined himself being sucked into the monster's vortex. "Help!" he cried, not expecting a response. Who was there to aid him? He just hoped his end would come quickly.

What came instead was a glow of light dropping downward from the heavens. At first it seemed like a shooting star. Then to Jotham's amazement, he saw it was a bird. In a blur of white wings, it soared out of the darkness straight toward where the creature had been.

One last blazing bolt sliced through the blackness, spotlighting bird and beast on a collision course. As Jotham stared in horrified fascination, the bird flew straight through the monster! Then suddenly there was no monster, only raindrops and the bird glowing at him in the darkness. It was a dove!

Jotham stood transfixed. A strange impression seized him. Were this dove, the bird at the crossroads, and the one in his room all one and the same? But how could that be? And what was this strange glow that framed the bird like a halo? Had the lightning flashes left some lingering effect on Jotham's vision? Yet the bird in his room had been framed by a halo too.

Blinking, Jotham gazed at the dove again. The glow remained. For an instant the bird hovered, fixing its gentle gaze on him. Then it soared upward, vanishing into the sky. As it did so, the cloud curtain parted just enough to provide a sliver of moonlight once more.

Feeling somewhat relieved, Jotham pushed ahead. So the monster was only a mirage in the mist, a formless incarnation of his fears! How grateful he was that the dove had revealed the truth!

A sudden memory jolted Jotham. What was it the widow had warned about Abaddon and his forces? *"They will try every means to frighten and turn back would-be travelers."* This must be the road to the border after all, and the monster had been one such trick. Jotham shivered, his mind turning against his will to the ruler whose nature and powers were shrouded in mystery even to those who knew him best.

One thing seemed certain to all who lived in Withershins. Though Abaddon seemed human, he could not be mortal. After all, he had ruled ever since the long, long before times. And though he had fought in many a battle, death seemed not to touch him. Historical parchments were rife with tales of swords and spears passing through him. Yet they had not harmed Abaddon nor even drawn blood. Nor had plague or fever or any infirmity ever laid him low. Why, no one knew, and no one dared to ask.

Then there were Abaddon's strange powers. It was rumored that he could appear and disappear at will. Some said he was able to assume other shapes. There was even talk of vast unseen forces he could marshal against those who opposed him. It was almost as if he lived simultaneously in this world and in some other dimension.

And yet, mused Jotham, *if Abaddon and his forces have been at work this night, they have not prevailed against one small dove. I wonder why?*

ELYMAS THE frog, watching from the shadows, well knew the dove's great power. His bulging eyes gleamed at the figure whose black robes blended with the night. "You see, Sire? It is as I said. Great wings of protection shield the boy. Surely you do not fault me now."

"If you had watched him more closely, you leather-skinned lout, it might not have come to this," his master snapped. "But the journey is far from over. I shall have my chance at him. The storm will soon pass, but the battle still rages. We will yet win."

"WE WILL YET win!" the widow murmured in her cottage far away. "Though I could not go with Jotham, I can battle here. I am the King's child. He will hear me. His Book says so, and it does not lie."

She bowed her head. "Oh, King and Father, hear my plea. Bring Jotham safely through the storm. Guide him in the wilderness. Lead him to Prince Morning Star and prepare his heart to receive the gift."

AT LAST, THE rain stopped. The ground was soaked, but Jotham's weary legs could go no farther. Sinking down at the side of the road, he fumbled in his satchel for bread. Swaying from fatigue, he broke off a morsel and raised it to his lips.

Suddenly, the bread slipped from his hand. But it did not fall. It floated. It was bread no longer. In the air before Jotham a banquet was spread: kidney pie, rare prime rib, goose-liver paté, peach custard. He reached for the food, but it drifted away down the road, back toward Acrasia. Voices called from the darkness: those of Alfric and Gwyneth and Magnus. "Come back!" Hands beckoned. Jotham wavered. He moved to follow.

Suddenly he recalled the widow's words. *"And though their evil ruler strove to hold them captive still, some saw the truth and fled."*

As if wresting himself from the grip of some mighty, invisible chain, Jotham turned away and took a halting step toward the border. He found his path blocked by a shop standing in the road. Letters blazed from its signpost: "Jotham's Woodcraft." All around him a multitude of voices rose in chorus, praising his work. One voice sounded above the rest. "All this can be yours, and more, if you will just return."

Jotham longed to obey. He could have his own shop. He would be recognized and honored. What could satisfy him more?

"And this great King will be a Father to those who have no father."

The Book's words echoed in Jotham's soul, stirring his deepest longings. With sudden resolve, he strode toward the shop as if to mow it down. It vanished, replaced by a regal figure in a white robe. Jotham knew him from the widow's portrait. It was Prince Morning Star. The Prince stepped forward, arms outstretched in welcome.

Jotham's own question to the widow echoed in his mind. *"To be free one must accept a gift? What gift?"*

As if sensing his thoughts, the Prince held out a beautiful golden box. Jotham's heart sang. He reached to take it.

Then he heard Alfric's voice in his head. *"I have told you the Book is nothing but lies and nonsense!"*

Even as the words were spoken, the box became a frog. Its eyes bulged with evil. Now it spoke, not with Alfric's voice, but its own guttural croak. "It's a trick! There is no King! Fly while you can, you fool!"

"Keep your wits about you!" The widow's words shouted in his memory.

Jotham snapped awake. He lay pitched forward on the damp road. His crust of bread floated in a rain puddle beside him. Dawn streaked over the horizon. He must have dozed. It had all been a dream.

Or had it? For the barest instant, from the corner of his eye, Jotham thought he glimpsed the leering face of a giant frog. It was gone in an eye-blink. But the crawling on his skin remained. Every nerve end tingling, Jotham struggled to his feet, seized his satchel, and pressed on again, not even stopping to eat.

The morning light revealed that Jotham was surrounded by a vast wilderness. The trees and shrubs were a tangle of strange twisted shapes. Jotham fancied that they were woven into an evil net that some unseen hand might fling over him without warning.

The wind had died. The air was thick with a menacing stillness. But it was not silent. A strange snapping and crackling filled his ears, keeping pace with his own hurrying footsteps. When he stopped, it did also, as if the sound was stalking him. Yet when he forced his weary eyes to scan the endless grayness, he saw nothing and no one.

Jotham thought of the frog, and terror gripped him, more paralyzing than before. But then he recalled the dove and the false monster in the storm. Perhaps these mysterious noises were equally harmless, made by some small creatures native to this bleak terrain. Jotham pushed his fears aside. He kept walking.

Though the strange sounds continued, nothing else went amiss. Jotham took a greater interest in his surroundings. Suddenly, he saw something that made him gasp in wonder.

Peeking out from beneath a twisted bush was a brilliant splash of color, red with a hint of blue and yellow. Having grown up in the country, he was familiar with wildflowers. He thought perhaps some seeds had been blown here by the wind and had somehow taken root in this unlikely landscape.

Curious, Jotham stepped off the path to take a closer look. But his eyes had fooled him. The flowers were farther off the path than he had thought. He must go a few more paces... and a few more still.

Only then did Jotham begin to guess that it was not his eyes that deceived him. The color itself was moving, luring him from the road. Normally, he would have known this at once, but his brain was sluggish from exhaustion. No more! An alarm sounded deep within him. *Run!*

It sounded too late. Even as he turned, he felt something loop around his foot. He looked down to see himself wrapped in the brilliantly colored coils of an enormous snake. The creature raised its head to strike.

"Noooooooo!" The cry ripped from Jotham's throat. He braced for the tear of the snake's teeth. Instead, he felt his leg released. Looking down, he saw the snake whip aside as if to flee. Jotham spied a swirling funnel of wind spinning toward the creature. Jotham caught a glimpse of a glow in its center, like the halo of the dove. Then the funnel lifted the snake high, flinging it down headfirst upon a large rock.

Seizing his chance, Jotham fled toward the road, not stopping to look back. If he had, an odd sight would have greeted him. The creature reared up once more, eyes flaming in fury from its crushed head... then simply melted into nothingness.

From then on, Jotham kept to the road. He saw no more snakes nor any other creatures on or off the path. Yet the noises persisted, and there seemed an odd heaviness around him, like the air itself was turning solid. It seemed to form a wall of resistance straining to hold him back. But each time he thought he could go no further, something sliced through this strange wall and made a way for him.

"OH KING, your Book is a sharpened sword! May its truth cut Jotham free!" cried the widow urgently. The white-haired man beside her read aloud from its pages, as if slashing with a weapon. He had come to visit the widow in her cottage and had stayed to labor alongside her.

"What is your sense of the battle, Maldwyn?" she asked him when at last he paused.

Maldwyn's voice was grave. "Though Jotham makes progress, I perceive the struggle is great. And opposition will grow as he nears the border. His greatest danger lies ahead. But we will fight with him!"

BY NIGHTFALL, Jotham had managed to put the wilderness behind him. The strange sounds were left behind, also. Now the road wound its way between thick shrubs and ferns. *It can't be many more hours to the border*, he thought. Fearing to attract unwanted attention, he refrained from lighting his torch. Despite a thickening fog, for the moment the moon was still bright enough to guide him.

Nor did Jotham pause for food, though he'd eaten only a few bites all day. His appetite had left him as anticipation heightened. Would the fairy tale come true? Would Morning Star heed his call? What mysterious gift of adoption would he offer? And if Jotham took it, would a great King welcome him as a son? What would this King be like?

Suddenly, a figure in a shining crown swept out of the

darkness. His face was kindly, his arms outstretched. Jotham's heart leaped with gladness. Had the King somehow learned of his journey and come to meet him?

Pulsing with eagerness, Jotham quickened his step. All at once, the face before him changed. It grew cold and angry. The crowned figure glared at Jotham in loathing. Jotham froze, Alfric's words ringing in his ears. *"Be glad you never had a father! He could have been like mine!"*

Now the figure spoke in an icy voice that stabbed Jotham to the core. "Lowly orphan! Why have you come?"

Jotham swallowed hard. "If it please Your Majesty, I heard you might want to adopt me."

The figure laughed cruelly. "What would I want with you? Be gone!"

Jotham took a step backward. Tears choked his throat. He had been prepared to find no king, but not this king! He had none of the attributes the Book or the widow had described! Jotham strained to remember the widow's paintings. How had the King looked there?

Then Jotham's breath caught in his throat as the truth slammed into his consciousness. *There had been no King in the paintings!* The widow's voice echoed in Jotham's mind. *"He can't be looked upon, or drawn."*

The film of falsehood dropped from Jotham's eyes. He glared defiantly at the figure before him. "The King cannot be seen! You are not the King! Nor will you keep me from him!"

Jotham took a step forward. The strange figure towered higher, lip curling, eyes flashing scornfully. "Insolent fool! Do you think you can withstand me?"

A sense of overwhelming dread flooded over Jotham. He felt he could not prevail... at least not alone. A thought sprang into his mind. *If only the dove were here!*

Suddenly, it was. Swooping down from the heavens, it

darted between Jotham and the false king. The glow surrounding the dove brightened to a blinding light. Jotham turned his head to avoid the glare, hearing as he did a dreadful sound, part hiss and part snarl. When he dared to look again, the false king was gone.

Jotham might have wondered greatly at this, but he had no time to do so. A new figure hurried toward him out of the fog. The dove turned and darted at Jotham, startling him. He stumbled backwards, tumbling off the road and landing in a heap, his satchel flying from his hand.

Fortunately, Jotham's fall was muffled and cushioned by mossy ferns. As he peered cautiously from among the fronds, a soldier with a lantern strode into view. "Perhaps your ears were playing tricks. I see nothing," the fellow shouted.

A second soldier lumbered out of the darkness. Jotham shuddered. There was something dreadfully familiar in the brutish stride. The soldier's voice confirmed Jotham's suspicions. Here, by some awful chance, stood his old tormentor, Ragnar.

"My ears are never wrong. We must investigate further," Ragnar barked to his companion.

"We must obey our orders," the other countered. "We have been commanded never to leave the guardhouse unattended!"

"Go back then, Cadel. I'll search alone," growled Ragnar.

"Not as long as I'm in charge," Cadel snapped. "This place is frightful enough without getting separated."

"Just a little farther and I'll give it up," Ragnar wheedled.

"Oh, all right!"

Jotham lay still, barely breathing, as the lantern's light passed over his hiding place. A moment later, Ragnar's cry of triumph rang out of the mist.

"Look here! A satchel!" A pair of eyes peered into Jotham's own. Had the soldiers found him?

No! Wings brushed Jotham's face. It was the dove! An almost audible voice vibrated through Jotham's being. *Now!*

Jotham sprang forward after the bird, bursting through the fog, flinging himself past a wooden guardhouse toward a high stone wall. Behind him, the soldiers turned and gave chase. Their feet pounded in Jotham's ears, coming closer, closer. He reached the wall and frantically clawed his way up the chinks in the rocks.

The guards were directly under him now. Lantern light swept the wall. He heard someone climbing below. As his fingers reached the wall's top, a hand seized his leg. Its cruel grip tightened, pulling him down. Against his will he turned.

The face below him broke into a gaping grin. "Is it Jotham?" Ragnar chortled in evil delight. "Well, well! So the woodcrafting wonder is a traitor! You cost me some irksome hours with a broom when last I saw you. And now I shall answer each broom stroke with the lash of a whip on your hide!"

Ragnar howled in glee, unleashing a gust of the old familiar foul breath into Jotham's face. The stench ignited a fierce fire in Jotham's breast. He would not be this brute's whipping post! In one last supreme burst of effort, he wrenched free, flung himself over the wall, and landed sprawling on the ground below.

For an endless moment, Jotham lay still, unable to move, the wind knocked out of him. He felt certain that at any second the guards would be upon him. At last he managed to raise his head . . . just as a hand reached over the wall. He was finished!

But no! Just as quickly, the hand was yanked back. A voice broke the stillness.

"Leave him, Ragnar! Why risk our lives by chasing after this fool? Let whatever horror lurks beyond these stones take vengeance for you! It will punish him far worse, and finish him also!"

"I suppose you're right," Jotham heard Ragnar answer. His voice sounded somewhat regretful. Nonetheless, two pairs of footsteps receded. The soldiers, at least, would not pose any further threat.

Jotham struggled upright. The dove had once more vanished. Beyond him, the ground sloped downward toward some structure he could not quite distinguish. With rising excitement—and fear—Jotham walked forward. Was it to his doom, as the soldier claimed? Or was it to deliverance, as the widow said? Jotham knew he would find out soon—very soon!

CHAPTER 8

Confrontation at the Bridge

❦

HEART POUNDING, Jotham picked his way down the slope as if descending into some vast pit. Fog and silence closed over him, swallowing him up. The grim words of Ragnar's fellow guard echoed in his mind. *"Let whatever horror lurks beyond these stones take vengeance for you!"*

Alfric's warnings bubbled up from Jotham's memory. As he reached the bottom of the slope, Jotham wavered for an instant. Then the widow's voice rang in his head, drowning out the others. *"To become a child of the King you need only go to the border, call for Prince Morning Star, and receive his gift."*

Taking a deep breath, Jotham called into the moonlit mist. "Prince..."

"Go no further!" thundered a voice at his elbow.

Jotham spun around. He stood transfixed at the sight of the face before him. He had seen it countless times on coins and flags and frozen statues, but this was no frozen statue. "Abaddon!" he gasped.

The prince moved swiftly, blocking Jotham's way. "Forsake this madness and return with me! I command you!"

Jotham's knees quivered, but his feet stood firm. He had come too far. He would not turn back now. He stared into Abaddon's eyes, unflinching, determined. "Let me go!"

"Do you know what awaits you? You are making a terrible mistake," the evil ruler argued. "The King beyond my lands is harsh and demanding and cares little for his subjects. But I care for the least of mine. Who do you think secured your post in Magnus's shop?"

Jotham felt a sudden shock of comprehension. "It was you who recommended me?"

Abaddon's eyes gleamed. "Indeed! I keep a watchful eye on those with talent. Now return to serve me and enjoy my favor. You are young. Others have deceived you. This will not be held against you. Come, my boy. I have always tried to make my subjects happy. What is it you want that you do not have?"

A wave of longing surged through Jotham. "A father," he sighed.

Abaddon's words poured over Jotham like syrup. "I could be a father to you, my boy. And doubtless a far better father than the one you lost."

The words sent a chill up Jotham's spine and an image spinning into his brain. He saw his mother rising up from her sickbed, gasping with her dying breath. *Your father was a good man!*

Jotham turned burning eyes on the prince. "I want nothing from you except my freedom!"

Abaddon feigned surprise. "What do you mean? You are free already. You have always been free."

"Then stand aside!" Jotham blazed. Staring past Abaddon, he lifted his voice to a shout. "Prince Morning Star!"

For an instant, Jotham's heart stood still. Then it nearly burst from his chest as a majestic, white-robed figure emerged from the mist a short distance away. A glow surrounded the figure, as it had the dove. Jotham knew him at once. He looked just as the widow had drawn him. Yet there was a presence about him that no brush could capture.

"Jotham! I knew you would come some day!" Morning Star cried joyfully.

How different was this white-robed Prince from the false prince on the road! Jotham tried to dodge Abaddon and run toward him, but Abaddon grabbed his hand in a viselike grip. "Foolish lad!" he snarled. "You cannot go to him. There is a chasm."

With his free hand, Abaddon seized a stone and tossed it into the blackness. The sound of rock hitting rock echoed up from far below. Jotham realized to his dismay that, this time, Abaddon spoke the truth.

Prince Morning Star's voice pierced Jotham's fears. "There is indeed a vast chasm between our two kingdoms. But you can cross safely. Behold!" Morning Star raised his arm. A bright light radiated from it, revealing that the structure Jotham had seen from a distance was a wooden bridge.

Jotham took a step toward it.

Abaddon's grip tightened. "Do not listen. The bridge is faulty. It will not hold your weight."

Morning Star called to Jotham again. "It will. I know. I built it myself. Trust me!"

Jotham struggled to pull free of Abaddon's grasp. Morning Star's voice grew stern and commanding. "Release him, Abaddon! I have paid his ransom. You know that."

Morning Star lifted his arm again. A blinding light flashed from it, striking Abaddon. As he recoiled, shrieking with pain and fury, his clawlike grip on Jotham's arm loosened for the merest instant. In that moment, Jotham pulled free and lunged toward the bridge. Abaddon sprang after him, but a second blast of light from Morning Star knocked him backwards, toppling him to the ground in a crumpled heap.

In seconds, Jotham reached the bridge's edge. He hesitated, then stepped onto its planks. They held. He took another step, and another. He began to walk, then run toward the outstretched arms of Prince Morning Star. With a burst of joy, he flung himself into the Prince's waiting embrace.

Morning Star held him close. Jotham felt an indescribable warmth envelop him, engulfing every fiber of his being. For one incredible, eternal moment, Jotham drank in a depth of love he had never known.

At last, Jotham raised his brimming eyes to Morning Star's shining ones, words tumbling from him in his eagerness. "Is it true? Can I really be a child of the King?"

Morning Star beamed down at him, and the glow on the Prince's face seemed brighter than a thousand suns. "Yes, Jotham." The Prince's eyes grew probing. "Are you ready to be brought before him?"

Jotham opened his mouth to say "yes," but something in the Prince's gaze made him hesitate. He glanced down at himself. In a crush of despair, Jotham saw what until then he had been too preoccupied to notice. The journey had taken a terrible toll. His clothes were caked with mud and moss; they were torn and tattered, grimy and smelly. Nor did he have others. His satchel was gone. He hung his head, too ashamed now even to look Morning Star in the face.

"I cannot go like this. I am filthy," he groaned.

Morning Star took Jotham's face gently in his hands. "I know. That is why I must give you my robe. Will you take it?"

Hearing his words, Jotham recalled what the widow had read from the Book. *"... go to the border, call for Prince Morning Star, and receive his gift."*

"Is . . . is that the gift I must accept to be adopted?" Jotham stammered.

Morning Star smiled. "Yes."

"Stop, Jotham!" Abaddon's voice boomed harshly from across the bridge. He had risen to his feet and stood towering at the chasm's edge. "Do not touch the robe," he warned, "or you will die! Morning Star himself died when he came to Withershins long ago. He is but a ghost. If you wear the robe, you will become like him."

A flicker of doubt stirred in Jotham's heart. He searched the Prince's face. In Morning Star's eyes, he saw the same look of deepest sorrow mixed with deepest love that the widow had captured in her painting.

"It is true that I died," the Prince said gravely. "It was the only way to free you."

Jotham stared, uncomprehending. "But I thought you bought our freedom. The widow said so. She said you paid a ransom."

"Yes, Jotham. And that ransom was my life."

For a moment, Jotham could not speak. When he did, his voice choked. "Your life? But...why?"

Morning Star sighed deeply. "Only then could the debt be paid and the people cleansed from the taint of evil."

"Then...you are a ghost?" shivered Jotham.

Morning Star's voice rang with triumph. "A ghost? No, Jotham! Though I died, I rose to live again. And because death could not hold me, the dark prince cannot hold you. If you put on the robe, you will die to your old life, but you will gain a new one. Will you receive the gift?"

Morning Star removed his robe and held it out. Jotham reached for it, even as Abaddon shouted one last time. "Is this what you have come to, Jotham? That you take handouts, like a beggar?"

Jotham's cheeks burned. His arms dropped. He might be an orphan, but a beggar he would never be! "I cannot accept such a gift. I must earn it," he said. "Only tell me how."

Morning Star pierced Jotham with his gaze. "If you mean

to earn this robe, you must be perfect. You must live your whole life unblemished with no hint of evil, no fault. You must keep yourself completely pure and holy. Have you done so?"

Jotham's old smudged feelings flooded over him. Well he knew how often he had fallen short of such a mark. His heart sank. "No, Your Highness," he whispered in a hollow, hopeless voice. "I see now that I can never earn the robe. Nor am I worthy of it. I do not deserve adoption!"

"No one does," Morning Star said gently. "Nor can new-born babes do anything to merit their parents' love and care when they are born naked into the world. Yet their parents give these helpless beggars what they cannot earn. So, too, those who come helpless and humble to the King, he will make his heirs. For indeed, this adoption is a birth as well ... a second birth. Will you take the robe?"

Once more, Jotham gazed into Morning Star's eyes. In his deepest being, he knew the Prince spoke true. Overflowing with gratitude, Jotham fell at his feet. "Yes! Yes, I will! Oh, thank you!"

Morning Star knelt and draped the shining white robe over Jotham. As its soft folds engulfed him, a strange thing happened. It was as if the robe not only covered him, but cleansed him—and not just his outside, but his inside too. It seemed to reach right down deep to his old smudged feelings and wipe them away.

Gently, Morning Star raised Jotham up. Jotham fingered his garment, awestruck. "I have never seen any fabric so clean and pure. What is it?" he marveled.

"It is the cloth of righteousness," the Prince replied.

Jotham saw that Morning Star's garments beneath the robe seemed to be made of the same material. These garments now gave off a glow that cloaked the Prince. This glow became a new white robe identical to the one he had given away.

In a flutter of wings, the dove flew out of the mist, landing lightly on the Prince's head. Then, for the first time, the bird flitted onto Jotham's shoulder. Morning Star took Jotham's hand. "Come, I will bring you to our Father." He led Jotham away, the dove soaring before them.

Across the chasm, Abaddon watched, shading his eyes from the receding light. His face was filled with wrath. "The wretch has been adopted! I cannot change that now," he muttered. "But I will not lose his great talents, as I did his father's. I will turn Jotham's heart against the King and bend him to my purpose. Alfric will be my tool in this. My hold on him is sure. He will do anything for his birthright!"

A look of indescribable evil spread over Abaddon's face. His next words dripped with dark promise. "The battle is just beginning!"

CHAPTER 9

Reflections on a Winged Horse

⁓⫘⁓

ALFRIC STOOD in Bogdan's grand hall once more, frowning at the mirror Jotham had fashioned. Gwyneth's carved eyes stared back unblinking from its frame. He had spoken little with her since Abaddon's departure. With Bogdan's help, they had calmed the black stallion and unsaddled the other horses. Then they had returned to the main house, and a servant had shown Alfric to a guestroom. He had passed a sleepless night, hope and fear wrestling in his heart, his mind tortured by unanswered questions. Now in the cold light of morning, one thought rose above the rest. By telling Abaddon about Jotham, had he ruined his chances with Gwyneth?

Alfric glared at the wooden features before him, muttering aloud. "I couldn't help telling Prince Abaddon about Jotham! He asked questions. He ordered me to answer. How could Gwyneth expect me to defy him? Yet I'm sure she's angry with me."

"No, I'm not!" Gwyneth's auburn curls appeared in the glass. As Alfric spun to face her, she added, "I realize you could not have done any differently."

"Well, I'm glad to hear it!" exclaimed Alfric, relieved. Then his face clouded over once more. "About this mirror..."

"Yes?" Gwyneth's face was questioning.

Alfric fought to keep his voice calm as hot pangs of jealousy stabbed him. "It is masterful work. Even I did not dream that Jotham was so gifted. How did you discover his talent? Did he show you samples of his craft after you had met at Cuthbert's?"

Her answer amazed him. "Oh, no! Jotham had not been to Cuthbert's then. I had never seen him or his carving. Prince Abaddon bade me try him. He had heard of Jotham's skill and wished to test it. I guess Abaddon had thoughts of commissioning Jotham to do work for him. Of course, once the carving was complete, I told His Highness how pleased I was with Jotham's efforts."

"Is that so!" Alfric's voice rang with relief. Perhaps the jealous fears that had gnawed him in the night were groundless. Yet one last question plagued him. "Still, I'm puzzled Jotham never told me of the mirror."

"He didn't?" Gwyneth shrugged. "Perhaps he didn't think it that important."

Whether that was so, Alfric didn't know, but he let the matter pass. "Have you heard any news of Prince Abaddon, or Jotham?" he asked. "When I rose, I questioned the servants, but there'd been no word."

"Nor has there been since," frowned Gwyneth.

Alfric's face grew downcast. Seeing this, Gwyneth's heart was moved. She took his hand. "Come, be of good cheer. Surely Prince Abaddon will bring him. Meanwhile, since our ruler bade you remain here, you must try to enjoy our hospitality."

Alfric brightened. "Will you show me the grounds, then?"

"I fear I must attend to other duties," she said gently. "But perhaps you wish to explore them on your own. You will find them quite lovely, I think. And should you grow hungry, tell the servants, and they will set food before you. We have no formal meal here except at night. And now, by your leave, I must go."

Alfric kissed her hand and released it. She hurried away. He gazed after her for a moment, then stepped outside. Trees and shrubbery were jeweled with droplets from last night's rain. The storm-swept air was fresh and clean to his nostrils. Although the day loomed long and lonely, it would not be entirely unfruitful. What he saw of Gwyneth's home might tell him more about her. Alfric strode off through the trees, eager to explore.

How long he wandered among well-groomed vegetation and burnished battle statues, Alfric knew not. At last he followed a side path to a bridge that spanned a babbling brook. Crossing it, he passed through a gap in a hedge to a secluded spot where a stately woman stood captured in bronze among towering trees and elegant topiary. The statue's arm was flung over a magnificent winged horse. The bronze woman made him think of how Gwyneth might look fifteen years from now.

Alfric stood riveted, recalling the winged horse he had seen Jotham carving. All at once he became aware of another figure, still as stone, so straight and stiff it seemed like a sculpture also. Alfric realized with a jolt that it was Bogdan. He was staring at the statue. Now he spoke, half to himself, half to the bronze lady. "Oh Cerys, how different things might have been if only you'd stayed faithful!"

Scarcely daring to breathe, Alfric turned, intending to draw back through the hedge and slip away unnoticed. It was then that he saw Gwyneth crossing the bridge. Somehow he did not want her to find him here. He crept behind a spreading shrub and waited.

Gwyneth passed through the hedge. Not until she was almost upon Bogdan did she see him. She gasped in surprise. "Father?"

Bogdan looked up, startled. Gwyneth searched his face. "I did not know you came here."

"Only when I'm troubled about you," Bogdan sighed. His face grew stern. "This Jotham. If indeed he returns, you must have no more to do with him!"

Gwyneth's face flushed. Her eyes flashed fire. "What cause have I given you to mistrust my judgment? I have always chosen my friends well!"

"No traitor is a friend!" Bogdan flared.

"Jotham is no traitor!" Gwyneth cried. "He has been deceived. You heard Abaddon say so. He can be made to see his error."

"I doubt that!" Bogdan's voice was grim. "I learned that bitter lesson with my own friend, long ago. Wise though he was, once the King's lies took root in him, he would not see reason. Earnestly did I plead with him, but he heard me not. Instead, he tried to sway me toward the King. Until..." Bogdan bit his lip and was silent.

"Until what, Father? What became of him? You would never say."

"I arrested him!" Bogdan cried. "In front of his wife, and she with child! Her face still haunts me. You shall never know such pain."

Gwyneth stood frozen with shock. Then she mastered herself. Taking Bogdan's hand, she spoke to him in a reassuring tone. "Really, Father! You make far too much of this. I have no deep interest in Jotham. I like his work and his conversation. That is all."

Bogdan looked somewhat mollified. "I am glad to hear it. Still, it would please me to see you more attentive to the young nobles who seek your hand."

Gwyneth's face grew scornful. "Spoiled laggards, all! Nor could any match me with a bow or sword. And I suspect if once I bested them, they'd soon lose interest in me."

Bogdan's voice grew playful. "I don't know. You once bested Alfric in horseshoes, but he does not seem deterred."

"When?" frowned Gwyneth, puzzled.

Bogdan smiled. "Long ago, on the palace lawn, when you were children. I shall never forget how furious his father was. Lord Killian couldn't abide his son being beaten by some snip of a girl."

Gwyneth laughed. "I'd forgotten that. As I recall, Alfric took the loss rather well. I liked him for it. Indeed, there is much to like about Alfric. Still, he lacks the wealth and status to win my hand from you. No, it is just as Mother said. I must wait for my Prince Charming on a winged horse."

Gwyneth pranced over to the winged sculpture, curtsying low. Bogdan caught her by the shoulders. He gazed at her intently. "There are no winged horses, Gwyneth, despite your mother's stories. Nor are there Prince Charmings, just mere mortals with human failings."

Gwyneth's voice grew tender as she met her father's eyes. "Mere mortals can become Prince Charmings. You're one, Father. Mother used to say so, till her heart was blinded by the fool's gold of false lust. Only find me one like you, and I shall marry soon enough."

Bogdan swallowed hard. He hugged Gwyneth tightly. Arm in arm, they passed back through the hedge and over the bridge.

Once they'd disappeared, Alfric crept from hiding. His heart was pounding. Gwyneth liked him. She had said so. As for wealth and status, he might gain those if he gained his birthright. And now Abaddon had given him cause to hope he might earn it after all. Then perhaps he, too, could become a Prince Charming, just like Bogdan had.

Alfric stared at the winged horse. An impulse seized him. He flung himself aboard the statue's back. For one magical moment he posed there, lost in thoughts of glory. All at once, he realized how silly he must look. Turning scarlet, he slipped to the ground and hurried off, grateful no one had seen him.

⚜

ANOTHER NIGHT dropped its dark curtain with still no word or sign of Prince Abaddon. Alfric found himself summoned to a formal meal. Few words were spoken. His hosts seemed preoccupied with their own thoughts. Alfric sensed that anxiety for Jotham weighed heavily on Gwyneth. Alfric shared her concern, but knowing Bogdan's mind on the matter, he did not feel he could speak with her openly about it. The worry and awkwardness weighed on his appetite. Though the delicacies far surpassed those of Cuthbert's, he ate little. Instead, Alfric squirmed in his chair. *How ironic*, he thought. *Now that my longed-for dinner with Gwyneth is happening, I can hardly wait for it to be over!*

At last, it was. The three retired for the night once more. No one had slept well the previous evening, and now exhaustion prevailed. Despite their cares, sleep crept upon them. One by one, they fell into fitful slumber.

⚜

WHAT SEEMED only moments after closing his eyes, Bogdan found himself roused by a servant. "Has morning come so fast?" he marveled.

"No, master. It's only an hour after midnight. But there is news," the servant told him.

A palace guard stood at the servant's side. The guard saluted, then held out a sealed parchment. Bogdan read the message. He looked up gravely. "It shall be as His Majesty commands. Wait for us at the coach."

The guard saluted once more, then followed the servant away. Bogdan dressed quickly and hurried down the hall to Alfric's room. But before he could reach it, another form in a flowing robe swept toward him, blocking his way.

"What is it, father? Is Abaddon back? Where's Jotham?" Gwyneth asked urgently.

Bogdan gazed at her gravely. "I do not know where Jotham is. But Abaddon has returned. He has summoned me to the palace. And he bids me bring Alfric."

Gwyneth's eyes grew steely with determination. "I am going too!"

CHAPTER 10

Alfric's Mission

THE ROYAL coach gleamed black in the moonlight as its team of jet-colored steeds swept it upward toward the grim, stone-faced walls that rimmed the hilltop. Just ahead, the dark gates of Abaddon's palace loomed like a vast iron mouth. At a signal from the guard who rode beside the driver, its cold jaws were flung wide to swallow the visitors, its metal teeth slamming shut behind them with a resounding clang.

Glancing out the carriage window, Bogdan felt a shiver run up his spine. As familiar as he was with these grounds, even he did not relish being here at this late hour. Like its master, much about the palace was forbidding and strange.

Although Abaddon's domain bordered Bogdan's own, by some strange quirk of nature, its habitat was eerily different. Despite being perched on a hilltop, part of the land was a swamp. Foul mists rose from it even on the clearest days. They thickened the air with a loathsome fog that made seeing difficult. Bogdan could only guess what might dwell there. He himself had noticed nothing more frightful than oversized frogs and lizards, but he had a sense that far more ominous life forms lurked deep below the surface and beyond his gaze. At times, the swampy earth seemed to bubble as if creatures in some vast subterranean abyss were struggling to burst forth. And the air seemed alive with odd sounds —shrieking noises and buzzings and hissings as if from a legion of snakes.

The soil immediately surrounding the palace was not swampy. But it was plagued by a deficit of its own. For some mysterious reason, it refused to sustain normal growth. The path to the palace door had been lined with trees transplanted from all over Withershins, but none would blossom or fruit. The leaves they put forth were without exception stunted and deformed. Even the grassy lawn sprouted sickly yellow, rather than the normal vibrant green.

There was, however, one plant that seemed to flourish in this odd soil. This plant was a night-blooming vine found nowhere else. When in flower, it was covered with a multitude of colorful red and yellow blossoms from which came its name of "dragon plant." But though beautiful to look upon, these dragon blooms gave off a terrible stench. The people called it, appropriately, "dragon's breath." Fortunately, the vine's blooming cycle was limited to a few days in early spring and early fall.

As the coach pulled up to the palace entrance, Bogdan realized to his dismay that one of those blooming cycles was happening now. Red and yellow flowers crawled up the walls of the towering black marble structure. The vines had even wrapped their tentacles around the two freestanding black marble columns that framed the palace doors. The flowers partially covered the golden bejeweled snakes coiled around the columns. It seemed as though the reptiles were peeking out from beneath the flowers, spying.

"Beware of the dragon's breath," Bogdan warned as the coachman held the carriage door open. But Alfric and Gwyneth, preoccupied with their own thoughts, were caught off guard and could not react in time. Unprepared for the horrid smell that assaulted their nostrils, they gasped and gagged as they were helped to the ground. The guard escorting them hurried them through the palace doors with Bogdan close behind.

For a moment, Alfric was too busy choking to take in the scene around him. When he did, he almost lost his breath again. Although he'd been on these grounds with his father, he had never set foot in the palace itself. Its opulent splendor was even more overwhelming than he had imagined.

The great hall in which Alfric and his companions now stood was a vast shrine to Prince Abaddon. The black marble floor was inlaid at intervals with his image. The walls, paneled in rich dark woods, were carved with murals of Abaddon receiving tribute from his lords and nobles. The carvings were gilded with gold and encrusted with precious gems. The room was lighted by enormous oil lamps on stands, each bearing the fanciful shape of a dragon's head. There were eighteen in all, arranged in three rows of six. One row stretched across the front of the hall. Two more columns of six were stationed like sentinels along the length of the room on either side.

Alfric thought he had never seen any place so magnificent. He felt blinded by the splendor around him—and blinded he was. His untrained eye did not spot the signs of rot and fungus in the rich woods around him. Nor did he realize that the light from the dragon lamps was hazy and murky. It dulled the luster of the gold and gems and gave the place an eerie, cloudy feel like that of the swamp nearby. But Alfric noticed none of this.

What he did notice was a magnificent black silk curtain at the far end of this vast room. It was embroidered with Prince Abaddon's crest—a red and yellow dragon with a multicolored snake coiled atop its head. Beside the curtain stood a palace guard in full dress uniform. Bogdan strode toward this curtain with Gwyneth; Alfric followed.

Catching sight of Bogdan, the guard saluted, speaking in a deferential tone. "His Majesty awaits you, sir. And the young man also." The soldier glanced at Gwyneth, hesitating. "But he did not mention your daughter."

Gwyneth's eyes flashed. "If you think to keep me out..."

Abaddon's voice boomed from behind the hanging, cutting short her protest. "Show them in at once! All of them!"

"As you wish, Your Majesty." The soldier pulled the curtain aside.

The curtain functioned as a room divider, screening the last section of this huge hall from view. In the center of the floor, mounted on a raised platform, was a dazzling golden throne. Rising above it on either side, as if guarding this seat of power, were two strange, ornately carved creatures plated with gold. Their bodies were like giant locusts. Their faces seemed human, yet not human. Below these figures, seated on the throne, was Prince Abaddon himself, cloaked in a black velvet robe richly decorated with embroidered and bejeweled dragons and snakes.

Alfric was so overcome with awe he could neither move nor speak. Bogdan approached, bowing low, followed by Gwyneth, who curtsied gracefully to the Prince as she had in the stable. Then striving to seem calm, she asked the question that was burning in her heart. "If you please, Your Majesty, where is Jotham? Have you had good success with him?"

Abaddon's face clouded and his voice was grave. "I overtook him at the border. But he would not be dissuaded from his actions. He has crossed into the realm of our enemy the King. And I fear he is in terrible danger, my dear."

Bogdan's eyes flashed. "If so, it serves the traitor right!"

He turned to Gwyneth. "Did I not warn you it would be thus? I hope now you will put this deserter out of your mind. He cannot be turned from his course."

Gwyneth's eyes blazed. "That can't be so!" She shifted her

gaze to Abaddon. "Is there nothing you can do, Sire?"

Abaddon answered with a partial truth. "I could not, and would not, force Jotham to return against his will. But there is one among us who may yet convince him and save him."

Gwyneth drew her tiny frame up to its full height. "If you mean me, Your Highness, I will go at once!"

Bogdan flared at her with a sternness born of panic. "You will do no such thing! I forbid it!"

Gwyneth's cheeks burned red in defiance. "You cannot forbid it if His Majesty commands it!"

The prince raised his hand, talking in a soothing tone. "Fear not, Bogdan. I would not put your only daughter in such danger. And Gwyneth, though you make a noble offer, it is not of you I speak."

Abaddon looked past them at Alfric, who was still rooted to his spot. "The one who must go is Alfric," said the prince.

Abaddon's words sent a shock wave of hope jolting through Alfric. Until now, he had listened to the conversation with increasing despair. *Not only is Jotham doomed,* Alfric reasoned, *but surely I will be ruined too!* The prince was sure to blame him for Jotham's fate. There would be no talk about Alfric's future, no army commission, no birthright, no chance with Gwyneth, ever. The sand in his hourglass had run out! He was finished, a failure, just as his father had predicted.

But now Abaddon had chosen him to bring Jotham back! The hourglass had been turned over. He had another chance. Or did he?

Abaddon's voice broke into his thoughts once more. "Come here, young man."

Trembling, Alfric approached the throne. The prince gazed at him intently. "Tell me what is on your mind. I command you!"

Alfric would rather have kept silent, but Abaddon's eyes

compelled him. "It's no use! Jotham no longer listens to me," he groaned. "I could not keep him from leaving. How, then, can I convince him to return?"

"By speaking my words to him," the prince replied. "I will school you in what to say."

Abaddon rose from the throne, placing a hand on Alfric's shoulder. "You must make him remember who he is," the prince continued. "The King and his followers will fill Jotham's head with lies. They will make him think he is a whole different person—a prince, an heir to riches. Except they're not riches at all. They're things of no value—like eternal life. As if any mere mortal could live forever!"

Alfric shook his head in amazement. "I don't understand," he frowned. "How could Jotham fall for such nonsense?"

"He'll be brainwashed by the King's words and his Book," Abaddon explained. "And they'll put a white robe on Jotham that has strange effects on its wearers. Like making them think they're strong when they're weak and they're blessed when they're poor in spirit. It's all part of the King's ruse to keep his subjects under his thumb."

Abaddon gave Alfric a piercing look. "You must be very careful not to let them put a white robe on you," he warned.

"Don't worry!" Alfric vowed. "I shall heed your words carefully! I swear it!"

Abaddon smiled approvingly. "Excellent, my boy!"

Alfric gathered his courage. "And if I succeed..."

"You will succeed!" Abaddon thundered. "And when you do, *this* shall be your reward!"

The prince clapped his hands. A servant appeared with a tray bearing pen and parchment. Abaddon dipped the quill in ink and wrote for a moment, then read his words aloud. "By order of Prince Abaddon, Alfric son of Killian is hereby granted an officer's commission in the royal army."

Abaddon fixed Alfric with his gaze. "All that's needed to make this official is my royal seal. I shall affix it as soon as you accomplish your task. You realize, of course, what this means?"

Alfric fought for breath. "When I gain my commission I shall meet my mother's condition for claiming my birthright."

Abaddon smiled. "Yes. The birthright shall be yours."

Alfric scarcely dared to believe his good fortune. For the moment, the dangers of his mission flickered dim beside the flame of his promised reward. "Thank you, Sire," he whispered, too overcome to say more.

"There is no time to lose," Abaddon added, growing somber. "The King is a harsh taskmaster. He expects absolute perfection from his children. Your friend Jotham will never measure up, and when he fails, he will feel the King's wrath!"

Abaddon turned to Gwyneth and Bogdan, who stood by listening intently. "I myself shall see Alfric to the border and teach him as we go."

Gwyneth seized Alfric's hands in her own, gazing into his eyes as if to infuse him with her own fierce resolve. "You can do this! I know it!" she exclaimed.

For an instant, Alfric's heart stopped. Could it be that this girl he desired believed in him? And if he succeeded and rewarded her faith, would she one day consent to share his life? How he longed to believe that this was possible! Yet he could not quite silence the small nagging echo of his father's doubts about him.

But if he could not silence it, he could certainly ignore it. He returned Gwyneth's gaze. "I won't disappoint you!"

MOMENTS LATER, the black coach tore through the jaws of the iron gate once more. Prince Abaddon had joined its original occupants. After taking Bogdan and Gwyneth home, he and Alfric would continue to the border.

Bogdan, bouncing on the seat beside his ruler, thought this not a bad result. He doubted Alfric had much hope of succeeding in his mission, but sending him might placate Gwyneth long enough for her to lose interest in Jotham. As far as what happened to Jotham himself, Bogdan did not greatly care.

Gwyneth cared very much. Abaddon's words had thoroughly alarmed her. Still, she believed Alfric had the passion and concern that inspire men to greatness. Perhaps he would accomplish this rescue after all. But if not, she had no intention of leaving Jotham at the King's mercy. She was not sure just what she would do to try to free him—but she would do something!

CHAPTER 11

In the Presence of the King

JOTHAM'S FIRST steps in Dominus felt like a waking dream. He was so overwhelmed by what had happened at the bridge and so exhausted from the rigors of his journey that his senses failed him. He fancied he was floating in his white robe, numb to all except the gentle tug of Morning Star's guiding hand. And then for a time, even that feeling faded, and he knew nothing.

When Jotham came to himself, he was draped across the Prince's back. Morning Star was carrying him. He had veered off the path and was striding toward a small country cottage. Before Jotham could gather his wits to speak, the Prince carried him over the threshold and laid him gently upon a soft bed inside.

"Where are we, Your Highness?" Jotham murmured thickly.

"In the home of a humble shepherd. He is always glad to welcome weary travelers," the Prince said softly.

Jotham saw no shepherd. But Morning Star slipped a pillow beneath his head and tenderly covered him with a blanket. As he drifted into sleep, the Prince's words whispered in his ears. "Rest now, little brother, and fear not."

WARM SUNLIGHT shining through a window caressed his face as Jotham awoke the next morning. He still saw no sign of the shepherd, but the Prince was already up and about.

"Are you hungry?" Morning Star asked.

Jotham's stomach spoke before he could. He reddened. "I haven't cared much for food these past days. I've been too excited," he answered. "But now it seems my appetite has returned."

The Prince smiled. "That is good. Still, your first food must be easy to manage. I think you will find this meal quite nourishing." He gestured to a small wooden table set with a chair, a glass, and a pitcher of milk. "Sit down, and I will serve you," he told Jotham.

Jotham stared openmouthed. This great Prince who had ransomed him was now going to serve him breakfast? "Please," he whispered finally, "shouldn't I be serving you?"

"The time will come for that," Morning Star replied gently. "Right now, you must eat."

"But..." The protest froze on Jotham's lips. Radiating from the Prince's face was that same indescribable, infinite love he had felt the night before. Mixed with it was a joy that shone more brightly, if possible, than the sunshine itself. Without another word, Jotham took his place at the table.

The Prince poured a glassful of milk and set it before him. "We give thanks to our Father the King for this food," he said. Then Jotham drained the glass in deep, delicious swallows.

"How did you like it?" Morning Star asked him.

"No meal has ever left me feeling so strengthened," Jotham replied. "It's so good I'd like some more, if you don't mind."

The Prince, looking not at all surprised, filled the glass a second and a third time until the pitcher was empty.

Sitting at this breakfast table, Jotham thought of another table in the Widow Nessa's cottage. Was it only two days since they'd read her Book together? And what had become of her when the soldier led her away?

The Prince saw Jotham's stricken face. "What is wrong?" he asked gently.

"I'd forgotten all about the Widow Nessa," Jotham groaned. "She meant to bring me here, but we missed our meeting. I last saw her with a soldier, and I fear she's been imprisoned."

"No, Jotham, she is safe," the Prince assured him. "And though she could not travel with you, she labored like a midwife for this second birth of yours."

Jotham stared in amazement. "How could this be? She is far away, in Acrasia."

"Not all battles are fought in time and space," the Prince replied. "But this knowledge, like heavy meat, is more than you can manage now. Later, you will understand."

"Tell me, please, does she know I've been adopted?" Jotham wondered.

Morning Star beamed at Jotham. "Yes. And she rejoices greatly."

The Prince led Jotham outside. They were instantly surrounded by a small flock of sheep. The animals bleated and rubbed affectionately against the Prince's robe. He patted their heads, spoke to them softly, and fed them, even as he had Jotham. To Jotham's amazement, although the sheep had dirt on their coats, not a single smudge rubbed off on the Prince's clothing.

Then it was time to resume their journey. For the first time, Jotham began to notice this new land he had entered. The darkness and fatigue of the night before, and this morning's meal, and even the feeding of the sheep had distracted him. But now a flood of impressions and images dazzled and amazed him.

His senses were so overwhelmed that Jotham would have stumbled if the Prince hadn't held him tightly by the hand. And no wonder! Having spent his whole life in the misty grayness of Withershins, Jotham was completely unprepared for what he now experienced in Dominus.

It was almost as if he had lived since birth with a film or cataract over his eyes, blurring and dulling his every perception of his world. Now suddenly, on the brightest of days, in the most glorious of gardens, this film was lifted. As Jotham beheld the richness of light and color and life that surrounded him, he felt dazed and blinded by the unaccustomed brilliance.

There had been flowers in Withershins, but none like these! They carpeted the fields, stretching beyond the horizon like a never-ending rainbow, shimmering from the sunlight reflecting off the dew on their petals. Their scents wafted upward, blended by a gentle breeze into a fragrance finer than the finest perfume. Around and among these myriad blooms, lush grass glistened emerald green. At intervals, tall trees stretched their leafy limbs to the sky. Their branches were jeweled with birds in bright-colored plumage, lifting tuneful voices in a chorus of praise. It seemed to Jotham that here in Dominus, the very ground pulsed with joy. A sense of thanksgiving and gladness filled the air like incense. He felt as though he was seeing the world for the first time ... as it was supposed to be!

Or perhaps, thought Jotham, *I'm dreaming it all, and none of this is real.* For an instant, he was flooded with disappointment. Then he bit his lip and felt a reassuring jab of pain. *It's real all right! But why is it happening to me?* he wondered. *Never could I possibly deserve such incredible good fortune!*

As these thoughts passed through Jotham's mind, he and

Morning Star continued on their way. Now and then they met other travelers, or people dwelling nearby ran up to greet the Prince. Jotham was struck by the deep affection between Morning Star and his subjects. Although they showed him great reverence and respect, there was no terror in their manner. In fact, they spoke freely to him about their lives. The Prince always listened intently and seemed to take a great personal interest in each of them.

Nor did the Prince fail to introduce Jotham to all they met. "This is Jotham, a new child of the King," he would tell them. This news was always greeted by expressions of delight and great rejoicing.

This, too, puzzled Jotham. Why would all these strangers be so glad to see him? And why, for that matter, would someone as important as the Prince take time to be his personal guide? Surely he had done nothing to merit such attention and caring.

Yet it continued. As lunchtime approached, people gathered on the grass. They begged Jotham and the Prince to join them and share their provisions. As he sat among them, Jotham noticed the great diversity of the King's subjects. People of every racial and ethnic origin gathered around them. *They are like a human rainbow*, Jotham marveled. *And I am part of it!*

Refreshed by their meal, Morning Star and Jotham traveled onward. After some time, Jotham spied what looked like a hill rising on the horizon. The traffic seemed heavier now, and everyone seemed to be going in the same direction they were. The people's mood was festive as if they were headed for some kind of celebration. As they drew nearer to the hill, Jotham saw that a city was built at its base and a gleaming palace crowned its top. It made him think of the painting on the Widow Nessa's wall.

"This must be where my new Father the King lives!"

Jotham cried, his heart racing in anticipation. "And the King must be having a party. Oh, I hope I am invited!"

"Yes, Jotham, there will be a party," Morning Star told him. "And of course you will be invited. It cannot be otherwise."

"Why is that? What are they celebrating?" Jotham asked.

The Prince smiled mysteriously. "You will see soon enough." Before Jotham could press him further, they entered the city.

It was a beautiful city, especially at this hour. The setting sun bathed the white stone streets and buildings in deep hues of gold. The sky was awash in color, as if someone had taken the flower carpet from the roadside and hurled it across the clouds. There were wonderful shops, a market place, and lovely little houses with gardens. And flowing down the hill and through the city was a river with the clearest water Jotham had ever seen.

Morning Star led Jotham up a path along the riverbank toward a wall surrounding the palace, made of marble so pure and white it almost seemed transparent. The river passed under a solid gold gate that was flung wide open in welcome. Still following the stream, Morning Star led Jotham upward through a series of courtyards paved in gold and shaded by stately trees laden with lush fruit.

At last they reached the uppermost courtyard. Here they found the river's source, a vast crystal-clear pool from whose center water bubbled up like a fountain. *Is the river fed by a spring?* Jotham wondered. *If so, what kind of spring could provide so much water?*

Morning Star spoke as if in response to Jotham's thoughts. "The spring that feeds this river knows no limits. Its living water could quench the whole world's thirst, if they would only drink of it," he sighed. "But come. The King awaits."

In wordless wonder, Jotham followed the Prince toward a palace magnificent beyond his wildest imagination. It was built of gold so pure it sparkled like diamonds. The structure was set on a platform of gold with steps of gold leading upward to its entrance doors. Framing these doors on either side were two towering golden pillars. Jotham marveled at their exquisite craftsmanship. The pillars were carved with lilies and pomegranates encrusted with precious stones. The golden doors themselves were carved in a palm branch motif. They sprang open at the Prince's touch, and Jotham entered.

He found himself in a great hall blazing with light. As his eyes adjusted, he realized that this light came from a series of towering, solid-gold lampstands. There were three rows of seven, one row across the front wall and two others stretching backwards down the sides of the building. The lampstands were set at equal intervals, and each had seven golden cups of oil.

The floor of this hall was gold. The walls were paneled in a wood Jotham's carpentry training told him was the choicest cedar. The walls were adorned with inlaid carvings gilded with gold. The carvings were of flowers, palm trees, and strange figures Jotham had never seen before. They had wings and four heads and watchful expressions, like guardians.

For a moment, Jotham became lost in contemplation of these strange figures. But the Prince's gentle touch nudged him forward, past the lampstands toward another doorway at the far end of the hall. It seemed this entranceway had been covered with a curtain at one time. But now the curtain was ripped down the middle and pushed aside.

Jotham was shocked to see such a flaw amid such elegance. He turned to the Prince. "How was that curtain torn, and why wasn't it replaced?"

Morning Star looked at once pained and joyful. "The curtain was torn when I died. It was left as a reminder of the ransom I paid."

Now Jotham saw that some great light infinitely more intense than that of the lampstands poured from beyond the curtain. So pure and bright was this light, Jotham felt he could not go a single step closer.

Morning Star seemed to understand his dilemma. The Prince draped one arm around Jotham's shoulders and raised the other in front of the lad as if to protect him from the blinding glare. Thus shielding and guiding him, Morning Star led Jotham over the threshold and into the throne room of the King.

There, framed by two enormous gilded carvings of the same winged creatures seen before, was a golden throne ablaze with precious stones, their reflection forming a rainbow of light. From the throne itself emanated a Presence of such indescribable and overpowering light that Jotham would have toppled on his face had the Prince not kept a steady hold on him. As it was, he fell to his knees and dropped his head, completely overcome.

"This light is the radiance of our Father the King," Morning Star explained gently. "He is so holy it is impossible for you to look upon him. But he can look upon you, and embrace you now that my robe is upon you."

Indeed, numb with awe as Jotham was, he could feel the King's great joy and infinite love surround and embrace him and bathe him in warmth as intense as the light and as gentle as the Prince's touch. Tears flooding his eyes, Jotham whispered the only word he could utter. "Father?"

The King's response seemed to penetrate to the depths of Jotham's heart. "Dear Jotham, as much as you longed for a father, how much more have I longed for you, my son! You are my precious child, and you will be mine forever. I have made you a prince, a citizen of my kingdom, and an heir to all its riches. But you are not ready to receive your full inheritance yet. For now, Prince Morning Star will hold it in trust.

But I have given you my Spirit as a sign and seal of what will someday be yours."

Jotham dared not utter what his mind now wondered. But the King seemed to know and spoke gentle reassurance.

"Fear not to ask questions of me, my child. You wonder who this Spirit is? It was he who freed you from the prison of your room and drew your heart away from the greater prison of your life in Withershins. It was he who showed you which path to take at the crossroads. It was he who exposed the mirage of lies and fear that would have turned you back, and it was he who saved you from the soldiers."

Jotham's eyes grew wide. "The dove?"

"He only appeared as one," the King explained. "But now I have put him within you, to comfort and guide you and lead you into truth. And he will empower you to do my will. As a token of your sonship and a symbol of the Spirit's presence, receive your royal ring."

Jotham, still kneeling with bowed head, felt the Prince slip something on his finger. He stole a glance at his hand and found he now wore a shining band of purest gold.

The King's voice sounded again, reaching to his inmost being. "This ring can never be removed. It will serve as a window to your heart. Your character must become like that of my Son, Prince Morning Star. But sometimes your heart may rebel and stray from purity and righteousness. When it does, the ring will blacken as a sign of the Spirit's sadness."

Jotham gasped in horror. New tears stung his eyes as he clutched at Morning Star in despair. "It's no use. I'm nothing like you," he whispered. "I will surely fail, and then the King will disown me."

The King's next words rang with such authority, yet such love, it seemed for an instant the whole universe trembled in response. "No, Jotham! Most assuredly I shall never disown you! I will correct and discipline you, as I do all my children.

But it is for your good, that you may become all you were meant to be. And it is a mark of your adoption and an evidence of my great love, a love you cannot lose—no matter what you do! And now I commend you to the care of my beloved Son, Prince Morning Star."

Morning Star gently raised the half-dazed boy to his feet and led him back through the great hall, out the golden doors, and down the golden steps.

Jotham gazed once more at his golden ring, gleaming in the last fading rays of the setting sun. Still worried, he turned to the Prince. "How I long to please the King! Yet I fear I will never be holy and pure, no matter how hard I try," he murmured.

Morning Star's expression grew more tender than ever. He gestured to a glorious tree nearby, bending under the weight of the marvelous fruit it bore. "Tell me, Jotham," he asked, "did this tree grow strong and tall because it tried?"

"No, of course not," said Jotham.

"Then how did it happen?" the Prince pressed him.

Jotham thought for a moment. "Good food and water, and this wonderful sun, I suppose."

The Prince smiled approvingly. "Yes, and in the same way you must be fed and nourished by the truths of the Book and watered by the Spirit. And you must spend time with me and all the King's children so that our love and support and encouragement may shine upon you. Then your character will grow strong and bear much fruit, just as these trees have.

"But first," the Prince beamed, "we must celebrate!"

Jotham saw that crowds of people streamed through the courtyards and up toward the palace. Some carried trumpets and cymbals. "I'm in time for the party after all!" he exulted. "Now will you tell me what it's all about?"

"It's a birthday party," the Prince smiled, "to celebrate

your adoption. Nothing causes greater rejoicing in all of Dominus than a new child of the King!"

A flood of emotion washed over Jotham. Tears of joy ran down his cheeks. His fondest wishes had come true. And then, amidst his joy, he felt a twinge of sadness. If only Alfric were here to share this moment with him! Jotham felt certain that if Alfric met the King, he would surely change his mind about fathers and be adopted too. And then they would truly be brothers.

Little did Jotham know that at that very moment, Alfric was indeed poised to join him in Dominus. But it would be in a very different way than Jotham envisioned, and for a very different purpose.

CHAPTER 12

Lost and Found

A SPINE-CHILLING shriek rose above the eerie crackling noises of the border road. The black steeds shied in terror, jolting Abaddon's coach. Alfric gripped his seat, his knuckles white. The prince took no notice. He just kept on hissing venom into Alfric's ears. But Alfric didn't know that his mind and heart were being poisoned. He drank in Abaddon's words, shuddering with horror at his ruler's ominous warnings about the deceptions of Dominus.

"Do not trust what you see or hear in the King's realm," Abaddon cautioned darkly. "Its beauty is only a mirage, and the people's contentment is the fruit of trickery. The King's subjects think he is loving and just, but such is not the case. He and his evil Son, Prince Morning Star, are stingy and cruel. Why, they even make their citizens live chiefly on bread and water. But because of the robes their subjects wear, they imagine this meal is a banquet."

Abaddon uncovered a basket on the seat beside him. "Now here is a banquet—cold roast, filled pastries, and cake from my palace kitchen! You'd best dine while you can! You will find no such fare in the King's land."

Alfric felt his stomach tighten. He waved the food away. "Thank you, Sire. But how can I feast when poor Jotham must be starving?"

"He is starving indeed! Yet he thinks he is filled," sighed Abaddon, "for they've stuffed him with lies."

"He shall soon spit them out if I have my way!" cried Alfric hotly.

"Well said! I like your spirit," beamed Abaddon, devouring a pastry. "But you shall need more than that to pry Jotham from the clutches of the King. Now listen closely. I have much to tell you."

The prince talked on as Alfric strained to absorb everything Abaddon said. So intent was he on their conversation that he heeded little else. Though the road was bumpy, high winds whipped the carriage, and the horses spooked often, still the hours passed quickly. Daylight faded to twilight. Then as night dropped like a curtain, suddenly the horses stopped. They had reached the border.

The coachman sprang to open the door. Abaddon leaped to the ground. Alfric followed, feeling his heart quicken. Ragnar and Cadel hurried toward them, bowing low. "We are at your service, Sire," Cadel murmured.

"And poor service you have done me, letting someone scale the wall," the prince snapped harshly.

Ragnar bridled. "Had it been up to me, Your Majesty, I would have chased him to the border and beyond!"

"Then be glad it wasn't. You would not have been up to the task," Abaddon barked. He gestured to Alfric. "This man will go after the truant. And when he returns, you must speed his way to Acrasia. Now return to your post, and beware of any further lapses in your duty!"

The soldiers saluted and slunk away, Ragnar looking very sullen. The coachman handed Alfric a pouch packed with food and drink for his trip. Then he lit a lantern and gave it to the prince. It was in the shape of a dragon's head, like the lampstands in Abaddon's palace.

Motioning to Alfric, Abaddon led him to a far part of the wall out of sight of the coachman and the soldiers. Holding up the lantern, he shone it on a spot of cold gray stone. The lantern's yellow glow poured from the dragon's mouth like a tongue of fire. As it licked the barren stone, there appeared on its surface the outline of a coiled snake. Abaddon pressed his hand against the serpent and a portion of the stone wall swung inward.

Alfric followed the prince through this secret door down the slope toward the bridge to Dominus. Even as he did, he felt his courage flicker like the lantern's light. But he tried to put on a brave face as Abaddon gave him a few last instructions. "You must take the road that begins on the far side of this bridge and make your way to the King's palace. When you reach it, you will soon find Jotham. All deserters from Withershins are brought there to be indoctrinated. Make haste! And beware of the light!"

"The sunlight?" frowned Alfric.

"No. It is brighter than sunlight," Abaddon replied. "This light will pierce you, and blind and confuse you with its glare. You must shield yourself from it at all costs."

"Don't worry. Nothing will confuse me, Sire. I shall soon snatch Jotham from the King's hand and return with him," vowed Alfric.

"And when you do," smiled the prince, "your birthright shall be yours. Now go forth and claim your destiny!"

Heart pounding, Alfric strode across the bridge and into Dominus. His mission had begun!

AT THE PALACE of the King, the celebration had started. With great clanging of cymbals and heraldic blasts of the trumpets, the crowd gathered around the crystal pool. Morning Star led Jotham to the water.

"We have a custom here," the Prince explained. "When the King adopts children, we dip them into this pool. And they proclaim they belong to him and his kingdom."

"It is true! I'm a child of the King! I'm a child of the King!" Jotham sang out joyfully.

Then the Prince helped Jotham into the pool, dipped him into the water, and raised him up as the crowd cheered approval. Though the air was cooler now that night had fallen and Jotham was wet, he felt no chill. Rather, he was wonderfully warmed from the inside out.

At a signal from the Prince, hot cakes of unleavened bread were brought and a great golden cup of ceremonial red wine. "This special food and drink is the banquet of adoption," Morning Star explained. "This feast is celebrated often by all the King's children. The cake is the bread of life, and the wine is the cup of promise."

Then Jotham and all those gathered around him partook of the banquet together. "What a marvelous meal!" he raved. "I would rather eat this bread than any meat I ever tasted back in Withershins. And this wine seems to purify, like a tonic."

Morning Star beamed with pleasure. "I am glad you like it, Jotham. And now, there is someone you must meet."

The Prince turned and beckoned with his hand. A young man joined them from out of the crowd. He was Jotham's height, but more muscular with deep blue eyes and hair the color of ripe chestnuts. "This is Evan," Morning Star told Jotham. "I have asked him to care for you. He will be your host and guide in Dominus and will answer your questions."

Morning Star embraced Jotham once more, then strode off into the crowd. Jotham turned to Evan, looking a bit wistful. "With all the Prince has to do, I doubt that I shall see him soon."

"You shall see him sooner than you think and whenever you have need," Evan reassured him gently. "He is never too busy for even the least in his kingdom. But now you must come home with me. Surely you are weary from your journey, and you must rest again."

⌒⫻⌒

EXHAUSTED, Alfric trudged along the path into Dominus. Though he longed to rest, he dared not. *I must travel as far as I can before dawn*, he reasoned. Even on a moonlit night like this, he would be less visible than in broad daylight. He was also less likely to meet others on his way. Abaddon had warned him that the King's subjects, while seeming friendly, were not to be trusted. "Speak little to them, and avoid them when you can," the prince had commanded.

So Alfric pressed onward like a hunted rabbit, jumping at the slightest sound until he reached a place where his road split into three. He stared in confusion. *Which path should I take?* he wondered.

"If you wish to know, it shall be revealed," said an unexpected voice.

Alfric jumped in alarm, his eyes darting about. "Know what? Who said that?"

A shepherd emerged from a grove of trees with a baby lamb in his arms. "It was I. I am the good shepherd in search of lost sheep. You seem lost too, and hungry. Come friend, let me feed you some of my bread and water. You will not taste a finer banquet anywhere!"

The shepherd set the lamb on the ground, reached into a pouch tied around his waist, and pulled out a flask of water and a flat cake of bread. Alfric suddenly realized he was starving and parched with thirst. At the moment, this shepherd's bread and water looked like a feast indeed. Then Alfric remembered Abaddon's warning. *How silly*, he thought. *This simple fare is no banquet. Abaddon was right. These peo-*

ple are terribly deceived! And who knows if the food may be poisoned? "Thank you kindly, but I brought provisions of my own which suit me better," Alfric answered. "And besides, I cannot stop to eat now. I am in too great a hurry."

"What will your haste gain you if you hurry down the wrong path?" asked the shepherd. "Perhaps I can help you find your way."

Alfric thought this sounded like a good idea. A shepherd would know the terrain. "Very well. Which of these roads leads to the King's palace?" he asked.

The shepherd gazed at him intently. "All three will take you there. But only the truth will lead you to the King. Follow me, and I will show you. I am the way."

Alfric scowled. What kind of double talk was this? It was just as Abaddon said. These people could not be trusted! Alfric stared at the three paths winding off in different directions. One sloped upward toward some hills rising in the distance. *It looks like a more difficult route, which might mean fewer travelers and less chance of trouble,* Alfric decided.

He turned to the shepherd. "You needn't bother. I think I can find my own way, after all. Good evening, sir." Alfric turned and walked swiftly down the path he had chosen.

The shepherd gazed after him with an expression of immense sadness. "How can you find your way?" he sighed. "You are blind and confused. You hunger and thirst, yet you refuse the food and drink I offer. You count me an enemy when I am your greatest friend. You reject what you need most, for you know not what you do."

A radiance softer yet brighter than the moonlight shone from the shepherd's face and robe. Stooping, he lifted the sheep tenderly in his arms. "Alfric needs a shepherd just like you do. He is lost." The shepherd's face lit up with joy. "But Jotham is found."

CHAPTER 13

The Crowns That Could Not Be Stolen

THE DAY AFTER Jotham's adoption banquet, he was in a stupor of exhaustion. The barrage of emotions he had felt since leaving Acrasia took their full toll at last. He found he could barely move or think. Evan seemed to understand. He fed Jotham small amounts of milk and bread and a nutritious soup and let him rest. But by the next morning, Jotham's strength was returning and he was eager to begin exploring his new surroundings.

"What is the name of this city?" Jotham asked as he followed Evan through the sunlit streets.

"It is called Azriel, though it has other names," Evan answered. "Some simply refer to it as The City of the King. For indeed, the King's presence has transformed this place down to the very stones. Have you noticed?"

Jotham had. The air felt different to breathe, so pure it made even the freshest breezes of Withershins seem like stale fumes. Jotham sensed his hearing and vision sharpened and even his clarity of thought marvelously heightened in this rarified atmosphere.

For some moments, Jotham followed Evan in silence, drinking in great draughts of this pervasive goodness through his very pores. The streets and shops around them teemed with white-robed figures, all appearing quite busy. This prompted a new question from Jotham. "What work do people do here?" he wondered. "Is it different from that in Withershins? And how do they spend their free time?"

"Those who live in this place labor at many things," Evan answered. "But there is a difference. All our efforts are bent toward honoring and serving the King. Because we delight in him, our burdens are light even when they are heavy. As for our leisure hours, our greatest joy is to study the Book and discuss it together."

"Where do these discussions take place? In people's homes?" Jotham wondered.

"Yes, Jotham, but more often in the courtyards of the King. People love to meet there for this purpose. Nor need they leave to sup, for food and drink are provided there for all the King's subjects at every hour of the night or day. Perhaps you would like to go there now and read the Book together."

Jotham felt a hunger gnaw at him that had nothing to do with food. His heart leaped. "Oh, please!"

LIKE FIELDS abloom with clusters of flowers, the palace courtyards were bursting with small clumps of people all gathered to study the Book. There were plenteous copies stacked in receptacles placed at intervals throughout the grounds. Evan took one, then sat with Jotham on a stone bench, laying the Book between them.

"Surely you must have many questions about this new life you are beginning," Evan said as he opened the volume. "The Book will answer them. What would you like to know first?"

Jotham hesitated, paralyzed by possibilities, like a famished soul staring at a table laden with delicacies. "I don't know! There's so much! Do you have a suggestion?" he pleaded.

Evan nodded, eyes twinkling. "Perhaps you would like me to tell you about your inheritance."

"Yes, do!" cried Jotham, his face shining with excitement. "The King spoke of it, but he didn't explain what it was." Jotham's face grew pensive. "I never dreamed I would have an inheritance. My parents left me only a handmade quilt. Though I count it very precious, I could not bring it with me. I am hoping a friend will keep it safe. Still, who knows what may happen to it before I return, if ever I do. The quilt may be lost to me forever." Jotham sighed deeply.

Evan seemed not at all surprised by these words. "Such is the way with the treasure people value in Withershins," he replied. "But your inheritance from the King is much different. It cannot rot or decay or get lost or stolen."

"What is it, then?" cried Jotham.

"The King has endowed you and all his children with eternal life and infinite spiritual blessings," Evan smiled.

Jotham looked rather puzzled. "But the King said I was heir to the riches of the kingdom!"

"Those are the riches of the kingdom," Evan told him. "And they are more precious by far than the finest gold or costliest jewels. But perhaps a tale from the Book will explain this better. Let me read the story of 'How a Rich Man Lost His Treasure.'"

Evan found the page and began. Jotham listened intently.

Once there lived a great lord whose chief passion in life was amassing a vast fortune. He raised crops in abundance and sold them for gold and jewels. Soon the vaults of his castle overflowed with these riches. Still, he was not satisfied. He ordered a great treasure house built and filled that as well.

Now the peasants who worked for this lord were poor folk and received but a meager wage. At last they came to him, pleading for his favor. "We have worked for you faithfully," they said, "and we are starving. Won't you give us a bit of extra grain? We will bless you for it. And truly, if you sold it for more gold, you would have no place to put it."

Then the lord grew angry. "If I need more room for gold, I shall build a bigger treasure house," he cried. "Now enough of your impudence! Be off!" And he chased them away.

But that night he died, and his treasure was lost to him.

"It seems to me his treasure was lost to him long before that," mused Jotham. "It did him no good. It just made him greedy and cruel. He would have done better to share it with those who had need."

"Which would have gained him riches indeed," smiled Evan.

"Don't believe him!"

Jotham gasped at the sound of the voice. "Alfric?!"

Sure enough, Alfric strode angrily from behind a nearby tree. Jotham grabbed his friend's hands, beside himself with joy. "Oh, Alfric, I can hardly believe you're here! I'm so glad you've come! The King is nothing like you think. But you will see for yourself when you meet him. Prince Morning Star can arrange it. You need only put on his white robe..."

"Never!" Alfric broke in angrily. "Besides, I did not come to meet your King. I came to bring you to your senses. How can you believe this nonsense they are telling you? Who ever heard of becoming rich by giving things away? And what kind of riches is eternal life anyway? Or spiritual blessings, for that matter? This new friend of yours says you have this marvelous inheritance...but it's all lies! You have nothing!

You are still an orphan!"

"No, Alfric! I'm a prince!" cried Jotham, stung.

"Is that so?" sneered Alfric. "Then why don't you have a crown?"

Evan looked thoughtfully at the pair. "He will. Would you like to see it?"

Jotham's eyes sparkled. "Yes! Where is it?"

Evan rose. "I will show you. Come."

Alfric felt certain this new talk of crowns was just one more deception. But he followed behind Jotham as Evan led them into a building adjacent to the palace.

There, in treasure chests lining the walls, they beheld gleaming golden crowns adorned with jewels of breathtaking size and brilliance. "They're . . . they're magnificent!" Jotham stammered.

"These are crowns of the kingdom," Evan explained. "One of these will be yours some day."

Alfric too was dumbfounded, but he quickly recovered. Surely this was but one more deception, and he would expose it. "Why can't Jotham have a crown now?" he bristled. "Why must he wait?"

"The time is not right for him to receive it," Evan answered. "But you are both free to look at them as long as you like."

"So we shall. And I hope you will leave us now," Alfric snapped. "We would like some private moments together."

Evan looked questioningly at Jotham, who hesitated, then nodded agreement. "Very well," said Evan gently. "I shall come and find you later."

Evan reluctantly walked away. Alfric waited to be sure he was really gone, then turned to Jotham, speaking in an urgent whisper. "Now's your chance. Take a crown."

Jotham's eyes grew huge with horror. "You mean, steal it?"

"You're not stealing," Alfric snorted. "Evan said one of these crowns was yours."

"No, he didn't," countered Jotham. "He said it would be mine some day."

Alfric's eyes flashed. "Well, I'll wager that day will never come! The King will likely just dangle the crown before you to make you do his bidding. His Book talks about sharing treasure, yet he will not give you one lone crown from all his plenteous store. If this wonderful King is really your Father, he shouldn't begrudge you that. It's one thing for him to say you're a prince. It's quite another to mean it."

"He does mean it!" Jotham insisted.

Alfric threw up his hands in disgust. "Have you lost your wits completely? Since when do you take someone's word untried? I thought you were more clever than that, and so did Gwyneth!"

Jotham felt his heart flutter. "Gwyneth? Then she knows I'm here?"

"Yes, and it has quite distressed her," Alfric snapped. "She hoped I might save you. Little does she realize how deceived you are!"

"I am not deceived!" Jotham's cheeks flamed red.

"Then prove it!" Alfric pressed him. "Put the King to the test. Take a crown, and see what happens."

"Fine! I will!" Jotham reached into a chest and tried to seize a crown. He strained and grunted, then turned to Alfric, amazed. "I can't budge it."

"Don't be silly! It can't be that heavy," Alfric frowned, reaching in to help. But tug as they might, it would not move an inch.

"Try another," panted Alfric.

But that crown would not move either, nor would the next.

Suddenly, a voice sounded behind them, freezing them. "It's no use, Jotham. You must have much greater strength of character to lift a kingdom crown, much less wear it."

Hearts sinking, they turned to face a majestic, white-robed figure. "Prince Morning Star!" Jotham cried before Alfric could speak. "I meant no harm, Your Highness!"

"Why did you try to take a crown?" the Prince asked softly.

"Because...," Jotham faltered. "To test the King," he admitted. "But I see no wrong in that."

It seemed to Jotham that Morning Star's eyes pierced to his very soul. "Your ring says otherwise."

Jotham dropped his eyes to the gold ring on his finger. It was streaked with black. Panic rose in his throat as he turned to Morning Star once more. "All right. Perhaps it was wrong. But it's not my fault! Alfric told me to do it."

The Prince locked Jotham in his gaze. "Did you have to listen?"

Jotham glanced at his ring. To his horror, it had turned blacker. Morning Star's voice rang in his ears, like a knell of doom. "I think you know the answer. You have erred. And you must go before our Father and confess it."

Alfric's face blanched. He seized Jotham's arm. "Don't do it, Jotham!" he urged. "The King will punish you. He'll beat you, just like my father beat me. You must believe what I tell you."

Jotham hesitated, torn. "I... I don't know," he stammered.

"No, I suppose not," snapped Alfric, "because you're wearing that white robe. Prince Abaddon said it would muddle your thinking. Well, I'll fix that!"

Alfric grabbed Jotham's robe and gave it a tremendous tug. To his shock, he could not budge the garment. Jotham pulled loose and backed away from both Alfric and the Prince, looking confused.

Morning Star understood the boy's dilemma. He moved toward Jotham, hand outstretched. "Come..."

Alfric darted between them, giving Jotham a quick shove. "Run!"

Jotham hesitated, quivering like a trapped deer. Then... he fled.

Alfric sensed a figure looming over him—Prince Morning Star. A brilliant light emanated from the Prince. Alfric felt himself frozen, captured in its glare. He looked up, blinking in terror, certain he was doomed. "You're going to cast me in chains, aren't you?" he gasped.

The Prince's answer caught Alfric off guard. "You are in chains already. I wish to free you."

For an instant, Alfric wondered if this could be true. Then, Abaddon's warning rang in his mind. *Beware of the light. It will blind and confuse you.*

Alfric raised one hand to shield himself against the brightness. With the other, he gestured to the crowns, mustering his courage. "If you wish to save me, give me from your myriad crowns but one gem!" he cried.

Morning Star looked at Alfric with inexpressible sadness. In that moment, it seemed that the weight of all the evil and sorrow in the whole universe rested on the Prince's shoulders. "You think a jewel will solve your problems?" he sighed. "Very well." Effortlessly, the Prince pulled a sparkling gem from a crown and handed it to Alfric. "Take it. You are free to go."

Alfric stared incredulously at the jewel in his hand. He backed away a step, expecting Morning Star to seize him. But the Prince merely stood still and silent as if he would weep. Heart pounding, Alfric turned and ran. Morning Star watched him go, knowing what Alfric could not guess—that Alfric had gained nothing and was fleeing from hope to hopelessness.

CHAPTER 14

The Ring Does Its Work

THE COUNTRYSIDE passed in a blinding blur under Jotham's racing feet. He had no clear idea of where he was going or what he would do. His one thought was to flee Morning Star and the King. Now the flower-perfumed air choked his throat, and it seemed that even the birds accused him. He fancied he could understand their chirps, "Thief! Thief!" Desperately, he flung himself forward until the green meadows gave way to a more wooded landscape. For what seemed an eternity, he ran headlong through the trees. At last, stumbling from fright and fatigue, he tripped and tumbled to the ground.

For a moment, Jotham lay deathly still. He was sure he would hear footsteps pounding in pursuit. No doubt the King would send soldiers bent on dragging him back to be beaten, just as Alfric had warned. But the wood was silent except for his own breathless gasps.

Then his ears picked up something else—a soft gurgling sound. Hesitantly, he struggled to his feet and followed the noise. Just beyond some nearby trees he came upon a small brook skipping along the forest floor.

Jotham knelt beside it, a hazy plan forming in his mind. If he could somehow wash his ring clean, there would be no visible proof of his wrongdoing. Should the King's men stop him, he might then convince them that they had the wrong culprit. And so he might manage to avoid arrest until he could reach the border and escape back into Withershins.

Jotham plunged his hand into the water, scrubbing frantically at the ring. To his unspeakable horror, it only grew blacker. He rubbed at it with renewed fervor, groaning to himself. "It must come clean! It must..."

"Your ring won't come clean until you do, Jotham," warned a sober voice behind him. Jotham turned to see Evan coming toward him through the woods.

"Prince Morning Star told me what happened. He sent me to find you," Evan added. "You were not hard to catch. You've been running in circles. And you will continue to do so until you confess to the King."

Jotham jumped up and backed away, filled with despair. "But he'll beat me! Alfric said so. And why endure it? I'll just do something else wrong and get beaten again. It's no use. I can't measure up. Alfric was right. I never should have come here. I'm going back. Tell the King I don't want his crown, or his kingdom, or his ring!"

Jotham yanked at the ring to pull it off. The ring refused to yield.

Evan looked at him with tender concern. "You can't remove it, Jotham. And you can't go back—at least not the way you think. You belong to the King, and nothing and no one can change that. Not even you."

"That's not true! I'll find Alfric. He'll help me," Jotham insisted.

"I'm afraid he cannot help you," Evan replied.

Jotham's heart sank. "Why? Has Prince Morning Star seized him? Are they dragging him before the King?"

Evan shook his head. "No, Jotham. Prince Morning Star let Alfric go. He is on his way back to Withershins."

"Then I will find him, and he will help me!" Jotham cried. He plunged back into the woods.

Evan watched him go. "No, Jotham, it is you who must help Alfric," he murmured. "But you don't see that now."

As ALFRIC'S feet climbed upward, his spirits soared. He had managed to find the path that had brought him to the palace. Backtracking, he rushed homeward, hardly feeling the ground beneath him, buoyed as he was by his growing sense of triumph.

"This business with the crowns has surely exposed the King's falseness to Jotham!" Alfric gloated. "Doubtless he is fleeing to the border even now and will soon be back in Withershins. And I will be close behind—just in time for Abaddon to praise me and reward me with my army commission, and my birthright."

An image rose in Alfric's mind of Gwyneth and her father standing by the winged horse sculpture in their garden. What was it she had said to Bogdan about Alfric then? *"Still, he lacks the wealth and status to win my hand from you."*

Alfric's chest swelled with pride. *Well, I'll have the status now!* he exulted. *And the wealth!* His hand closed on the gem in his pocket, stroking it in worshipful caress. *When Bogdan sees this priceless jewel, he will gladly give me Gwyneth's hand in marriage. We will live in splendor. Likely Bogdan will become my mentor. And I will rise ever higher in Abaddon's service. Indeed, some day I may be as powerful as the mighty Bogdan himself!*

Alfric reveled for a time in such grand ideas until a lingering mystery nagged him. *Why did Morning Star give me the stone? It is simply one more trick*, Alfric reasoned. *Morning*

Star may have sought to appear kind and good so I would come over to the King's side. But I am much too smart for that!

The sound of running footsteps shattered Alfric's blissful mood. Never once on his way to the palace had he met a single soul on this solitary road. Who could this be? And why such haste? Was the runner chasing someone?

Chasing me! This thought burst into Alfric's consciousness. *That's it, of course!* he groaned. *I'm being chased by Morning Star's men. He has no intention of letting me take this jewel across the border. He's told them I'm a thief and ordered them to seize me. But they must catch me first!*

Alfric doubled his pace. A faint voice floated to him on the air. "Alfric!"

Ignoring it, he ran all the faster. *I will not let this chance for happiness slip away!* he vowed to himself.

FRANTIC AND desperate, Jotham had run until he'd lost all sense of direction. He'd become so confused that he'd feared he would never find the border. Finally, he'd stumbled on a narrow dirt path that led upward, connecting at last with a twisting, hilly road. Then just ahead, disappearing around a bend, Jotham had spied his old friend. With his last burst of strength, he had rushed forward, calling Alfric's name. "Alfric! Alfric!"

To Jotham's horror, Alfric had fled without even looking back. Jotham faltered, swaying. Dark thoughts engulfed him like a cloud of doom. *Doubtless Alfric wants no more to do with me! He's disgusted, and I don't blame him. Now I've lost my one friend and advocate in Withershins. Surely, I can't look to the widow for help. Her loyalty is to the King. It seems that Evan was right after all. I cannot go back. Nor can I go forward. What am I to do?*

Stunned and numb with panic, Jotham fell to his knees and buried his face in his hands. "Help me! Somebody, help me!" he cried.

Jotham felt a gentle touch on his shoulder. A soothing warmth enveloped him, like a hedge of protection. He looked up to find Morning Star bending over him like a parent comforting a frightened child.

"I have waited and watched and longed to help," the Prince said in a soothing voice. "Are you ready now to turn to me and heed my words?"

Jotham spoke in a plaintive whisper. "I have no one else to turn to. I called to Alfric, but he fled."

"It was not from you he fled," said the Prince.

Jotham stared in surprise. "From who then?"

"From no one," Morning Star said softly. "As it says in the Book, 'The wicked flee when no one is chasing them.' Alfric was running from the specter of his own groundless fears. Just as you are."

Jotham frowned. "But if I tell the King about the crowns, won't he punish me terribly?"

"No, Jotham," the Prince reassured him. "My robe, which you wear, will protect you. It covers all your imperfections. The King will see only my righteousness. Besides, he already knows what you have done."

Jotham was puzzled. "I don't understand. If he knows about the crowns, why must I tell him?"

Morning Star looked grave. "So we can all agree that it was wrong. Such behavior is like a fungus that eats at your heart. It will stunt your character growth, just as real fungus stunts a tree's growth. That is why you must repent and turn from it."

The Prince's gaze grew, if possible, more tender. "And you will not have to face the King alone. I will go with you," he said gently.

"How I long to believe you," sighed Jotham.

"Then do," Morning Star urged firmly. "Did I lie to you at the border?"

"No," Jotham admitted.

"Nor will I now, or ever," the Prince promised. "But you must continue to trust me, as you did then."

Morning Star held out his hand. This time, Jotham took it. "I am ready to go to the King," he said resolutely.

The Prince smiled joyfully. "And he is waiting for you."

CHAPTER 15

Baubles, Bangles, and Quilts

⌖

"CLOSE YOUR eyes, Gwyneth!" Bogdan's voice echoed down the hall to her room. Gwyneth, seated on her bed, halfheartedly obeyed. Normally, she'd have loved a surprise from her father. But these days, a pall hung over her, dampening her spirits. It was partly concern over Alfric and Jotham and partly the gloom of inaction. Her temperament was one that would rather face danger than be left to wait and worry. "Sometimes I wish I had been a boy!" she muttered absently.

"I have something that will soon change your mind!"

Gwyneth jumped, startled by her father's voice close at her elbow.

"No peeking!" Bogdan cautioned. "Almost ready! Now!"

Gwyneth opened her eyes, then blinked in amazement. Flashing up at her was a sea of glittering jewels. There were bracelets, brooches, necklaces, earrings, and rings of every description. All were wrought of fine gold or the purest silver. All were set with precious gems: brilliant rubies, sapphires, emeralds, diamonds, and a host of lesser stones. They were nestled on velvet in a vast wooden jewel box.

Gwyneth was lost in delight, fingering the baubles, holding them against her skin, and preening in a mirror. At last she turned to her father. "Where did they all come from?"

Bogdan beamed. "They are your inheritance, my dear. Many of these pieces have been handed down for generations. At length they passed to your mother, who wore them until..."

Bogdan's voice choked off. He took a deep breath. "She left them for you. I'd planned to present them on your wedding day. But I think now is just as good a time. Perhaps you will keep them in your hope chest."

Gwyneth bit her lip. "I'm not sure when it will be finished."

"Why, it's finished already!" cried Bogdan. "Didn't I tell you? Magnus sent word. He bids you come to his shop and inspect it. If you are satisfied, he will have it brought here."

Gwyneth leaped to her feet. "I shall go at once!"

*   *   *

MAGNUS'S GREEN eyes sparkled from beneath snow-white brows as he watched Gwyneth stroke the wooden veins on the winged horse's head. "I thought you would be pleased," he murmured.

Gwyneth's hand wandered to the wooden wings. "It's wondrous work!"

"The last Jotham did before leaving," Magnus sighed. "I shall miss him sorely. A talent like his is rarely seen."

Gwyneth nodded. "I could not agree more. I had hoped to commission additional pieces. Now I shall wait, in hopes he will come back. If he does, and can find a position..."

"He has a position!" Magnus's voice rang through the shop. Other workers looked up, startled. Seeing this, Magnus lowered his tone. "If Jotham returns and you learn of it, send him to me at once! I shall hire him back in an instant!"

"Nor will you soon be sorry," Gwyneth smiled, satisfied she'd achieved her objective.

"Now, will you also inspect the chest's interior workmanship?"

Magnus raised the lid and drew in his breath sharply. "Why, what's this?" Intrigued, Magnus pulled out a folded quilt. He turned twinkling eyes on Gwyneth. "Does Jotham have more talents than I knew?"

Gwyneth stared in amazement. A tingle ran through her. "I doubt he made this," she murmured. "But I have an idea who did."

"Look! There's a note!"

Magnus unpinned a paper attached to one corner. He handed it to Gwyneth. She read it aloud.

> My esteemed friend Gwyneth...
>
> Having no one else to ask, I beg a favor of you. Would you hold safe in your keeping this quilt, which was wrought by my mother? Knowing how you value handwork, and also mothers, I hoped you might not be offended by this bold request. I trust it shall not be too great a burden. You shall have the undying gratitude of your faithful friend...
>
> Jotham

For a long moment, Gwyneth said nothing. Then she laid the note aside. Wordlessly, she unfolded the quilt, draping it across the chest. Stem-twined daisies laughed up at her from its fabric. "How charming!" she cried.

"Quite a whimsical pattern," chuckled Magnus. "Now I see where Jotham gets his magic...from his mother. It is not a far leap from dancing daisies to winged horses."

"The winged horse is my mother's magic," laughed Gwyneth. "I bade Jotham carve one on the hope chest."

"Your mothers should have met. They might have found much in common," Magnus smiled.

Gwyneth's face grew pensive. "But that will never be."

Pulling back the quilt, she turned her attention to examining the chest once more. She ran her hand across the interior wood, nodding in satisfaction. "The craftsmanship is beyond reproach. Please have this delivered at once," she told Magnus.

"And what of the quilt? Do you wish to leave it inside? Or would you prefer to take it with you?"

Gwyneth frowned. "I'm not sure..."

"Someone, help!"

The breathless, frantic cry came from a young soldier who burst into the shop. His clothes were askew, his face pale, his eyes panicked. "Please, does one of you own that horse outside?" he gasped.

Gwyneth stepped forward quickly. "She is my mare. You are Devlin, aren't you? I've seen you at the fortress. What is wrong?"

Devlin's words tumbled out in a flood. "My wife, Brie. She's with child. And it's coming sooner than we thought. The Widow Nessa had promised to attend her. I was on my way to fetch her when my mount lost a shoe."

Devlin hesitated. "Please... may I borrow yours?"

Gwyneth's answer was swift. "I will fetch the widow myself. Tell me where you are quartered."

"On the grounds of the fortress, in the soldiers' housing," Devlin gasped. "The guard at the gate can direct you."

Gwyneth nodded. "I will find it. Meantime, you must hurry back to your wife."

She turned to Magnus. "Will you find someone to take him? As for the quilt, you may leave it in the chest after all. And please let my father know I may be delayed. If the widow needs help, I may stay to assist in the birth."

"As you wish, Lady Gwyneth," Magnus said, and sprang into action.

MOMENTS LATER, Gwyneth galloped her horse down the street, her heart pounding with new purpose. No longer would she sit idle, waiting for news. In case Alfric failed in his quest to free Jotham and she had to take action herself, she would be well prepared. She would learn all she could about this King. And who better to probe than the Widow Nessa, a Person of the Book? While helping the midwife with the birth, she would also ask questions. Hopefully, she would learn something useful.

CHAPTER 16

A Jewel of No Price

TWISTED BY pain and bathed in sweat, the soldier's wife looked aged and wraithlike in the flickering lamplight. Gwyneth found it hard to believe that Brie was scarcely older than she was herself. How fragile Brie seemed, tangled in the bed sheets, clutching the Widow Nessa with one hand and gripping her husband's arm with the other.

"Courage, Brie," urged the widow. "Just think of your new little baby. Come on. Breathe!"

Brie gasped and grunted for a few moments more, then fell back on her pillow. Gwyneth knew what that meant—a lull in the labor pains. But it wouldn't last long.

"Don't leave me, Devlin," Brie moaned to her husband.

"I won't." Devlin reached up to take the cold compress Gwyneth was holding. "Let me do that. Rest a moment."

He turned to the widow, mouthing his words so Brie wouldn't hear. "Will she be all right? It's been nearly a day since her pangs first began. Do these things always take so long?"

She patted his arm. "They do sometimes."

But the widow was worried. Examining Brie, she had realized something Devlin did not know. The baby was turned the wrong way. Instead of the head emerging first, the feet or buttocks would. This heightened the risk that the cord connecting the unborn child with the mother might get pinched in the birthing process, cutting off the infant's air. There was also a chance of the baby's head getting stuck. As the widow well knew, both mother and child could be in grave danger.

Striding to the window, she pulled back the curtain. The night was ending, its blackness melting into the first streaks of dawn. Yet in her own heart, the shadows of concern were deepening. "My Father and King, give me guidance," she pleaded.

"How could you call this enemy your King?"

The question caught the widow by surprise. She turned to find Gwyneth staring at her with an outraged expression.

"Don't you realize such words are treason?" Gwyneth blurted. "Prince Abaddon is your ruler. And besides, this King is far away. How could he even hear you?"

"He is never far from me, and he always hears my voice," the widow answered.

Gwyneth frowned. "Even if he could, what do kings know about childbirth?"

The widow spoke reverently. "My King has all knowledge. He is the source of all true wisdom."

"That can't be!" exclaimed Gwyneth. "My father doesn't know your King. But he's probably the smartest man in all of Withershins!"

"He may be very smart, yet not be wise," the widow told her gently. "One who is smart knows information, but one who is wise knows how to live. There are many smart fools."

The widow's answer gave Gwyneth pause as had happened many times in these past hours. The more they'd talked, the more the widow's words made Gwyneth question her own perceptions. Did her father know how to live? Or was he a smart fool? He had a brilliant mind, but that very brilliance made him terribly intolerant. He tended to be hard on others, and harder on himself. Nor did he show much mercy to those who failed him. Was such harshness wise? Was this partly why her mother left?

"Ohhhhhhh..."

Brie's agonized cries sent Gwyneth and the widow racing back to her bedside. The pains were coming again, fiercer than ever. Devlin squeezed her hand.

"Push, Brie," the widow urged.

Gwyneth blotted streams of perspiration from the young woman's forehead as she strained to obey. The baby's buttocks appeared. The widow reached in and freed the infant's legs, clearing the passageway for the birth to proceed.

"Push again! Harder now!" The widow's voice rang with urgency.

With a great grunt of pain, Brie complied. The baby's torso emerged. Just the head was still inside.

"Almost there. Once more. Now!"

Gathering all her strength, Brie pushed once more. The widow pulled. Nothing happened!

Gwyneth felt her chest tighten. She knew something of such births. *Is the baby's head stuck?* she wondered with a shiver of dismay.

"Keep trying! Quickly, Brie!" The widow's voice was taut.

Brie screamed in agony, clutching wildly at her husband and the midwife. Gwyneth saw the terror in Devlin's eyes and the anguish in the widow's. To her horror, Gwyneth wondered if this woman, not much older than herself, might die—and her baby with her.

Then the widow began to speak to this King of hers again just as if he was right there in the room with them. "Oh, mighty King, spare this mother and child by your power and grace. Show them mercy. Give them comfort and peace. Calm us now, by your presence, in the name of your Son, Morning Star."

The widow's words soothed the soldier's wife. She relaxed for a moment. Then with one last groan and push, the baby's head was free.

For a fleeting instant, Gwyneth dared to hope the danger had passed. Then, to her horror, she realized it hadn't. The child was not pink, but deathly pale. The cord joining it to its mother was wrapped around the infant's neck. Had the baby strangled?

Gwyneth turned away, unable to watch, as the widow moved like lightning. Could the baby be saved? Would it breathe? Scarcely breathing herself, Gwyneth waited. An eternity passed. Or so it seemed. It was really less than a minute till the lusty squall of the baby's first cry rang in Gwyneth's ears. She glanced back in relief to see the widow holding up a pink, wriggling mass of arms and legs.

"You have a little girl," she said smiling, as the parents wept for joy. "Just let me clean her up, and you can hold her."

Gwyneth helped make the new mother comfortable. Then she went to the widow, who had bathed the infant and was wrapping her in a blanket. "I see now why your midwife skills are in such demand. For a moment, I feared the worst."

The widow's face grew grave. "I did also, my dear."

Gwyneth looked somberly at the midwife. "Have you ever lost anyone in childbirth?"

"Yes, it has happened," the widow sighed as a faraway look crossed her face. "Years ago, I lost my dearest friend."

"That must have been hard," Gwyneth murmured, taken aback.

The widow nodded. For a moment, there was silence.

When the widow next spoke, her words caught Gwyneth off guard. "And how is your friend?"

Flustered, Gwyneth reddened. "Which friend do you mean?"

"The young man who came with you to my cottage," the widow smiled.

"Oh, you mean Alfric!" Gwyneth's flush faded. "I don't know. I haven't seen him lately. He's gone off on an errand for Prince Abaddon. If he succeeds, the prince will give him his birthright."

"Is that so?" asked the widow, fighting to keep her surging anger from showing in her face. *Poor Alfric,* she seethed to herself. *He will never receive his birthright from that prince!*

Gwyneth's voice broke into the widow's thoughts. "If you think you can spare me, I really should be going."

The midwife placed the infant in her mother's arms, then took Gwyneth's hands in hers. *How fond I have grown of this girl!* she mused. Of course, the widow realized Gwyneth might have had mixed motives for staying. Still, she had cared deeply about Brie and the baby and worked tirelessly to help. And their talks of the King had touched Gwyneth's heart... of this, the widow felt certain. The door they had opened between them must not close!

"I am so deeply grateful for all you have done," she told Gwyneth, smiling warmly. "In just a few hours, I have found myself feeling toward you as I would toward a daughter."

Gwyneth struggled to swallow the sudden lump in her throat. She had grown unexpectedly fond of the widow, too. But as her father often warned, it was not wise to like your enemies. However, there was no point being rude to them, either. "Thank you for your kindness," Gwyneth said simply.

Then Gwyneth bade farewell to Devlin and Brie, who also showered her with thanks, and hurried away.

Devlin bent to stroke his child's tiny head, then turned to the widow, speaking in a voice choked with emotion. "I am glad I did not arrest you that night at the crossroads. You saved my daughter's life—and perhaps my wife's as well."

"It was not my doing," the widow protested. "Thank the King. It was by his grace."

Devlin felt discomfort and confusion at these words. Even speaking about this King was treasonous, he feared. And he wished to be a loyal soldier. Even so, what if the widow was right and this King had indeed saved his child's life? "Who is your King? And what is grace?" he asked at last.

"My King is the ruler of all," the widow explained. "And grace means he gives good things to undeserving people. But you can read more about him in the Book."

The soldier whispered to his wife. She nodded. He turned back to the widow. "Perhaps we shall read your Book sometime," he said. "And I think we shall name our daughter Grace."

⇛·//·⇝

GWYNETH TURNED her horse toward her father's house, her mind churning from all that had happened and all she had learned. *Not until now did I guess just how formidable a foe this King is,* she fretted. *Nor did I dream he has such a powerful hold on his subjects. The widow seems completely dependent on him. Imagine thinking some far-distant sovereign could help in a troubled birth! Yet that is exactly what the widow believed. Can Alfric pry Jotham loose from an influence so strong?*

Even such troubled thoughts could not keep Gwyneth awake when at last she reached home. She'd slept little during the birthing and her energy was spent. Stretching fully clothed upon her bed, she fell into instant slumber.

It was hours later when she was roused by a servant's

eager knock. "I'm sorry to disturb you, m'lady, but I thought you'd want to know. Alfric has returned. And he has important news."

"Where is he?" gasped Gwyneth.

"He is waiting below."

Gwyneth sprang up. "I am coming."

She ran down the stairs, searching for Alfric as she flew. He wasn't in the entry hall or the drawing room. Gwyneth hurried outside. A white horse stood riderless in the late afternoon shadows, munching grass. She started toward it. "Alfric?"

A tall form crept from a nearby bush and grabbed her from behind. Before she could turn, Alfric covered her eyes with his hand. "You'll never guess what I've brought you!" he crowed in triumph.

"Yes, I will!" gasped Gwyneth, trembling.

"No, you won't!"

Alfric lifted his hand. Gwyneth stared, blinking in the glare of the sparkling gem he held out to her. Never had she seen such perfection in a jewel. For a moment she stood speechless, overwhelmed by its beauty and brilliance.

"So, what do you think of it?" he beamed proudly.

"It's...it's magnificent," she stammered. Gwyneth glanced around, her face falling. "But...where's Jotham?"

Alfric's heart sank. He'd thought Gwyneth would be so dazzled by the jewel, all else would pale by comparison. But it seemed she was not as impressed as he had hoped. He shoved the gem in his pocket and turned to her, flustered. "I ...I don't know where Jotham is. I assume he is somewhere in Acrasia. He started for the border just ahead of me. At least, I thought he did! When the guards said nothing, I figured he sneaked across. But the soldiers lent me a horse to ride, and Jotham was on foot. So perhaps I passed him on the road..."

Alfric paused, overwhelmed by a sudden realization.

"Though it seems I would have seen him..."

"Fool!" burst out Gwyneth. "Why didn't you stay with him? Who knows what has happened to him now? I don't know why Abaddon sent you in the first place."

Stabbed by her words, Alfric flared back. "I did my best! Don't you think I care about Jotham? He's more my friend than yours."

Alfric paused, eyes narrowing. "Or is he? Why is Jotham so important to you, anyway?"

"Why indeed, Gwyneth?" asked a voice from behind them both. They turned to see Bogdan walking toward them. His eyes searched his daughter's face. "You told me your friendship with Jotham was a casual one. So why such distress?"

Gwyneth's mind raced. "My distress is not so much for Jotham, but for Prince Abaddon," she said quickly. "He has ruled us well and deserves our loyalty. I hate to see Jotham turned against him by the King's lies."

"Well, I assure you, Jotham is deceived no longer," Alfric added hastily. He recounted the story of the crowns and how he had made Jotham see that the King's promises were empty.

"Well done!" exclaimed Bogdan. "It seems you have had more success with your friend Jotham than I once did with a friend of mine. You have much to show for your trip."

"More than you know," said Alfric, producing the gem. "Behold the spoils I have brought!"

Bogdan's reaction was much more to Alfric's satisfaction than Gwyneth's had been. He could not take his eyes off the gem. "It's breathtaking!" he gasped.

"And it will doubtless bring a breathtaking price," beamed Alfric. "Perhaps Abaddon himself will buy it."

"Buy what?" Suddenly Abaddon was standing beside them as if appearing out of thin air.

Where did he come from? Alfric wondered. But there was no time to ponder the question. He held up the gem for the prince to admire. "The jewel I brought back as booty from Dominus."

Abaddon eyed it greedily. "Let me see that!" He snatched the stone, then let out a yelp as if holding a burning coal. He dropped the gem, which disintegrated in a blaze of fire.

Abaddon confronted a stunned and disappointed Alfric. "The jewel was from one of their crowns, wasn't it?" he barked.

"Y-yes, Sire," Alfric stammered. "How did you know?"

"They use special stones," Abaddon snapped. "At first they seem harmless and beautiful, but in time they burn like fire. They're terribly noxious."

Alfric felt a wave of self-disgust wash over him. "I can't believe I fell for Morning Star's trickery!" he groaned. "Perhaps Gwyneth was right, and I should have stayed with Jotham."

Abaddon's eyes narrowed. "What do you mean?"

Alfric told Abaddon the saga of the crowns and how he had made Jotham fear the King's punishment. "But even though Jotham fled, what if he was intercepted?" Alfric fretted. "What if Morning Star deceived him into going to the King after all? Perhaps Jotham is suffering some cruel and awful punishment even at this moment!"

Gwyneth listened to all this in silent horror. She was only partly comforted by Abaddon's response. "Or perhaps not," frowned the prince. "The greatest trick of all would be to let the boy go free. The lad has spirit. The King may think him useful against me. So he may not punish Jotham at all. He may pretend to forgive him!"

CHAPTER 17

First Fruits and Second Chances

ONCE AGAIN Jotham knelt quivering in the presence of the King. As before, Morning Star shielded him from the glare of the King's glory. Even so, Jotham felt exposed. It seemed as though the King's holiness was a searchlight that plumbed his soul. What it revealed to Jotham only confirmed what the ring had shown.

Eyes downcast, Jotham whispered words of confession and repentance. "I'm sorry, Father. I should never have tested you. It was wrong to try to take a crown, and even worse to blame it on someone else. Prince Morning Star says you will forgive me. But I don't deserve it. I realize now I must pay the price for what I did."

Then Jotham waited, uncertain what punishment might befall him. Perhaps he would indeed get a beating—or something far worse.

What did happen was the last thing Jotham expected. A light emanated from Morning Star. But this light was deep red, and it washed over Jotham's robe. As it did so, the robe turned as red as blood for one brief instant. Then it glowed white—if possible, even whiter than before. The glow engulfed Jotham, who felt at that moment as if a great weight had been lifted from his shoulders.

Then the King spoke. "You could never pay the price, my child. But it was paid already—when Prince Morning Star ransomed you."

For the first time, Jotham lifted his eyes, hope stirring in his chest. "Forgive me," he begged.

The King's voice engulfed him like a soft warm blanket on an icy winter's morning. "I already have. And I love you as much as ever!"

"Thank you, Father," murmured Jotham, overcome with gratitude.

Jotham turned to the Prince. "Oh, thank you! Thank you so much!"

A joyful smile spread over Morning Star's face. Gently, he held Jotham's hand up for the lad to see. "Look at your ring," the Prince urged.

Jotham did so. "It's gold again!" he cried. "It's gleaming just as brightly as ever!"

For a long, thoughtful moment, Jotham stared at the ring. Then he turned to Morning Star, his face growing pensive. "I wish my ring would stay like this always," he sighed. "But I fear I'll fail again."

Morning Star gazed at Jotham with a look of deepest understanding. In his eyes was the empathy of one who has been in life's crucible and endured its greatest pressures. "You may indeed stumble, and then you must promptly confess it to the King," he said gently. "But you don't have to falter. Remember, Prince Abaddon is your ruler no longer. You belong to our Father now. You must reject Abaddon's lies, and the lies of those who serve him. Beware of their traps!"

Jotham felt the old familiar tingling of his skin. "Will they still be watching me, then?"

Morning Star nodded gravely. "Yes, Jotham, and they will try to trip you. But I and my Father are greater, so fear not. Only listen to us, and do what we ask."

"Oh, I want to, with all my heart!" exclaimed Jotham.

Morning Star beamed approval. "Then your trust and obedience will bear fruit," he smiled. "Look in the pocket of your robe and show me what you find."

Eagerly, Jotham reached into his robe. He pulled out a large piece of fruit. It looked like an orange, but its skin was brown and prickly. Jotham stared at it, puzzled. "I've not seen this kind before. What is it?" he wondered.

"This fruit is called peace," the Prince explained. "The inside is delicious. But it often comes covered with a thick skin of rebellion, anxiety, and care. Only I can peel it. But if you will let me, you can enjoy the sweet fruit inside."

"Please peel it for me. I would love to taste it," Jotham begged, handing Morning Star the fruit.

With swift, sure strokes, the Prince stripped the stubborn skin away, revealing a luscious golden center. He handed the fruit back to Jotham. Jotham took a big, juicy bite. "What a marvelous flavor!" he cried. "I can't even describe it. I've never tasted anything quite like it before."

Then the King spoke. "You shall taste it often if you trust me and my Son. And now you must begin to discover the gifts I have given you."

Jotham reddened with embarrassment. "Gifts? Oh, no! I couldn't accept them. Not after what happened with the crowns. You don't have to give me anything, really. I've learned my lesson."

"You will learn many lessons, and the gifts will help you do so," the King told him. "I give gifts to all my children. You must take them and give them to others, and they must give their gifts to you. In this way, you will all be encouraged and strengthened, and your character will grow."

Once again, the King commended Jotham to Morning Star's care. As the Prince led him out of the palace, Jotham's heart was overflowing. He could hardly believe his good fortune. *First forgiveness, and now gifts!* he marveled to himself. He wondered what these gifts might be and where he might find them. And what would Alfric say to all this if he knew?

Jotham remembered how his friend had run from him in the woods. But the balm of the King's love and pardon soothed his hurt and resentment. Aching with concern, he turned to Morning Star. "Poor Alfric! I wish he could see how gracious the King is to his children!"

Morning Star nodded sadly. "I wish so, too. But though he saw, he would not see. Alfric looks at the King through the distorted glass of Abaddon's lies. Through that glass, light seems like darkness and a gift like a curse."

⚜

ALFRIC FELT he was living in a dream. Surely any moment now, this vast banquet hall, the elegant linen and china, the choice food set before him would all fade away. But it didn't. He was really here, being feasted by Prince Abaddon in the presence of Gwyneth and Bogdan.

"Let us lift our glasses in Alfric's honor," boomed the prince as Alfric glowed with pleasure. Abaddon raised his goblet and turned to Alfric, beaming. "To your courage, skill, and cleverness. And to Jotham's speedy rescue, and the birthright that will soon be yours."

"Hear, hear!" cried Bogdan, holding his own glass high.

Gwyneth said nothing, but she smiled when Alfric touched his goblet to hers.

Alfric hoped her opinion of him had been improved by Abaddon's praise. Although he'd failed to bring Jotham back, their ruler did not seem to think he was a failure. He was giving Alfric a second chance to complete his mission and had even thrown this banquet to reward his efforts.

"To our gracious ruler!" cried Alfric in a burst of gratitude.

Abaddon nodded and smiled as the glasses clinked again. Then he set his goblet down and leaned toward Alfric, a sly flicker in his eyes. "Now, we must plan your return to Dominus. I know the King has tightened his grip on Jotham's heart. Doubtless, he has promised Jotham gifts. And Jotham is thrilled. But he ought to be angry instead."

"Why?" frowned Alfric. "Will they burn up like the jewel from the crown?"

Abaddon's eyes narrowed. "No, my boy. It is something far worse. The King plays favorites with his children. He gives better gifts to some than to others. You must help Jotham see how unfair this is."

Alfric's stomach churned with anger. A scene from his past flashed before his eyes. He was standing in his father's stable. A man's laughter mingled with a child's giggles, searing Alfric's heart. Seething with resentment, he watched his father hoist his small half-brother astride a magnificent palomino pony. "This is your pony, Bowen. Happy birthday," Killian beamed.

The child clapped his hands and tossed his golden hair in glee. Then he turned to Alfric, eyes shining. "What should I name him?"

Alfric's anger burst like a dam. "You shouldn't even have him!" He turned burning eyes on his father. "Why should Bowen get a horse? He's only three! I'm much older, and you never gave me one! I don't know why you favor him so. It's not fair!"

Bowen burst into tears. Killian scooped him up and hugged him close. "Shame on you!" he stormed at Alfric. "See how you've hurt him? Say you're sorry!"

"Why should I, Father?" Alfric blazed. "You don't say you're sorry, and you hurt me all the time. First say you're sorry, and then I will."

"How dare you!" Killian stomped away with Bowen in his arms.

"Alfric? What's wrong?" Gwyneth's voice broke into Alfric's reverie. He met her gaze, bitterness bubbling up. "Just a bad memory."

Alfric turned to Abaddon, eyes flashing. "So this King whom Jotham now calls Father plays favorites too! How well I know the pain of that. I will do everything I can to make Jotham see the truth. But I fear the powers of his robe may blind him. And apparently, it won't come off."

"Nonetheless, the boy's ire can be stirred," Abaddon insisted. "When he sees how the King treats his children, he will turn against this new Father of his. And then, though he wears the robe, the King's influence over him will fade."

"Let us hope so, Your Majesty," Bogdan frowned. "But the King's hold can't always be broken. It could not with my friend."

"But it will with Jotham," Alfric vowed. "I shall do as you say, Sire. And don't worry, I won't disappoint you!"

Alfric turned once more to Gwyneth. "Or you, either," he assured her. "This time, Jotham shall return."

Gwyneth looked Alfric full in the eyes. "I know he will," she answered.

Alfric's face shone with pleasure at her confidence in him. But as Abaddon proposed one last toast, Alfric did not catch what Gwyneth whispered under her breath so low that none could hear. "Because this time, I am going to Dominus, too!"

CHAPTER 18

Gwyneth Meets the Shepherd

⟨━━⫘━━⟩

GWYNETH SAT staring into her lap, oblivious to the clink of crystal and clatter of dishes around her. The banquet was over, and servants were clearing the table. Her father and Abaddon were deep in conversation on matters of state. Alfric had already left to prepare for his journey to Dominus tomorrow. He would leave on a wagon bringing fresh supplies to the border guards.

But how will I manage my own trip to Dominus? Gwyneth fretted. *Father's made it quite clear he won't let me go after Jotham. If I invent some excuse for a journey, he'll insist I have an escort. Which leaves me no choice but to sneak away. But I hate to do that. He'll be so worried...*

Splat! Gwyneth jumped at the sudden noise. Had a servant knocked something over? Her eyes scanned the table. "Ugh!" she gasped, recoiling, as she pointed at a serving bowl. A pair of bulging eyes peered up at her over its rim.

"Don't worry, madam, it's only a frog. They slip in sometimes. I'll get rid of it." A servant reached in, grabbing for the creature. But the frog was too quick. Leaping high, it landed on Gwyneth's head. She shrieked just as a hand plucked the creature off.

"Cute little fellow, isn't he?" said Abaddon's voice behind her. "He must have come in through the window. I'll put him out myself."

Gwyneth watched as the prince strode to the window, frog in hand. But he didn't put it out right away. First he held it up before him, peering at it intently. The prince's face darkened. Gwyneth had a fleeting impression that the frog was somehow communicating with him. *If so, Abaddon must not like the creature's news. He seems quite displeased*, she mused. Then she scolded herself silently. *What a silly notion! Frogs can't talk!*

Still, Abaddon's mood had certainly changed when he joined them once more. When he spoke, his voice crackled with anger. "One more matter, Bogdan. We must deal more strictly with these treacherous People of the Book. It is not just Jotham they have deceived. I have word they are influencing others. And it seems their boldness is growing. They must be stopped!"

At Abaddon's order, a servant fetched him pen and parchment. He wrote for a moment, then read the result.

> By royal decree, I, Prince Abaddon, declare that the People of the Book are forbidden to assemble together. Nor may they seek to interest others in their writings. Those who do so shall be guilty of high treason.

The prince sealed the document with his signet ring. Then he handed it to Bogdan. "You yourself must announce this law throughout the kingdom," he commanded. "Impress upon our soldiers the importance of strictly enforcing the decree. You will leave at dawn."

"As you wish, Sire." Bogdan kept his voice calm, but his heart was troubled. This whole business with Jotham had left him quite worried about Gwyneth. Now was hardly the time for her to be home by herself. He turned to his daughter. "I fear this will take a few days. I don't like to leave you so long. Why don't you come with me?"

Gwyneth saw her chance. "Please Father, can't I visit Megan instead? I've not seen her for months. And you needn't fret about an escort, either. I can travel on a military wagon as Alfric is doing. They pass by her village all the time. And I'll ride one back as well."

Bogdan brightened. Gwyneth loved spending time with Megan, a cherished childhood friend who lived some distance from Acrasia. This was the perfect solution. "A splendid idea! You have my permission," he beamed. "When will you leave so I may give orders concerning your trip?"

Gwyneth's mind raced. She did not want her movements traced. "Tomorrow or the next day...I'm not quite sure. Why don't you just write me a letter of passage, Father?"

Bogdan smiled. "So I shall."

⚓

IT WAS STILL dark next morning when Gwyneth rose to wish her father a safe journey. Once Bogdan left, she wasted no time. Stopping only to pack a small bag and instruct the servants, she set out on horseback for the Fortress of Belial.

With Bogdan gone, Gwyneth might have ridden all the way to the border alone. But that would be dangerous. So she had conceived a better plan. On the pretext of seeing Alfric off, she would learn which wagon he was taking. When no one was looking, she would hide inside. She would be far safer traveling this way. And she would avoid a chance meeting with soldiers who might turn her back. Best of all, she could follow Alfric into Dominus.

But first, I shall have to find him, thought Gwyneth as she emerged from the fortress stables where her horse would be cared for until her return. Instantly, she was swallowed up in a teeming bustle of activity. The Fortress of Belial served as the chief base of military operations for all of Withershins. A vast army was stationed there. On its grounds were great storehouses filled with weapons and supplies. These, and contingents of soldiers, were constantly being dispatched to lesser outposts in the realm.

Gwyneth navigated through this sea of busyness, hurrying toward the storehouses where Alfric's wagon would surely be loading. Soldiers galloped by, their mounts kicking up dust. Horse smells mingled with the odor of sweating bodies. Shouts, whinnies, and the stomping of hooves blended in a tumultuous chorus of noise. Gwyneth strained her eyes, searching for Alfric.

"Gwyneth!" Alfric's voice rang like a welcome trumpet above the din. She turned toward the sound, and her heart sank in despair. His wagon was already loaded. Its cover was fastened down and a soldier sat on the seat, the horses' reins in his hands. Alfric, who was perched beside him, jumped down as Gwyneth hurried toward him.

"I hardly expected to see you here. Are you going somewhere too?" Alfric asked, eyeing Gwyneth's travel bag.

"Father left on official business so I'm going to see my friend Megan. I have passage on a wagon. But first I'd thought to bid you a last farewell."

Alfric glowed with pleasure. "You're just in time. We're leaving now."

Gwyneth grasped for a way to stall him. "So soon? I had hoped we might have a few minutes together. It's still early. Surely you have time for tea. There's a shop nearby that serves refreshments."

Alfric glanced up at the soldier on the wagon's seat. "What say you, Torin? Can we delay a few moments?"

Torin frowned and shuddered. "No. We'd best be off. Our route is frightful enough in daylight. The less we must travel after darkness falls, the better I will like it."

Alfric took Gwyneth's arm and led her a few steps out of Torin's view. He lowered his voice. "No time for tea, then. But perhaps a kiss?" He leaned his face toward hers. She reddened, stammering, caught off guard. "I . . . Prince Abaddon!"

Alfric froze, turning scarlet as he spied the prince approaching.

If Abaddon noticed the young people's discomfort, he ignored it. "I am glad I found you, Alfric," he said. "There is one last thing I must tell you."

Just then Torin leaned around the wagon. "Hurry Al . . ." His voice trailed off at the sight of Abaddon. "Your Majesty!" he gasped. Leaping from his perch, he fell prostrate before his ruler. "Torin, at your command, Sire."

Abaddon raised the trembling soldier to his feet. "Leave us, Torin. I must have a private word with Alfric. Go and fortify yourself for your journey with a tall mug of cider. By then we will have finished our business."

"Y-yes, Your Highness," Torin stammered, hurrying away.

The prince turned his attention to Gwyneth. "And you'd best be going too, or you'll miss your ride."

Gwyneth shivered, sensing some strange undercurrent in the prince's words. But there was no time to ponder the matter. She held out her hand to Alfric. "Farewell then, and may your errand prosper."

"Yours also." Alfric kissed her hand politely, then let it drop.

Gwyneth hurried away, glancing back just once to be sure she was not being watched. The prince and Alfric had turned aside, their heads bent, deep in conversation. Gwyneth slipped behind the wagon. Making sure no one saw her, she lifted the cover's flap and scrambled inside, crouching down between two crates.

It wasn't long before Gwyneth heard Torin's voice once

more and Alfric's in response. The wagon swayed slightly as
they clambered aboard. Torin shouted to the horses. Gwyneth felt a giant lurch as the wagon rolled into motion. She
was on her way.

⌒～⫯⟋～⌒

THE RIDE proved rougher than Gwyneth expected. Though
the weather in Acrasia had been calm, winds rose early in the
journey and grew worse as time went on. Fierce gusts battered the wagon, causing Gwyneth to be jostled by sliding
crates and boxes. She could almost feel the purple bruises
blooming on her soft, fair skin. But she set her jaw and
made no sound. She had learned a soldier's toughness from
her father. A few bumps, however nasty, would not deter her
from her goal.

But Gwyneth knew other obstacles might prove more
troublesome. Even as she sat cramped and confined, her
brain was racing. Her father was fond of saying that a soldier's best weapon was a well-armed mind. Now she armed
hers, probing every possible problem she might encounter.
She was determined that she would be ready for anything…
even the chance that Bogdan might stop the wagon and
search it himself.

This thought sent a shiver up Gwyneth's spine that had
nothing to do with the chilled blasts of wind screeching
under the flapping wagon cover. She did not know her
father's travel route. Still, it seemed unlikely he would pass
them. Even if he did, he would have no cause to search the
wagon, would he? Yet he might, prompted not by cause, but
by some canny instinct.

This possibility gnawed at Gwyneth as she huddled in
the wagon, drawing her cloak close for warmth. But she had
retired late and awakened early. Now her eyes drooped. All
thought was drowned out by the hypnotic clippety-clop of

horses' hooves. Then even that sound faded to nothingness.

How long the nothingness lasted, Gwyneth did not know. Suddenly, she became aware that the wagon had stopped. The flap was pushed aside. Gwyneth choked back a gasp of horror as her father's face appeared in the opening. His eyes scanned the boxes and crates. Would he spot her?

Gwyneth held her breath. At last, Bogdan seemed satisfied nothing was amiss. He began to pull back. And then, without warning, a huge jolt rocked the wagon. The boxes hiding her were thrown aside. She swallowed hard and looked up, expecting the worst. No one was there! Gwyneth realized she'd been dreaming.

Now she heard new voices shouting directions. Horses neighed. The wagon rolled backwards. They had reached the border! Any moment the soldiers would begin unloading. Unless she moved swiftly, she would be discovered.

Gwyneth groped for her travel bag but could not find it. The bumping and jostling of the journey must have flung it aside. She dared not linger to search. The wagon had stopped. Peeking outside the flap to make sure no one was watching, she dropped noiselessly to the ground.

Night had fallen, though a partial moon provided some light. The wind had mellowed to a mild breeze. Gwyneth melted into the darkness, taking refuge behind a tall shrub. Peering out, she saw that the wagon had pulled up to a small wooden building. *Likely that is both storehouse and sleeping quarters for the sentries*, she guessed. Her eyes searched the landscape. *And the border must be past the wall. Perhaps there's a way through. I must keep close to Alfric and see where he goes.*

Alfric and Torin jumped down from the wagon as two other soldiers joined them. "Stand watch, Ragnar, while I help Torin with the boxes," said one. He grasped Alfric's hand. "Good luck on your mission. May you fare better this time than last."

"Thank you, Cadel," cried Alfric.

Torin, too, wished Alfric well. Then both strode behind the wagon to begin their task. Alfric turned toward the wall, but found Ragnar blocking his path.

"So that sniveling traitor Jotham didn't crawl home after all! I thought as much! I doubted he could slip across the border without my knowledge. But tell me, why risk yourself again for that worthless coward?"

Gwyneth, watching from hiding, felt her stomach knot in anger. Alfric's tone was cold with fury when he answered. "He is hardly worthless if Abaddon bade me save him. Besides, Jotham is my friend."

Ragnar laughed scornfully. "You mean he has friends now? Surely he had none at Flotsam Manor."

"You knew him at the orphanage?" frowned Alfric, liking Ragnar less and less.

"Oh, no one really knew him," sneered Ragnar. "Quite a strange one, he was! With queer thoughts and suspicions..."

"Enough of this talk!" cried Alfric. "Stand back!"

"Good for you, Alfric!" Gwyneth muttered under her breath.

Ragnar moved a step closer, glowering. "How dare you give me orders! You are not my superior."

"Perhaps not now, but I will be soon enough," Alfric snapped. "Once I complete my mission, I'll be commissioned an officer."

Ragnar's voice rang with triumph. "Ah-ha! So that's it! You will get a commission for your trouble! Quite a handsome reward, I must say!" Ragnar's voice grew oily. "Perhaps you are not as dense as I once thought. Come, Alfric, we can help each other. You have failed once in your task. You may fail again. Let me go after Jotham in your place. I shall drag him back, even if I have to beat him! I've done so before. And when I become an officer, I'll aid your fortunes also."

Alfric's tone was taut. "I want no help from you except to

step aside."

Ragnar folded his arms across his massive chest, leering nastily. "Make me!"

Alfric's eyes flashed. His arm shot out without warning, shoving Ragnar aside. The bully, caught off balance, toppled to the ground. For a moment, he stared in shocked fury. Then he howled in pretend pain. "Owwww! Help! Seize him!"

Torin and Cadel rushed upon the scene. "Seize who? What's happened?" Cadel barked.

"Alfric! He attacked me!" Ragnar yelped.

"If I had, he'd be in far worse shape," snapped Alfric. "I just pushed him out of my way when he refused to move on his own."

"Next time, mind your manners, Ragnar," scowled Cadel, dragging Ragnar to his feet. "Now, put your bulk to better use and go help Torin. I'll stand guard. That's an order!"

Ragnar lumbered off as Cadel turned apologetically to Alfric. "I'm sorry. I fear Ragnar is nothing but trouble. Luckily, I'll be rid of him soon. His tour of duty at the border is ending. He's been reassigned to Acrasia. Torin will replace him."

"I'm sure you're relieved," smiled Alfric. He shook Cadel's hand once more, then strode off along the wall out of sight.

Gwyneth dared not follow until Cadel, too, had moved away. Bending low behind a row of bushes, she hurried as fast as she dared. Up ahead, she saw Alfric stop and draw something from his coat. A moment more and she caught a flicker of flame, as if from a candle, in his hand. He held the flame up, paused a moment, then pushed on the stone wall and walked straight through it.

There must be a doorway in the rock surface, Gwyneth thought. But when she reached the wall, she could not find a break. In the moon's pale glow, she saw nothing but gray sameness. Meanwhile the sound of Alfric's footsteps grew fainter. Swiftly searching for a place where the chinks in the wall were deeper, she began to climb.

It was no easy task. Her body ached from the bumpy wagon ride. Her skirts swirled around her legs, hindering her effort. Her heart pounded at the slightest noise, so fearful was she that she might be spotted. Nor did her fear lessen once she swung over the top. Though the soldiers would not see her now, Alfric might if he glanced back. But at last, having lowered herself part way down the wall, she let go, landing safely in a growth of ferns.

By now, she could barely make out Alfric's form. As swiftly as she dared, she followed his distant blur down what seemed to be a slope. By the time she neared what she now saw was a bridge, he had reached the other side.

Fearing that once again he might look back and glimpse her, Gwyneth waited until Alfric disappeared from view, then she stepped onto the structure herself. She gazed ahead at what must be Dominus. Then she turned and stared down at what seemed to be a vast chasm below. The full impact of what she was doing struck her like a blow. Despite her fierce determination, she felt her body tremble. For an instant, she faltered, swaying toward the chasm's depths.

In that very moment, something swooped toward her with lightning speed. Instinctively she pulled back, unconsciously correcting her balance. She glanced up just in time to see that it was some sort of bird. Then it vanished, soaring into Dominus in the same direction Alfric had taken. Drawing a deep breath, Gwyneth followed.

By this time, Alfric was nowhere in sight. But he had recounted his journey to the King's palace in detail the night of the banquet. Gwyneth knew he had taken the road that now stretched before her. Perhaps if she hurried, she might catch up enough to keep him in view.

She never did. But dawn found her at the place where the road became three. Alfric had described this spot, also. *Shall I take the hilly path, as he did?* Gwyneth wondered.

"Just because a friend chooses a certain road does not mean it is the right one," said a gentle voice behind her.

Startled, Gwyneth spun around to face a shepherd with a staff. "How did you know what I was thinking?" she demanded.

"The same way I know that you are hungry," the shepherd replied. "Why don't you eat the fruit that you brought with you from Withershins?"

"You're quite mistaken. I brought no fruit," she retorted.

"Look in the pocket of your cloak," the shepherd insisted.

Scowling, she complied, finding to her amazement that there was indeed a piece of fruit inside. Its skin was rosy, like a ripe apple, and it smelled delicious. Gwyneth's mouth watered. Wherever this strange fruit came from, it would make a nice breakfast! Gwyneth took a big bite. She chewed, then frowned and made a face.

The shepherd watched her intently. "What's wrong?" he asked.

"This fruit has little flavor and a bitter aftertaste," Gwyneth grumbled.

The shepherd nodded wisely. "I am not at all surprised. That fruit is called hope. If the tree it grows on is not rooted in the proper soil, it may prove quite disappointing. The very best hope fruit grows on trees planted in the courtyard of the King's palace. All his children are free to pick and eat as much as they want. Would you like me to give you some?"

Gwyneth's stomach rumbled. How she longed for that fruit! But just in time, she remembered what she'd heard of the deceptions of Dominus. Gwyneth backed away. "N-no thank you, I'm not hungry anymore. Besides, I have to go. I'm looking for a friend."

The shepherd gazed at Gwyneth with an expression of inexpressible sorrow. "You are looking for more than a friend. But you will not find what you seek unless you follow me."

For a brief instant, Gwyneth felt herself drawn almost irresistibly to the shepherd. But then a chord of recognition sounded in her brain. Alfric, too, had spoken of a shepherd who wished to lead him. This might be the same fellow, probably an agent of the King. He had almost tricked her— but not quite!

"No, really," she said in a still firmer tone. "I seek only my friend. And I'm sure I can find him on my own."

The shepherd's sad eyes met Gwyneth's for one endless moment more. Then he gestured with his hand. A white dove flitted out of a tree, cooed at Gwyneth, and fluttered down a path. It was not Alfric's path, but so anxious was Gwyneth to escape that she hardly cared. She hastily excused herself. "I'll just follow that bird. Thanks anyway. Perhaps one day I'll see you again."

Gwyneth hurried after the dove. The shepherd watched her go. "You have not seen me yet," he sighed. As he watched Gwyneth disappear into the distance, a single tear glistened in his eye.

CHAPTER 19

The Gifts Unlike All Others

THE MORNING sun bathed Jotham in its glow as he sat lost in thought on a stone bench in the palace courtyard, a piece of fresh bread forgotten in his hand. A brightly colored bird alighted beside him, nibbling at the morsel. Jotham didn't notice, but Evan did. "Careful, friend," he chuckled. "Looks like someone's stealing your breakfast."

Jotham glanced down. Too late. With one final tug, the feathered thief pulled the crust free and flew off with its prize. Jotham cocked an eyebrow at Evan, smiling wryly. "Now I know why I can't discover my gifts from the King. I don't have them anymore. A little bird came and snatched them away."

"Now, Jotham, the King's gifts can't be stolen any more than spiritual riches can," laughed Evan.

"And no wonder, since they're so well hidden," Jotham bantered.

Evan's tone grew reassuring. "You will find them in good time. Even now, I see someone who may help you. Come."

Evan led Jotham toward a group of women sitting under

a tree. One among them held a copy of the Book and was speaking to the rest. She was sturdy of build with graceful features and skin like polished ebony. Jotham sensed a gentle authority in her manner that impressed him. "Who is that woman, and what is she doing?" he asked.

"Her name is Elsbeth," said Evan, "and she's giving her gift."

"What gift?" asked Jotham, puzzled.

"Her gift is called teaching," Evan explained. "The King has given her special insight into the Book and the skill to help others understand it."

Jotham studied the women's faces. "All the rest seem to look up to her."

Evan nodded. "Yes, Jotham. Good teachers are greatly admired."

Jotham thought of how people had admired his wood-carving in Withershins. Even Gwyneth had thought it quite special. He missed that.

"I do hope the King has given me this gift," he sighed. "I should like to be held in such high esteem."

"Though the gifts may bring admiration, they are not given for that purpose," Evan told him.

Jotham frowned. "Why not?"

Evan moved closer, listening to the teaching for a moment before turning to Jotham again. "I believe Elsbeth herself is about to explain this. Why don't I leave you to listen while I tend to some business. I'll return later."

Evan hurried away. Jotham turned his attention to Elsbeth. She was comparing the King's family to a body.

"We must work together for each other's good, like the parts of a body," she said. "The King has given us gifts to help us do so. But these gifts don't make us better than each other, only different. Imagine for a moment that we are all body parts. I'm an eye. One of you is an ear. Am I better because I see and you hear? Of course not! The body needs both."

Jotham nodded thoughtfully, pondering this, so intent on Elsbeth's words that for once he had no eerie sensation to warn him he was being watched.

"Each member of the King's family is unique," Elsbeth added. "Each of us has a role to play and a need to fill. As we serve the King and each other, we'll discover what our gifts are."

"Psssst!"

Startled, Jotham turned and looked over his shoulder. The noise was repeated. Jotham hesitated, then moved toward it. Without warning, a hand wrapped around him, muzzling his mouth and yanking him behind a thick tree trunk. One whispered sound hissed in his ear. "Shhhhh!"

Fighting back terror, he glanced up at his captor. Fear gave way to delight. As the hand eased off his mouth, he whispered a joyous greeting. "Alfric! I never dreamed you'd return! But I'm so glad you have. I told the King about the crowns after all. And he didn't beat me. He forgave me, just as Morning Star said."

He pretended to forgive you, just as Abaddon said, thought Alfric, fuming.

Glaring at Jotham, Alfric spoke in a strident tone. "The crowns are not what they seem. And neither is this King. He appears to be gracious. But in truth, he is terribly unfair."

"Surely, you are mistaken," frowned Jotham.

"No, I'm not!" Alfric's eyes flashed with indignation. "The King doesn't treat all his children equally. He gives gifts to them, but he plays favorites. Some of his children receive better gifts than others."

"But Alfric, all the King's gifts are good," Jotham assured him. "Just listen to Elsbeth and you'll see what I mean."

Alfric fell silent so they could hear Elsbeth speak. "The King's gifts are like no others," she was saying. "And though some may receive more attention, each is significant and necessary."

"That's nothing but drivel," Alfric scoffed. "Listen, Jotham. When I was a boy, my father dreamed of my being a champion archer. But I was more skilled with a pen than a bow. Yet Father cared little that I wrote fine essays. Such gifts were insignificant to him. He wanted me to win tournaments. I didn't. So he admired the boys who did, and I was overlooked."

Jotham bit his lip. His shoulders sagged. Alfric's words made sense. "In that case, I fear I may be overlooked here in Dominus," Jotham admitted. "Because here the gift of teaching is admired, and I doubt I have it. I could never explain things the way Elsbeth does!"

"Then I'd say you were cheated!" Alfric snapped, seizing his advantage. "And I'd wager Elsbeth has a swelled head. The boys who won those tournaments certainly did."

"I hate being cheated!" Jotham scowled. "I was often cheated at the orphanage. And if Elsbeth does have a swelled head, I doubt I shall like her."

Behind a nearby rose hedge, someone else was scowling, too. It was Gwyneth. She had reached Azriel late the previous night. Not wishing to seek lodging and risk being questioned, she had chosen instead to make her bed in a sheltered spot by the roadway. Her mind had been restless, and she had slept little. Rising early, she had slipped through the palace gates ahead of the morning throngs. Watching from hiding, she had seen Jotham enter, and her heart leaped with gladness.

But now that gladness was tinged with disappointment. *I thought I knew Jotham, but perhaps I don't*, she mused. *Why does he suspect that Elsbeth's conceited just because she's good at something? Must a woman be only an adornment? Can she not have talents and use them?*

Gwyneth felt a wave of sadness. She was used to men resenting her wit and skill. But in Jotham, she had sensed a different spirit. Now she wondered if she'd been wrong.

"Heed me, Jotham!" Alfric's words broke into Gwyneth's thoughts. She realized with a jolt that she'd become distracted. She leaned forward, focusing once more on what her two friends were saying.

"You must hurry back to Withershins with me," Alfric now urged Jotham. "Prince Abaddon will soon commission me an officer. I shall gain my birthright, and be rich and powerful. Then I'll be your patron and buy you a shop. And you shall be famous...more famous than Magnus. One day you will be the greatest woodcraftsman in all of Withershins."

"A famous woodcraftsman. I would like that," Jotham said wistfully. "Perhaps you are right."

"Of course I am," Alfric insisted. "I fear the King has given you a paltry gift at best. You shall win no great renown here. But in Withershins you shall have fame and fortune..."

"Farewell, Elsbeth."

The cheery voice turned Jotham's attention back to Elsbeth. He saw that the women with her were leaving. She watched them for a moment. Then she leaned against the tree, sighing deeply. Something in her demeanor stirred Jotham. "Elsbeth doesn't look conceited, just troubled," he told Alfric. "I must speak with her. Wait."

Jotham moved toward Elsbeth. Her face had the same soulful beauty as the Widow Nessa's. This inner beauty drew him.

"Excuse me. I am Jotham," he said gently. "I have listened to you teach. But now you seem burdened. What's wrong?"

Elsbeth spoke in anxious tones. "I long to give my gift well and honor the King. Yet I fear my efforts fall far short, and my gift will not be received."

"How could you think that?" cried Jotham, quite amazed. "Your teaching is so marvelously clear!"

Jotham's face grew thoughtful. "And if some do not receive it, why are you to blame? A gift may be spurned even though it is given well. Many in Withershins have spurned the King's gift of adoption. Yet surely that's not the King's fault, or Morning Star's."

"No, indeed," agreed Elsbeth. "Thank you for reminding me. And for giving me your gifts."

Jotham stared in amazement. "How could I give them?" he wondered. "I don't even know what they are."

Elsbeth smiled warmly. "You have the gifts of encouragement and wisdom. And I could not give my gifts without receiving yours."

Elsbeth's words set Jotham glowing deep within. "I'm starting to understand," he beamed. "These gifts somehow need each other to work right. It is like a body! I am significant and needed! And I have never felt so wonderful inside!"

Elsbeth nodded, her own face glowing. "Look in the pocket of your robe," she told him.

Jotham did so, pulling out a large round piece of fruit with a sunny yellow skin. "This is not like the peace fruit I found here before," he observed. "What is it?"

"It is joy," Elsbeth answered. "And it, too, has a wonderful flavor. Taste and see."

Jotham peeled off the skin. The fruit was in sections. He ate a piece. Its flavor set his heart singing.

FROM HIS HIDING place behind the tree, Alfric listened with growing dismay. He had nearly persuaded Jotham to return with him. But now it seemed Elsbeth would undo it all! He was nearly beside himself when Jotham rejoined him.

"You are not needed here! You are needed in Withershins! I need you, Jotham!" Alfric burst out before Jotham could speak.

"Oh, Alfric, don't you see?" cried Jotham. "It's the King you need! You must go for adoption. Then he will give you gifts and joy fruit, too."

"What would I want with joy fruit?" Alfric scoffed. "I'd rather eat steak at Cuthbert's!"

"If you taste this fruit, you will soon change your mind," Jotham countered. "There is nothing quite like it. Just try some."

Jotham handed Alfric a generous section of fruit. He took a big bite—then spat it out, gagging and choking. "It's awful!" he gasped.

Jotham's jaw sagged in shock. "But I tried some myself. It's delicious!"

"You think it's delicious because you're deceived," Alfric spat. "This King has so confused your mind that you don't know sweet from sour or friends from enemies. Once we were friends, Jotham. But I fear we are friends no longer."

Jotham stared in dismay. Hot tears burned his eyes. "What are you saying, Alfric?"

"We were so close, Jotham. We shared everything. We trusted each other. But now this King of yours has come between us like a wall. You don't care about me anymore!"

"That's not true! I care about you more than ever!" Jotham choked.

Alfric pierced Jotham with his gaze. "If you're really my friend, leave Dominus and come home with me."

Jotham recoiled in horror. "If you're really my friend, don't force me to make such a choice. All my life, I have sought a place of refuge. At last, I have found it! I am near my Father. I feel peaceful and safe. You have such a place of refuge too, near your mother. You find comfort there, even as I do here in Dominus. And I would never ask you to give up your special place for me."

"This land isn't special nor are you safe here. You've been tricked! Can't you see that?" But even as Alfric spoke, Bogdan's words echoed in his mind. *The King's hold can't always be broken. It could not with my friend.*

Suddenly, Alfric felt as though all his hopes, his dreams, his birthright, his future with Gwyneth were drowning, sucked into a sea of hopelessness. And he was drowning with them. His one hope, his lone life preserver, was Jotham. But Jotham was bobbing out of reach, being pulled away by the King. Alfric lunged at him in desperation, seizing his shoulders. "You must see! Come back with me, Jotham! For your sake! For my sake! You must!"

"I can't!" gasped Jotham.

Frenzied by passion, hardly knowing what he did, Alfric shook Jotham violently. "You must! You must!"

"Alfric, stop!" Jotham pushed him hard.

Alfric swayed, then toppled backwards to the ground. For an endless moment, Alfric stared in shock. A cold numbness seized him. He spoke with the voice of a doomed man. "It's no use! I'm leaving. And this time, I won't be back!"

"Alfric, please!" Jotham reached out his hand to help Alfric up.

Alfric spurned it, struggling to his feet. He hurled his last words like a slap. "You are dead to me!" Then he was gone.

Jotham sank to the ground, tears staining his cheeks. Never had he felt so helpless. Suddenly, a hand touched his shoulder. It was Morning Star. The Prince's face seemed to mirror the pain Jotham felt. "I saw what happened. You are deeply grieved for Alfric, aren't you?" he asked gently.

Jotham struggled for words, his voice breaking. "I wanted ... I pleaded. He won't be adopted. And the joy fruit ... I don't understand! He said it was awful. Is there something wrong with his tongue?"

"The problem isn't his tongue, it's his heart," the Prince sighed sadly. "When your heart is sour, the joy fruit puckers your mouth."

"Poor Alfric!" cried Jotham, his own heart going out to his friend. "How I wish I could help him! But I can't!"

"Perhaps you can," the Prince countered.

Jotham's eyes grew wide. "How, Your Highness?"

"Go back to Withershins," the Prince said softly.

Jotham reeled in shock. "That's what Alfric wanted! But I thought... Surely you don't mean...?" Jotham took a deep breath. "Leave Dominus? Desert the King?"

"No, Jotham. Do the King's work," Morning Star said gently.

As the Prince spoke these words, Jotham saw on his face a look of such infinite love that it took his breath away. Something in that look made him think of the Widow Nessa. A memory stirred, of a question he'd asked her. *Why didn't you stay with the King?*

Her reply echoed in his soul. *"I returned to tell others about him."*

And she told me, and now I'm adopted, Jotham realized with new understanding. A deep desire stirred within him. "Yes, my Lord, I will go back," he answered firmly.

Morning Star beamed approval. "This pleases me greatly, Jotham. You have heeded a high calling."

Jotham's face clouded slightly. "Still, I feel so unequal to the task. Perhaps if I could explain the Book, like Elsbeth..." His voice trailed off.

The Prince laid a kindly hand on his shoulder. "Fear not, Jotham. I am with you, and you have the King's Spirit to guide you. And when the King calls you to serve him, he provides what you need. I myself shall prepare you for your return to Withershins."

Jotham felt his spirits soar. "Oh, thank you!"

GWYNETH, who was watching from behind the hedge, felt her heart nearly bursting within her. *I was right about Jotham after all!* she exulted to herself. *He was able to appreciate Elsbeth's gifts once his better instincts conquered his first jealous impulse. Nor is he hopelessly in the King's clutches. His bond with Alfric is deeper than either of them guess. Once Jotham returns to Withershins, Alfric may yet break the King's hold on him. But Alfric must make Jotham see the King's deceptions. And to do so, he will need my help!*

Gwyneth felt a surge of new resolve. *Alfric gave up too soon. It is good that I came!* she thought. *I shall stay near Jotham, and listen closely to his so-called "preparation." If I am to counter the lies he is told, I must know what they are.*

And so Gwyneth followed stealthily as the Prince led Jotham away. Little did she dream Morning Star was aware of her presence. Nor did she guess the Prince wanted her to hear all he said. For Morning Star knew what Gwyneth did not: that the truths of the Book had their own way of working—even in the unbelieving hearts of those who mistook them for lies.

CHAPTER 20

Salt and Light

❦

THE CLEAR, cold water sparkled like diamonds in the noon-day sun and tinkled like bells as it filled the people's cups. Yet, though her lips cracked with thirst, Gwyneth dared not drink. She had sipped from streams along the road on her journey to Azriel, but this water was from the King's own spring. What if it had some strange effect on those who swallowed it? She could not risk dulling her senses. She must remain focused on the task at hand, learning all she could about what the Prince was telling Jotham.

Wrenching her gaze from the beckoning liquid, Gwyneth turned back to Jotham and Morning Star, who were lunching nearby. A line had formed of those who wished to greet the Prince. Gwyneth marveled at the time and care he took with each. She found herself fighting an impulse to like him. It was the same strange attraction she had felt toward the shepherd. And it brought to mind a caution of her father's: *"The most dangerous enemy is one who appears to be a friend."*

As she pondered these words, two others joined Jotham, the young man she had heard him call Evan and the woman named Elsbeth. Morning Star led all three up the palace steps. Then he faced the throng, who pressed closer, sensing something was about to happen. Gwyneth skirted the crowd, staying out of sight while drawing closer herself. The people fell silent as Morning Star began to speak. Though his words were directed to Jotham, they seemed meant for all his subjects.

"Heed my words, Jotham. Though you return to Withershins, you belong to it no longer. You are now a citizen of Dominus. Your first loyalty is to the King. And your task is to tell those in Withershins about him."

Gwyneth was horrified. *This is high treason,* she fumed to herself. *And no wonder! The Prince wants Jotham to switch his allegiance. He's to follow the King, not Abaddon, and urge all he meets to do likewise. For his trouble, he will doubtless be jailed or perhaps put to death. And how could he hope to sway others to join in such folly, anyway?*

As if in answer to her silent question, Morning Star held up a glass carafe filled with a fine white substance. *What is this?* Gwyneth wondered. *Some strange potion to confuse people's minds? Will the Prince ask Jotham to slip it into people's tea or porridge? If so, it would hardly surprise me!*

What did surprise her were the Prince's next words. "This is salt," he explained, pouring some into Jotham's hand. "It's quite valuable in Withershins, is it not?"

"Yes," said Jotham. "It's so highly prized, it's sometimes used as currency."

"Taste it," Morning Star urged him.

Jotham did. His face grew puzzled. "This salt has no flavor."

The Prince gazed at him intently. "Then what is its value?"

"It is worthless. It has no use at all," Jotham answered.

"Quite right," said the Prince. "And you are salt, Jotham. You must flavor Withershins with the King's ways. But if you become like Abaddon's servants, you will lose your flavor just as this salt has."

Gwyneth flushed with anger. *I am a servant of Abaddon,*

she seethed. *And Jotham won't be flavorless salt by becoming like me. Indeed, any influence of mine is sure to improve him!*

The Prince's voice broke into her thoughts. This time, he pointed upward to the sun, high in the sky. "And what is the sun's use, Jotham?" he asked.

"To give warmth and light," Jotham answered.

"And if the sun were darkened, what then?"

Jotham frowned. "It could not fulfill its purpose."

Morning Star gazed somberly at Jotham. "You are warmth and light. You must shine our Father's truth and love in the darkness of Withershins. Otherwise, you will be like a darkened sun and will not fulfill your purpose."

Gwyneth's stomach churned. She was outraged! How could Morning Star claim that those who served Abaddon were in darkness? Her own father was Abaddon's top official. There was no one more intelligent, educated, and enlightened than he. He had far more light than Jotham—or Morning Star for that matter.

It gratified Gwyneth that Jotham himself seemed to have some doubts about this. "But how can I do this?" he asked the Prince. "How can someone like me be salt and light?"

"You must follow the example of Oswin," Morning Star replied. "He lived in Withershins in the long-before times. His story is in the Book." Morning Star turned to Elsbeth. "Will you read it?"

Gwyneth felt her nerve endings tingle as Elsbeth opened a copy of the Book. She had not realized how curious she was about its contents. Though it was surely filled with lies, they must be clever ones. This intrigued her. Besides, she loved a good story. Her mother had often told tales beside the fire on long winter nights. Even now, an echo of her mother's lilting voice whispered in Gwyneth's memory. With a shiver of anticipation, Gwyneth leaned forward, listening intently as Elsbeth read.

Long ago, in a province of Withershins called Lemuel, there lived a lad named Oswin. His birth was noble, and his training nobler still. He learned of the King at an early age and came for adoption. His love for the King and the Book grew greater with each passing year.

Elsbeth continued, her words painting pictures in Gwyneth's mind.

In those times, local lords under Prince Abaddon often warred upon each other to increase their domains. One among them, Nagid, rose in power and prominence above the rest. At length, he conquered Lemuel and dragged off many of its youthful nobles to serve him. So it was that Oswin found himself uprooted from his homeland to live at Nagid's castle in the city of Baasha.

Gwyneth imagined a young man, perhaps Jotham's age, in an opulent foreign court, surrounded by strangers. *How did he feel?* she wondered. *How would I feel?*

Elsbeth's voice tinkled in Gwyneth's ears as she went on with the story.

But though most of those in Nagid's court followed Prince Abaddon's ways, Oswin would not do so. He never forgot he was the King's child and a citizen of Dominus. He remained true to the teachings of the Book and lived according to its precepts. So the King rewarded Oswin with the gift of wisdom. He was able to explain great mysteries to Lord Nagid. In time, he became one of Nagid's most trusted advisors. And Oswin gave the King all the praise for the insights he received. Because of Oswin, Lord Nagid himself was drawn to the King."

Gwyneth recalled what the Widow Nessa had told her about wisdom. She had said it meant knowing how to live. Did the story imply Oswin learned this from the King and the Book?

Elsbeth stopped reading. Jotham turned shining eyes to the Prince. "What a wonderful story! I can certainly see how Oswin was salt and light." Jotham's face grew thoughtful. "But did his loyalty to the King ever put him in danger?"

Morning Star nodded. "Yes. Later in his life, Oswin served a different lord whose name was Darrick. He too was impressed with Oswin and wanted to promote him. But others were jealous of Oswin's influence and sought to destroy him. They tricked Darrick into making it a crime for Oswin to communicate with the King."

"What did Oswin do?" asked Jotham, wide-eyed.

"He sought the King's guidance anyway," the Prince replied. "And Darrick was forced to obey his own law and throw Oswin into a den of wild beasts. But the King's mighty powers shut their jaws and kept Oswin safe. Darrick rejoiced and praised the King's greatness. Many came for adoption when they heard—all because Oswin was faithful!"

Gwyneth recalled hearing something about a long-ago figure who'd been thrown to wild animals and lived. But as any educated person in Withershins knew, it was merely a myth. It was ridiculous to suppose that anyone, even the King or his Son, Morning Star, could keep ravenous beasts from devouring a man who landed in their midst.

Or was it? At that moment, Morning Star turned and gazed in Gwyneth's direction. For one terrifying instant, she sensed overwhelming power emanating from this Prince. For that instant, it seemed to her that he could command, not just beasts, but Abaddon, the stars and planets, and all cosmic forces of the universe—even creation itself.

Morning Star turned back to Jotham, whose face now filled with yearning. "Do you think that Alfric will come for adoption because of me?" he asked.

"That is up to him," the Prince said gently. "All you can do is be a good ambassador, like Oswin."

"Will I also be protected like Oswin?" Jotham wondered.

"You will wear my armor," Morning Star replied.

What good will that do? Gwyneth scoffed from her hiding place. *How could any armor, no matter how skillfully wrought, save Jotham from the forces of Abaddon? One lone lad spouting treason will be easily overcome, no matter how he is dressed. It is not as if Prince Morning Star himself were there to give Jotham protection.*

A strange thought seized Gwyneth. *But what if he were? What if this Prince could be Jotham's armor? If that were so, Jotham might stand a chance after all.*

But as quickly as the notion crossed her mind, Gwyneth shook it off. *Thirst and worry must be clouding my judgment,* she thought. *This Prince has no special power. I have simply imagined it so. Nor can anyone wear someone else like armor. It's impossible!*

CHAPTER 21

The Meaning of Friendship

⚜

WITH A SAVAGE kick, Alfric sent a loose rock toppling over the hillside. *My life is just like that rock*, he thought bitterly. *Everything I hold dear is falling away. I've failed in my mission to bring Jotham back. Now I'll never claim my birthright or win Gwyneth as my bride. My future is shattered. And it's all Jotham's fault.*

Alfric sank to the ground, burying his face in his hands. Rejection and despair engulfed him like a flood. *Why even return to Withershins?* he wondered. *I've no reason to go there ... or anywhere!* Rare tears spilled from his eyes. "I have nothing and no one!" he sobbed.

How long he lay crumpled there, Alfric did not know. All at once, he became aware of a gentle cooing sound. He raised his head. Through tear-blurred eyes he saw a dove perched on a bush beside him. For some strange reason, Alfric found the bird's presence calming, even comforting. *But it won't last! Soon the dove will fly away*, he thought bitterly.

That prospect made Alfric feel even lonelier. He scrambled up, waving his hands, barking harshly at the bird. "Go away! You don't care about me. You'll desert me too. Just like Jotham did. And I thought he was my friend..."

"What *is* a friend?"

The voice startled Alfric. He spun around. A shepherd was walking toward him up the path. Alfric realized it was the same fellow he had met on his first trip to Dominus. In his present mood, Alfric had no wish for conversation. Yet something in the shepherd's eyes compelled him to answer.

"What it means... If you're someone's friend, you stand by him," Alfric stammered. "You're loyal to him. And you care about his happiness."

The shepherd's eyes searched Alfric's soul. "And this friend of yours, Jotham. Do you care about his happiness?"

Alfric flushed with indignation. "Of course, I do! That's why I wanted him to return with me to Withershins."

"And was he happy there?" the shepherd pressed him.

Alfric was about to say yes when the shepherd's gaze stopped him. He squirmed for a moment, then blurted, "Not completely. He was always longing for a father."

"And now?" asked the shepherd.

Alfric scowled. "He thinks he's happy. He fancies the King has adopted him and loves him like a son. But it's all a lie!"

The shepherd raised an eyebrow. "What makes you so certain?"

"Because Prince Abaddon said so," Alfric retorted.

"And how do you know that he's told you the truth?" frowned the shepherd.

Alfric had never thought about this. His mind flailed for a moment. "He's my ruler. I trust him," Alfric answered a bit lamely.

"Is that so!" The shepherd held Alfric in his gaze. "Can you always trust those who rule you? Could you always trust your father?"

"What do you know of my father?" Alfric sputtered, taken aback.

"What I know of us all," said the shepherd. "Our deeds reveal our character. Judge the King and Abaddon by that standard! You will know soon enough who is trustworthy, and who is not!"

Alfric looked a bit rattled. "I'm sure Prince Abaddon would not lie about the King. Still, I suppose that he could be mistaken. But if so, I don't dare contradict him. It's too risky."

The shepherd's face grew solemn. "Friends take risks. They make sacrifices for each other." He pointed downward to where Alfric had kicked the rock. "Do you see my sheep?"

Alfric now saw that stretching below them was a lush green meadow. A flock of sheep grazed contentedly on the grass.

The shepherd's tone grew tender. "I am a friend to my sheep. I've made sacrifices for them. I have even laid down my life that they may live."

These words puzzled Alfric. How could the shepherd have laid down his life? He was alive right now! Perhaps he just meant he was willing to lose his life, if that were needed. *Such a sacrifice is quite noble*, Alfric mused. *Would I do that? Would I risk my life for a friend . . . even such a friend as Jotham?*

A thought began to form in Alfric's mind—a thought so foreign he could scarcely believe it was his. *Maybe Prince Abaddon is wrong about the King. Jotham does seem happy in Dominus—happier than I've ever seen him. Nor does it seem likely he'll cause Abaddon trouble from this distance. Why not tell Abaddon so, and plead with him to leave Jotham alone?*

So absorbed was Alfric in this idea that he had not been watching the shepherd. Now he realized the fellow had gone. But the shepherd's words had given him a glimmer of hope. *I will go first to Gwyneth*, Alfric decided. *I'll make her see that Jotham is better off in Dominus. She is his friend too. She will want what's best for him. Surely she will help me speak with Abaddon on Jotham's behalf.*

Buoyed by this new purpose, Alfric set off on the path once more. As he did so, a flash of white wings crossed his vision. The dove had not flown away. It soared in and out among the trees, staying with him as he walked.

Maybe the bird won't abandon me after all, Alfric told himself. *And maybe Gwyneth won't, either. Perhaps our friendship for Jotham will bring us together. Or perhaps it won't. But for now, I can still dream!*

So Alfric walked on, dreaming of the future that might be while the dove fluttered beside him. He did not see the shepherd standing on a hill behind him, watching his progress. The shepherd's eyes brimmed with a mixture of love and pain. He knew Alfric's hopes full well. And he knew that indeed, Alfric's future might dawn bright with promise. But he also knew that looming over that dawn was an even greater darkness.

CHAPTER 22

A Different Kind of Armor

⟡

THE WIDOW NESSA'S cottage was dark except for a few flickering candles, the curtains tightly drawn against prying eyes. A short, round, balding man stood watch at a window, peering into the night. Across the sitting room, a knot of three others sat huddled together for comfort. The widow read to them from the Book as they listened hungrily. "The King will protect us. He is our fortress, our strength."

"I want to believe that, but I don't feel it! I'm so scared!" These words came in a choked whisper from a thin, frail young woman with a hollow, frightened face.

"You can't trust your feelings, Fidelia," said a kindly white-haired fellow. "But you can trust the Book!"

Their other companion, a motherly middle-aged woman, squeezed Fidelia's hand. "Maldwyn is right. Take courage, child. Your name means faith. Have faith in the King. He is our hiding place..."

"Hush, Ganya! I think I see something!" the balding man spoke. His next word sent a shock wave through the others. "Soldiers!"

The widow sprang up. "Out the back door! Quick!"

But it was too late! Soldiers' boots crunched outside. Fists beat against both doors at once. A harsh shout assaulted their ears. "Open up, in the name of Prince Abaddon!"

"One moment. I'm coming," the widow called, at the same time beckoning the others into the bedroom and throwing open a large wardrobe. She hustled them in behind the clothes. Fidelia was shaking so hard that her friends were forced to half-carry her.

The sound of boots kicking wood resounded throughout the cottage. The widow hastily closed the wardrobe and rushed from the room. "Wait! Please..."

With a thunderous bang, the back door gave way. Soldiers stormed inside. One grabbed the widow. Another flung open the front door for his comrades. The widow counted six men in all—an officer and five others. One was Devlin.

Despite the pain shooting through her arm from her captor's iron grip, the widow maintained her composure. She fixed the officer with her gaze. "If you had been more patient, I might have saved your boots some wear."

The officer scowled. "I doubt it was our boots you hoped to save." He motioned to his men. "Search the house!"

The soldiers scattered to obey. Devlin entered the bedroom alone. The widow's heart lurched. She sent up a silent plea to the King for help. Even as she did so, the officer shoved her toward the kitchen. "I am hungry. Find me something to eat. Then I'll look around to make sure my men miss nothing."

Meanwhile, Devlin was searching the bedroom and feeling quite distressed. *What a miserable turn of events!* he groaned to himself. *The last person I would wish to cause harm is the Widow Nessa.* Stooping low, he peered under the bed. Then he opened the wardrobe. His eyes scanned the hanging clothes, then dropped to a row of shoes. To his horror,

Devlin saw one shoe slide forward. It had a leg attached!

For one terrible moment, Devlin stood frozen. What was he to do? The sound of approaching footsteps jolted him into action. Devlin turned quickly, blocking the telltale leg from view as the officer entered, dragging the Widow Nessa with him. The officer crammed the last of a hunk of cheese in his mouth. "What luck, Devlin?" he mumbled, chewing.

Devlin swallowed hard. "No luck, sir. There's nothing here."

The widow caught the flicker in Devlin's eyes. Her heart beat faster. *He's noticed something*, she thought with a chill of apprehension.

The officer's eyes narrowed. "Are you sure? Stand back soldier!"

Devlin hesitated, then obeyed. The officer glanced around the wardrobe, his eyes coming to rest on the foot. The widow, observing this, steeled herself for the worst. But the officer showed no reaction; nor did he probe further. A moment more and he closed the wardrobe and strode from the room. With growing awe, Devlin realized his superior had seen nothing! Eyes wide with wonder, he turned to the widow, mouthing a one-word question, "How?"

The widow's lips formed a soundless answer, "The King."

By now, the other soldiers had also returned empty-handed. Devlin and the widow joined them.

"Would you like a cup of tea before you go?" she asked mildly.

The officer glared. "What I'd like is a reason to throw you in jail. I can't find one—yet. But you will be watched." He turned on his heel and stomped out with his men, slamming the door behind him.

The widow waited to be sure they were gone. Then she ushered her friends from the wardrobe. Fidelia, whose foot had slid into view when her knees had buckled in terror, was shaking no longer. Instead, her eyes were shining. "The King really is our hiding place!" she beamed.

"Nonetheless," frowned the bald man, "we dare not meet here again. Yet we have nowhere else to go."

The widow looked thoughtful. "Perhaps we do, Hyam. Long ago, in times like these, our people met in hidden places—ancient caverns just beyond the city. I have an old map on which the entrances are marked."

Maldwyn nodded. "It is at least worth investigating. We'd be safer from the soldiers there."

The widow grew solemn. "Still, we must be mindful that we do not battle against men only. Abaddon has other forces he can martial against us. And we cannot defeat these dark powers ourselves. We must rely on the King and Morning Star. And we must be careful to put on the armor we were given."

⚜

"TOMORROW YOU shall receive your armor," Morning Star told Jotham. "The King shall present it to you in his throne room in a special ceremony. Then I myself shall escort you to the border."

"As you wish, Your Highness." Jotham tried to sound brave, but he felt torn inside. How he hated to leave Evan and Elsbeth and this land of Dominus! Yet his longing for Alfric to become the King's child had grown stronger with each passing hour. That longing drew him to Withershins and spurred thoughts of his other friends there. *If only Magnus too could know the King, and Gwyneth also!* Jotham mused, a lump rising in his throat. *But doubtless they won't even speak to me now.*

His stomach tightened at the thought. A hand touched his shoulder. He looked into the gentle eyes of Morning Star. Jotham sensed that the Prince understood and had felt such rejection himself. Though the hurt did not lessen, Jotham found himself comforted.

"The hour is late," Morning Star said. "Go with Evan, and sleep. Meet me here in the morning at the palace doors."

GWYNETH, HIDING behind some shrubs, shivered with excitement. Her heart rejoiced to think Jotham would leave for home tomorrow. The King's influence, and Morning Star's, would surely fade once Jotham was back in Acrasia. Nor had she been idle. All afternoon as Evan and Jotham had spent time together studying the Book, she had listened. Already she was thinking of ways to counter the Book's falsehoods.

As Evan and Jotham joined a trickle of others leaving through the palace gates, Gwyneth wondered where she would spend the night. So intent had she been on Jotham, she'd forgotten her own plight. Now she became painfully aware of her parched lips and gnawing stomach. Her last meal had been berries picked on the path to the palace the day before. She'd been just as reluctant to eat the King's food as to drink from the palace spring. *I will find an inn. I must have food and rest, even if I am questioned,* she told herself. *I can't think what else to do. My head is spinning.*

A mere handful of people were left in the courtyard. Gwyneth slipped from hiding. She swayed. Suddenly, the world swam before her eyes. Then everything went black.

WHEN GWYNETH'S world slowly came back into focus, she was lying on a bed. A young woman not much older than herself sat beside her.

"Don't be afraid," the woman said softly. "I am Danya, and

my husband is Amyas. We were near you in the palace courtyard and caught you when you fell. We brought you to our home to care for you."

Lifting Gwyneth's head, Danya held a cup of water to her lips. Gwyneth drank deeply of the cool liquid. Danya spooned some nutritious broth into Gwyneth's mouth, speaking in a soothing voice. "It seems you are a visitor here. Please stay with us as long as you like. In Dominus, we love to entertain strangers."

"Thank you." Gwyneth closed her eyes, feigning sleep to avoid conversation. But she didn't need to pretend long. Within minutes, she drifted into a deep slumber.

When she awoke, the morning sun had risen high in the sky. Recalling Jotham's planned meeting with Morning Star, Gwyneth felt a surge of panic. "I am deeply grateful for your kindness," she told Danya and Amyas. "And I mean no rudeness, but I must leave at once. I have urgent business elsewhere."

Gwyneth feared her hosts might try to detain her and ply her with questions. But if they were curious, they did not show it. They only insisted she take a flask of water and a parcel of food for her later refreshment. Nor would they accept the payment she offered. After thanking them once more, Gwyneth hurried on her way.

If only I am not too late! she fretted as she hastened to the palace. *I must see this new armor of Jotham's and learn more about it. Like the white robe, it may be a tool the King uses to control his subjects.*

AGAIN TODAY, the palace grounds were teeming with people. Gwyneth's eyes searched in vain for Jotham's face among them. Were he and the Prince with the King even now? Or had they already set out for the border? Gwyneth wished there was some way to know.

And then, as she gazed toward the palace, Gwyneth realized something was different. This day, the golden entrance doors stood open. A steady stream of people flowed in and out, seemingly at will. Could Jotham have gone in also? Gwyneth hesitated, then slipped inside.

For an instant, Gwyneth was overwhelmed by the sheer magnificence of her surroundings. She wandered toward a golden lampstand, staring at it in awe. Nearby, some people broke into song in honor of the King. Other voices joined in, and she felt herself swept up in a sea of sound. As it subsided, she spied the Prince and Jotham not ten paces away. Being careful to keep her head down, she inched cautiously closer.

"Are you sure I'll be able to manage this armor?" she heard Jotham ask. "I'm unused to such things. Perhaps it will be too heavy for me. Might I not move more freely without it?"

"No, Jotham," the Prince assured him. "Quite the opposite. You will know the greatest freedom when you have it on. Nor will the armor weigh you down, but rather, lift you up."

Gwyneth tingled with excitement. *This armor must be made of a substance far stronger and tougher yet much lighter than any known in Withershins,* she reasoned. *Capturing such armor would be an important military coup.*

"Will I have a weapon as well?" Jotham wanted to know.

"You shall fight with the sword of the Spirit. There is none sharper," Morning Star replied.

Gwyneth was even more intrigued. *If the Prince's claim is true, this Spirit person must be a master weapon-maker like no other! I must find a way to seize the blade and test it!*

Even as she thought this, Morning Star was guiding Jotham forward toward a far doorway from which streamed a brilliant light. Melting in with the crowd, Gwyneth tried to follow. But while she was yet some distance away, she felt something push her back. It was as if some invisible force barred her way. And she sensed that the light itself was so potent, it might well consume her if she ventured farther.

Gwyneth felt herself gripped by a fear and awe such as she had never known. She reeled, trembling to her very core. This King must be more powerful than she had ever dreamed. She wished she could see him and hear what he said to Jotham. What twisted persuasion would he use to make Jotham fight for him?

ONCE MORE, Jotham knelt before the King's throne; Morning Star, as always, was standing by his side. The King's voice sounded in his ears and in his soul. "My precious child, the armor I give you is unlike any other. No weapon of Abaddon's can prevail against it. But you must wear it every day, for Abaddon and his forces lurk like beasts of prey, poised to pounce upon you when you least suspect."

The King's words reminded Jotham of the Widow Nessa's warnings and his old strange feeling of being watched. "I shall wear it faithfully," he promised grimly.

"So you intend," the King said gently. "Nonetheless, you will grow careless at times. Your armor will slip. Abaddon will strike. And you may be wounded. Still, you shall not be destroyed. My Son, Morning Star, saw to that long ago. Though the battle must be fought, the war has already been won!"

"I ... I don't understand," Jotham stammered.

"You will in time," Morning Star assured him. "Do not trouble yourself about it now. This day is for commissioning and sending."

The Prince's face shone with pride as the King began the ceremony.

"My child, it is time to receive your armor," the King proclaimed. "It is like a second skin, worn deep inside to protect your heart and mind. Each piece has a special name. Remember them well. Your belt is called truth. Your breastplate is righteousness. The shoes I give you are known as peace. Your helmet is salvation, and your shield is faith."

Jotham felt a glow as if some invisible "second skin" had indeed enveloped him. But wasn't there one more thing he must receive? "What about my sword?" Jotham asked. "The Prince promised I would have one. Does it have a name also?"

"Yes, Jotham," the King replied. "You know it already. And you have felt its sharpness, which has cut you loose from bondage to Abaddon's lies. Take it now, and use it well."

At these words, Morning Star handed Jotham the last thing he expected.

"Now go forth in my name, and Prince Morning Star's," the King commanded. "And we shall be with you."

SECRETED BEHIND a lampstand, Gwyneth waited anxiously, her body tense, eyes riveted on the throne-room doorway. At last, she saw Jotham and the Prince emerge. She nearly cried out in shock. Jotham wore no armor, just his same white robe. And he carried no sword, just a copy of the Book. *How can this be?* she wondered.

Jotham seemed to wonder also. "Please tell me, Your Highness," he asked, "how can this Book be a sword?"

"Its truth is sharper than any blade and can pierce what no sword can penetrate," Morning Star replied gravely.

Gwyneth flushed with anger. *Now I see,* she seethed. *The armor and sword are merely imaginary! This King does not wish the expense of outfitting Jotham properly for battle. Instead, he and his Son, Morning Star, have deluded Jotham. They have made him think he's protected, when in truth he's defenseless!*

Yet why would even this King and Prince send soldiers into battle unprotected? Gwyneth wondered. *It makes no sense!*

Neither did what happened next. A brightness surrounded Jotham, its glare so great that Gwyneth was forced to avert her eyes. When she turned back, it seemed for an instant as though Jotham were standing inside the Prince. It was as though Morning Star himself was Jotham's armor, just as she had fancied yesterday on the palace steps.

This impression lasted only an instant. In an eyeblink, Jotham looked as before. Gwyneth shook off the image. *My mind must be playing a trick on me,* she thought. *Or else it is some strange effect of this land of Dominus. Either way, I have no time to ponder it. I must hurry back to Withershins and find Alfric. I will tell him I've been here and what I have learned. Though he may not be pleased that I made the trip, surely he must admit its value. Together, we will yet bring Jotham to his senses. And when Alfric wins Abaddon's favor and his birthright, he will thank me for my efforts! But we must act quickly before Jotham further fuels Abaddon's wrath.*

Spurred by this purpose, Gwyneth tarried no longer, but set off hurriedly for home.

⟞⫘⟝

JOTHAM DID not depart just yet. When he emerged from the palace, he found Evan and Elsbeth waiting for him. Together with Morning Star, they shared one last meal in the courtyard. Then Jotham wrapped his friends in a fond embrace. "I hope I shall see you again."

"Most certainly you shall," Elsbeth smiled.

Evan gripped Jotham's hand. "And we shall think of you often."

Then Morning Star led Jotham through the golden gates and down the road toward the border. As they walked, the Prince told Jotham many things. Jotham listened eagerly, basking in the Prince's presence and drinking in his wisdom.

Once again, the Prince's subjects shared food with them. Their pace was unhurried, and it was after midnight when they reached the shepherd's cottage where Jotham had spent his first night in Dominus. He hoped he might meet the shepherd this time, but the cottage was empty as before. Still, they spent a cozy night there.

In the morning, the Prince served Jotham a breakfast, not just of milk, but of bread and a bit of meat. He wrapped extra food in a parcel for Jotham to eat on his journey. Once again, Morning Star fed the shepherd's sheep. It was midmorning when they set out again, and midafternoon when at last they spied the border bridge.

The Prince paused, placing a gentle hand on Jotham's shoulder. "Now that you are returning to Withershins, you must wear your robe and ring on the inside, as you do your armor."

At these words, Jotham's white robe and ring seemed to glow and melt inside him. He found himself clad in the garb he had worn when he first crossed the border. Yet these clothes, though no different in other respects, seemed marvelously freshened and cleansed.

Jotham stared at the bridge looming large before him. The bottom dropped out of his stomach. Suddenly, his time in Dominus seemed all too short. And besides, it was perilous to cross into Withershins in daylight, was it not?

"Perhaps I should linger here until dark. If I scale the wall at night, I've less chance of being spotted," he told the Prince.

"Fear not," Morning Star assured him. "The soldiers shall not see you. The King will blind their eyes."

But in truth, Jotham was fearful now that the time had come. Only his great concern for Alfric and his wish to please the Prince kept him from turning back.

Morning Star seemed to sense his struggle. Reaching into his pocket, he pulled out a new kind of fruit with a blood-red skin. "Eat this, Jotham," he urged. "It will strengthen you for the task ahead. It is the special love fruit I've told you about. You must give some to Alfric also, when the time is right."

"How can I?" frowned Jotham, puzzled. "If I eat it, there won't be any left."

The Prince smiled. "When you eat this fruit, it multiplies. You shall have all you need, and more."

Thus encouraged, Jotham feasted on the love fruit's fragrant goodness. Never had he tasted anything quite like it. Revived and refreshed, he thanked the Prince. "I am ready to cross now," he said.

Morning Star embraced him, speaking in a tone of utmost tenderness. "Remember, though you cannot always see me, I am always with you."

Jotham stared in amazement. "Always with me? I don't know what you mean!"

"I dwell in you, as in every child of the King. And I will not forsake you!" the Prince said firmly.

Mystified yet strangely comforted by these words, Jotham walked across the bridge into Withershins. Morning Star stood watching, his own heart overflowing. Well he knew the cost of seeking lost sheep as Jotham would now be doing. He himself had endured untold suffering to pay their ransom long ago. Now Jotham would share that suffering— but he would also share the joy!

CHAPTER 23

Abaddon's Fury

＊

COLD FINGERS of dread gripped Alfric's heart as he stood before Prince Abaddon. The air in the throne room seemed to mirror his mood. It was strangely chilled, as if made of vaporized ice. But the look Abaddon gave Alfric was icier still. "So you have failed!" he spat.

Things had not gone at all as Alfric had hoped though they had started well. The journey to the border had been quite pleasant indeed. The dove had remained at his side. And for the first time, he had met a few others on his hilly path. While Abaddon's warnings might once have made Alfric shrink from contact with them, the shepherd's words had changed that. Now he wished to discover for himself what these people were like. Moreover, his provisions were exhausted, and he hoped to buy more. But those he met would take no payment, freely sharing of their food and drink instead. He did not find it sour, like the joy fruit, but surprisingly tasty.

But when Alfric had reached the border bridge, his luck began to change. The dove turned away, vanishing into the falling dusk. And to Alfric's dismay, the first face he saw at the border outpost was Ragnar's. "The bully claimed you'd need help with Jotham," Cadel told him. "He said he must wait and escort you to Acrasia. He warned that if I refused and something went wrong, it would be my fault. I feared he might cause trouble for me so I let him stay."

Hearing this, Alfric had been relieved that Jotham wasn't with him after all. But the trip to Acrasia the next day was torture. It fell to Ragnar to drive Torin's empty supply wagon back to the capital. Alfric had no choice but to ride beside him on the seat. The bully bombarded him with endless taunts. Alfric only survived by distracting himself with thoughts of Gwyneth. Again and again, he rehearsed in his mind how he would persuade her about Jotham. Hopefully, she had returned from her trip. He would get a night's sleep, think through his argument one last time, then find her.

But it was not to be! No sooner had they reached the Fortress of Belial that night than Ragnar made a hue and cry. "Find General Bogdan!" he bellowed. "Tell him Alfric is back! He has been on a special mission. I am sure the general will want to speak with him."

Bogdan did. Alfric learned to his dismay that Gwyneth was still away. Moreover, he himself would be brought straight to the palace at Abaddon's command. Bogdan would accompany him. He must face the prince without Gwyneth's help!

Now, standing before Abaddon's throne on quaking limbs, Alfric mustered his courage and spoke through fear-parched lips. "If it please you, Sire, perhaps I have not failed. Jotham does not seem bent on causing you trouble. And he is quite happy in Dominus. Why not leave him there? What harm can it do?"

"Fool!" Abaddon spat out the word like the hiss of a snake as Bogdan looked on, scowling. "Know you not that whoever is for the King is against me? But then, perhaps you are a traitor, too!"

"I am no traitor!" gasped Alfric, horrified.

"Then at best you are a coward," snarled the prince. "You will never be an officer of mine! As for your birthright..."

Abaddon clapped his hands. A servant entered, bearing a strongbox. Abaddon lifted the lid and drew out a parchment. His next words slashed through Alfric like a knife. "Your inheritance is revoked!"

Alfric stood transfixed, his father's voice echoing down the corridors of time. *"You will never earn your birthright!"* Was this hated prophecy about to come true? A strange mix of shame and rage surged within him.

Then he smelled smoke.

Beside the throne was an oil lamp—a smaller version of the dragon-like fixtures in the hall leading to the throne room. Alfric saw that Abaddon held the tip of the parchment to its flame. An expression of utmost cruelty contorted his face as the long-sought birthright caught fire.

Alfric's pent-up passion burst like a dam. With desperate, reckless abandon, he lunged at the prince. So stunned were Abaddon and Bogdan that for one brief moment, they froze. In that instant, Alfric managed to wrest the burning document from the prince's grasp. Leaping away, he grabbed at the black throne room curtain, hoping somehow to smother the flames.

Instead, the curtain itself caught fire. Charred parchment melted into burning silk as thick, acrid smoke billowed upward. Instantly, confusion reigned. In that moment, Alfric hurtled toward the palace doors and flung himself out into the night.

The darkness engulfed him like a shroud. Unseen clouds hid the moon and stars from view. Alfric plunged blindly into the blackness, not knowing where he went. One lone thought pounded in his head like a drumbeat of doom. *What have I done? What have I done?*

Then suddenly, it seemed to Alfric that the blackness became blacker still. A foul odor burned in his nostrils. He felt the air thicken. The ground over which he ran seemed to suck at his shoes. With a chill of horror, Alfric realized where he must have wandered. An ominous bubbling sound and an eerie shriek confirmed his fears. He had stumbled into the dreaded palace swamp!

And now it seemed as though some strange battle swirled around him. Cold, reptilian tentacles grasped his flesh. Unseen creatures tugged him downward into the slime. He flailed frantically, sinking ever deeper.

JOTHAM WOKE with a start. An image rose before his eyes: Alfric flailing, struggling in the grip of some awful, unseen terror. As clearly as if words were spoken, Jotham knew his friend was in danger. But what could he do, alone at night on this dark border road? Suddenly, he recalled the words of Morning Star in the shepherd's cottage, his first day in Dominus. *"Not all battles are fought in space and time."*

Jotham had not understood this then—but he did now. He could fight for Alfric here with the sword the King had given him. Though it was too dark to see the Book, he knew some lines by heart. At Evan's urging, he had learned them on their last day together. Now he spoke them aloud, crying out to the King in urgent, pleading tones. "Oh King, you are our strength and shield. You deliver us from evil. Save Alfric now, I beg you! Help him, please!"

ALFRIC FELT himself sinking in the mire. It was up to his knees, his waist . . .

Then for a moment, the grip of his unseen tormenters faltered. In that moment, a memory flashed through his mind.

He was sinking in despair on the mountainside in Dominus. He had cried out for help. And a dove had come!

Fighting back the waves of terror, Alfric cried out in a choked voice, "Help!"

Suddenly, the darkness was lightened by a growing glow. All around him he saw frogs and lizards and snakes slither into the mud as if fleeing the light. And then, Alfric heard the gentle cooing of a dove. He realized in amazement that the glow was coming from its wings.

The dove circled once, then flew slowly forward. In its light, Alfric saw a narrow ribbon of firmer ground winding through the wetness. Struggling out of the mire, Alfric followed this path and soon left the swamp behind him.

But now the sound of running feet and shouting soldiers reached his ears. *No doubt, a full search has been launched to find me,* he groaned. But even as panic seized him, the dove's glow revealed a section of the palace wall not ten paces ahead. Tearing frantically at the jagged stones, Alfric willed himself upward. Swinging over the top, he inched his way down the other side.

Barely stopping for breath, he hurled himself into the night, knowing full well he was still in dire peril. Abaddon would comb the capital for him. But there was one place he might be safe—in his special place, his place of comfort.

Now Alfric threw his whole effort into reaching this place of refuge. Thankfully, the dove stayed close. With its help, he fled the Northern Heights on which the palace lay. Moving east and south, he skirted the city, staying under cover wherever he could. At last he was climbing again, the ground level rising beneath him. He had reached the eastern foothills.

By now, the first rays of morning light streaked the sky. As day dawned, the dove disappeared. Familiar landmarks now told Alfric he would soon reach the haven he sought. His muscles, tensed into knots, began to relax. He pressed forward eagerly like a runner with the finish line in view.

And then, suddenly, he was going not forward, but down! For a terrifying moment, he was lost in time and space. He was falling...falling! Then with a mighty splash, he sank beneath an icy wetness.

Kicking hard, Alfric forced himself upward. Sputtering and choking, he broke through the water's surface. He could breathe again.

But he could not see. He was smothered in blackness. Where was he? Was this real, or was he trapped in some strange nightmare? Fighting back a tide of panic, Alfric paddled forward. Splash! Splash! Bump! His hand hit something hard. He pulled himself out of the wetness onto stone.

As he crouched, trembling, a dim thought emerged from his fear-fogged mind. He must have fallen into some sort of underground cavern. Cautiously, he crawled ahead until he felt the outlines of a rock wall.

Alfric pulled himself upward, shivering with cold and trembling with exhaustion. Hands pressed against the stone, he inched his way along. He heard no sound except his own footsteps and the eerie echo of dripping water. Still, who knew what horrors lurked here hidden in this inky blackness? Alfric's ears strained. His eyes searched the darkness.

Suddenly, the blackness took shape and became a black velvet robe. Abaddon's face loomed above him, burning with fury. Alfric shrank back, squeezing his eyes shut. He would perish here in this tomb of rock, alone, friendless!

"I am a friend to my sheep." The shepherd's words floated through his mind like a gentle caress. The terror he felt seemed to ebb. Hesitantly, he opened his eyes. The angry prince was gone, a figment of his fears. Shakily, he moved onward.

How long he continued like this, Alfric did not know. The blackness seemed to swallow him up like some giant monster. Or maybe the monsters were lurking within it, sharp teeth waiting to tear him apart. Yet he could only go on, hand over hand, stone on stone, deeper, deeper. There was no escape!

Then suddenly, Alfric felt the wall curve. Moments later, something brushed his cheek—a breath of a breeze, a breath of hope! He had found an air current.

Gulping hungrily at that air, Alfric hurried forward. The breeze was his lifeline, his guide, his way out! Or was it? Alfric sensed that the space around him had narrowed. He stretched out his hands. He felt walls on both sides.

The walls were closing in on him. The air current was a cruel deception, a mere trickle from some crack in the stone. Any moment the walls would squeeze him, crush him.

"Nooooooo!" Alfric shoved his hands against the walls as if to force them apart. And then his hands pushed air, not stone. Alfric probed the rock. The walls turned off in opposite directions. Both ways, a faint breeze beckoned him.

Alfric's head swam. "Which way shall I go?" he moaned aloud. "Which path shall I trust?"

Two faces seemed to float in the darkness. Two princes beckoned him, Abaddon and Morning Star. *Which shall I trust?* The shepherd's words echoed in his memory. *"Our deeds reveal our character."*

An image rose in Alfric's mind of his birthright—burning, burning! In mindless horror, he flung himself toward the face of Morning Star. But there was no face, just darkness and cold rock beneath his feet. And then the rock gave way.

Alfric grabbed for the wall . . . to no avail. He felt himself swept downward on a sea of sliding stone. He covered his head and squeezed his eyes shut. He braced himself for the agony of being crushed and buried alive.

Splash! Alfric felt the shock of cold water that swept him into its flow. So swift was the current that he was powerless to resist it. He gasped and gulped, fighting for air. A strange roar reached his ears. And then he was tumbling again, swallowed up in a torrent of crashing spray and foam.

The flow of water he landed in this time was not quite as strong. With his last ounce of strength, he scrambled out, collapsing onto firm ground as consciousness left him.

Slowly, Alfric became aware of tall forms surrounding him. He tried to raise his head. Something smacked him... then another something. He sunk his face into the stone. The soldiers had found him. "I surrender!"

Alfric waited for harsh hands to seize him and bind him. Nothing happened. No one spoke. At last, hesitantly, he raised his head.

It was dark, but not as black as before. He was in some vast chamber. The tall forms were not soldiers but towering crystal formations. Some soared up from the floor. Others hung from the ceiling. Dark shapes fluttered among them and clung to the walls. Alfric recoiled as one brushed past him. Now he realized what had slapped against him—bats!

Alfric struggled to his feet, his eyes taking in the crashing waterfall down which he'd fallen and the underground river flowing past him through the rock. Then he noticed something else...a faint light that seemed to come from somewhere just outside the chamber where he stood. He moved closer. The roar of the waterfall receded. He heard voices.

Alfric felt his blood chill. He would have retreated, but his only path lay toward the speakers. Cautiously, he crept forward through an opening into a smaller, connecting chamber. He now saw that the light came from a pair of lanterns set on a rock ledge. Beside them, two people sat talking. The man, an elderly white-haired fellow, Alfric did not know. The woman was the Widow Nessa.

CHAPTER 24

The Truth About the Birthright

HEAD DOWN, heart pounding, Gwyneth rode through the gates of the Fortress of Belial. The last thing she wanted was to be recognized. She must trade her mount for the mare she had left here and rush off to find Alfric. They had precious little time to plan how they would keep Jotham out of trouble. *Though he left after I did and will be on foot, he can't be that far behind me,* she reasoned.

Unknown to Gwyneth, Jotham had actually reached the border first. He and Morning Star had traveled a shorter path. Nor could Gwyneth push her still-weakened body as fast as she'd hoped. But she'd quickly made up the time on the horse she had stolen—she would have said "borrowed" —from the tiny border outpost. The silent stealth she'd learned from her father had served her well as she'd crept through the darkness, loosing the steed from its tether. She had even managed to help herself to a torch and extra food and water. Though she'd felt a twinge of guilt at her actions, she'd pushed it aside. What she did was for a noble cause, the provisions she took were of little worth, and the horse would be returned soon enough!

And so Gwyneth had ridden for Acrasia, never knowing she'd passed Jotham in the night.

Dawn had found her approaching the western crossroads. It was then that Gwyneth had noticed the heightened presence of soldiers on patrol. It had taken all her wits to avoid being spotted. At first she'd thought the extra watchfulness must be due to Abaddon's decree. But now, as she threaded her way through the bustling fortress, she was not so sure. She felt a strange tension in the air as though something were afoot. A vague uneasiness gripped her. What was wrong? Eager as she was to be on her way, she must try to find out. But first, she must make herself look more presentable.

Moments later, having freshened her appearance and left her tired mount to be cared for, Gwyneth quizzed the stable boy saddling her own mare. He babbled excitedly in response to her questions. "There's a flap, all right! They're looking for someone. Quite a hunt, I hear..."

"Gwyneth!" Bogdan's voice, harsh and shrill, pierced her ears. Gwyneth turned as her father raced to her, gripping her shoulders, his haggard face staring into hers. "I have been so worried!"

Gwyneth fought for composure. What did all this mean? Were they looking for her? Had her father found her out? Did he know she had not been with Megan?

"Worried? Why?" Gwyneth asked, dreading the answer.

"Alfric!"

Gwyneth stared in amazement. "Alfric?"

Swiftly, Bogdan recounted the events of the night before. "I must go now and join the search," he told her. "And you must stay home under guard until Alfric is captured."

"Surely you don't think he would harm me?" Gwyneth gasped, incredulous.

"We cannot be certain of that," Bogdan frowned. "He's

already attacked Prince Abaddon. I fear the young scoundrel's gone mad. Who knows what he might do? You will follow my wishes."

Gwyneth saw that there was no point protesting. "Yes, Father," she conceded, her heart sinking.

JOTHAM HURRIED anxiously toward Acrasia, consumed by concern for Alfric. Some inner voice told him that the crisis that had wakened him was past. But that same voice warned him his friend was still in trouble. Alfric needed him. He must hurry!

Thankfully, the road that had once held such terrors for him did not frighten him now. Jotham knew he was not alone. Morning Star was with him—he had promised he would be. And though the night was dark and moonless, a lone star shone down from the sky as if sent to guide him and light his way.

Only once had uncertainty gripped him—when approaching hoofbeats sounded in his ears. He dove for cover beside the road, not sure if it was friend or foe. But the unknown rider passed without trouble, and Jotham encountered no one else.

The star left at dawn, but not Jotham's sense of comfort and protection. All through the morning he hurried onward, talking silently to the King, crying out on Alfric's behalf and pleading for wisdom.

It was afternoon when he saw the dwellings of Acrasia poke above the horizon. A strange feeling seized him—one of being home, yet not home. He thought again, briefly, of Magnus and Gwyneth and wondered how they'd treat him now. But his sense of Alfric's danger soon pushed such concerns aside.

Then a new reality seized him. *Am I in danger too?* he asked himself. *Have I been marked as a traitor? Are soldiers waiting to drag me off, even as they did my father?*

A strange, hunted feeling crept over Jotham. *Was this how my father felt?* he wondered. *Did he suspect his danger beforehand? Will I too be captured before I can even help Alfric?*

A wave of hopelessness washed over Jotham. For a moment, he regretted his decision to return. But then the memory of the love fruit surged up within him. In his mind, he tasted once more its exquisite sweetness. He thought of Alfric and he remembered the armor the King had given him.

Hopelessness gave way to fresh resolve. *No, I am not sorry!* he decided. *But I must be careful and keep my wits about me!*

The border road was ending now, blending back into the main thoroughfare. It was as busy as always, and there were more soldiers than ever. Jotham kept his head down, melting into the bustle. But he did not choose the road through the city to Odd End. Instead he chose a path that circled Acrasia. *If I'm to help Alfric, I cannot risk being seized myself,* he reasoned. *I need safe haven and wise counsel. I will go to the Widow Nessa. She will help me.*

THE LAST RAYS of daylight had faded away when Jotham walked through the Widow Nessa's gate once more. His friend the squirrel chattered excitedly in welcome. The widow's face flooded with tears of joy when she answered his knock. Pulling him swiftly inside, she hugged him tightly.

"Oh Jotham, I'm so glad you've come!" she cried. "Alfric is in terrible trouble! Soldiers hunt for him everywhere, even as I speak."

"I feared as much!" groaned Jotham, telling her of his strange prompting in the night. His eyes searched her face as guilt clutched his heart. "Is this somehow my doing?"

The widow laid a hand on his arm. "I think perhaps it is the King's doing," she murmured. "Alfric's heart has changed. He realized you were happy where you were. He begged Abaddon to leave you alone. Abaddon flew into a rage. Cruel as always, he seized a parchment and set it ablaze. Alfric thought Abaddon was burning his birthright. He lunged to save it. A curtain caught fire, and in the confusion, Alfric fled."

Questions tumbled from Jotham's lips. "Did he tell you this? Is he all right? Do you know where he is?"

"He told me this, but I have not seen him since."

The widow explained about the decree and the search of her cottage. "We thought we might meet in the caverns instead," she told Jotham. "Early this morning, I was exploring them with my friend Maldwyn. Suddenly, Alfric appeared, frantic and disheveled. Apparently he stepped into a hole, overgrown with brush, and fell through to the chambers below."

"He begged us to show him a way to the surface," the widow continued. "As we did so, he told us of his confrontation with Abaddon. He ranted and railed. I tried to speak, but he gave me no chance. We did manage to press on him some bread we had with us. When we reached the entrance, he scrambled up ahead of us and vanished."

The widow's eyes filled with yearning. "If only he had listened, I could have told him the truth!"

Jotham looked puzzled. "The truth about what?"

"His birthright," the widow sighed.

"Abaddon burned it. You said so," Jotham frowned.

"I said Alfric thought he burned it," she corrected him.

Jotham's eyes widened. "You mean, he didn't?"

The widow's next words shocked Jotham. "He couldn't. He never had it."

Jotham stared, incredulous. "How do you know?"

For answer, the widow rose, disappearing for a moment. She returned with a parchment. "Alfric's mother wrote this letter to her unborn child," she told Jotham. "She asked me to keep it in case anything should happen to her."

"You knew her?" he gasped.

She nodded. "Karissa was one of us."

Jotham gaped in surprise. "Alfric's mother was a child of the King?"

A faraway look crossed the widow's face. "Yes, Jotham. She loved the King greatly, though it displeased Alfric's father. Killian was jealous. He did not understand."

"And how did she die?" asked Jotham.

The widow's face filled with sorrow. "In childbirth. I myself attended her, but I could do nothing."

Jotham frowned. "Did you ask the King for help?"

"Oh, I begged..." The widow's voice broke. Her eyes grew moist. "But though I pleaded, Karissa slipped away. I confess I was angry with the King. I did not understand. But I have learned to trust the King even when I cannot know his purpose."

"Did Killian blame you?" Jotham wanted to know.

"I'm sure he did," she sighed. "And in a way, I think he blamed Alfric. I suspect that is why he was always so hard on his son."

"What of the birthright?" Jotham wondered.

"It is in a safe place. The letter explains this also," the widow said softly.

"And you've never told Alfric?"

"I dared not," she explained. "He was taught to believe the Book was false and all of us were liars. I feared he would think the letter a fraud. So I've kept it, hoping some day the time would be right." Her face fell. "And now it is, but I know not where to find him."

Jotham looked thoughtful. "Perhaps I do. There's a special

place Alfric goes for refuge when he is troubled. He took me there once. It's in the eastern foothills. There's a small deserted cabin and a graveyard."

The widow's face flooded with understanding. "No wonder Alfric happened upon us! He must have been on his way there. The place of which you speak is just beyond the hidden caverns. I know it well. That is where Karissa is buried."

CHAPTER 25

More Revelations

GWYNETH PACED her room like a caged animal. She must wait. Not until tonight when all the servants slept could she make her move. If she slipped away then, perhaps her absence would not be detected till morning. And the more time she gained, the more chance she might find her friends.

But waiting was agony! Gwyneth's mind whirled with unanswered questions. What had possessed Alfric to act as he had? What would happen to him? What would happen to Jotham? What should she do? What could she do, guarded as she was?

All afternoon, these questions battered her tortured brain. At last she fell into fitful sleep. But even in slumber, she found no rest. An image rose before her, a gaunt figure languishing in a cold, dank dungeon. The figure turned. Gwyneth saw to her horror that it was Alfric. Now the face changed. It was Jotham. Alfric...Jotham. The figure reached out to her as if pleading for help. All at once a sword slashed the air.

"Ahhhhhhhh!" Gwyneth woke with a scream.

A servant rushed through the door. "What's wrong, m'lady?"

"N-nothing," Gwyneth stammered. "Just a nightmare."

"Don't you worry," soothed the servant. "That Alfric fellow won't get near you! The watch at the gate has been doubled. Now, why don't I bring you some supper?"

Gwyneth wasn't hungry, but she let the servant bring a tray. If she were to be of use, she must keep her strength up. As she picked at her food, she wondered where Alfric might hide. All at once, a phrase floated through her mind. It was something Jotham had said to Alfric when they'd argued in Dominus. *"You have a place of refuge too, near your mother."*

Perhaps he's gone to his place of refuge. If only I knew where it was, Gwyneth groaned to herself. *But I don't. Only Jotham does. And who knows? He himself may be seized when he arrives.*

Gwyneth's stomach churned. A wave of anguish gripped her chest. She breathed deeply to calm herself. *Jotham's wits are sharp*, she reasoned. *Doubtless he will notice the heightened patrols, just as I did. He too may seek out a safe place... or a safe person.*

The Widow Nessa! Some inner voice fairly shouted the name. That's where Jotham would go—and where she must go as well. Once the servants slept, the guards would be easily handled. Gwyneth knew of an herb that, in concentrated form, induced a rather sound slumber. There was some in the kitchen. It made a nice tea. She would bring the sentries a hot drink to warm them. They would never suspect!

Before this night ends I'll be speaking with Jotham, Gwyneth told herself. She felt gladdened... and yet regretful. She had only bad news. How she wished she had words to cheer him!

All at once, her eye fell on the hope chest. Her spirits rose. She lifted the lid, gazing at what lay inside. "At least I can tell him his mother's quilt is safe."

Gwyneth smiled once more at the whimsical pattern, idly tracing the outline of a laughing daisy with her finger. All at once, she realized its petals were not fully sewn down. She leaned closer, pulling back a petal and peering beneath. Much to her surprise, she found a letter "J" embroidered in thread.

In quick succession, she lifted the flower's other petals. Her smile widened. She chuckled. "What a clever idea!"

<hr/>

"WHAT A SILLY idea!" grumbled Elymas as his bulging frog eyes peered from beneath the sodden leaves of a dew-drenched shrub. "Even Alfric is not fool enough to venture onto Bogdan's land. Why my master ordered me to watch here, I will never know."

Yet Abaddon had been adamant. "Keep an eye on Gwyneth."

So Elymas crouched in the greenery, looking on by the light of the sentries' torches as Gwyneth poured tea for the guards. He found himself missing the challenge of spying on Jotham. At least that had tested his skill. This was boring!

The soldiers seem bored too, thought Elymas. Even as Gwyneth left them, they were yawning. Now one guard's head drooped, and he slid to the ground in slumber. Another followed. Soon all four lay prone and snoring.

Elymas caught his breath, snapping to attention. Something wasn't right! As he stared, Gwyneth crept back through the gate and closed it behind her. She was leading a horse.

"Keep an eye on Gwyneth..."

Slipping onto her mount, Gwyneth seized a torch and galloped into the night. A frog leaped unseen behind her. Elymas was bored no longer!

<hr/>

GWYNETH TETHERED her horse a short distance from the widow's cottage. *Better to proceed on foot*, she thought. *There's less chance I'll be seen, and the place may be watched. After all, the widow is a Person of the Book.* Extinguishing her torch, she crept toward the light of a lantern hung beside the cottage door. Was she right? Was Jotham there? Her heart beat faster.

All at once, the door inched open. The lantern's light went out. Gwyneth froze, her breath catching in her throat. Faint footsteps broke the stillness. The gate creaked. Skirts swished. A candle flickered. The widow's vague form hurried into the night. Perhaps she was going to Jotham—or Alfric.

Gwyneth followed, never guessing she also was being followed.

IT WAS WELL past midnight when Jotham reached the weathered wooden cabin that sat like a battle-weary sentinel at the entrance to the graveyard. The deserted cemetery had belonged to Karissa's family. Except for Alfric, they were all long dead or had moved far away. The cabin, once a caretaker's dwelling, had lain vacant for years.

Jotham desperately hoped it was not vacant now. He called Alfric's name and knocked. No one answered. There was no light except for the candle Jotham clutched in his hand. He tried the door. It resisted for a moment, then swung open.

The spare one-room dwelling was bare of furniture except for a table and chairs and a cot against one wall. The cot's rumpled mattress was sprinkled with a few lonely breadcrumbs. It looked as though Alfric had been here. But was he still?

Leaving his Book behind on the table, Jotham walked back outside. He turned his steps toward the graveyard, overgrown with weeds. Eyes searching the darkness, he wound his way among worn headstones. He saw a faint glimmer of candle-light. And then he heard it—a jagged, choking sound.

A moment later, Jotham spied a bent form crouched be-side a simple gravestone. It was Alfric, sobbing and speaking all at once. Jotham crept closer, listening.

"Forgive me, Mother," Alfric was gasping in a tortured voice. "I tried to serve Abaddon as you wanted. But I couldn't! I could not hurt Jotham! I'm his friend! And now Abaddon has burned my birthright, and your hopes for me are lost. All is lost..."

"All is not lost!" Jotham sprang from hiding.

Alfric fell back in shock, staring at him as if seeing a ghost. "Whatever possessed you to come back?" he sputtered at last.

"What you said in Dominus. You said you needed me. And I care about you. I wanted to help," Jotham answered earnestly.

"You have taken a terrible risk."

Jotham nodded. "I know. But I had to! I'm your friend, too!"

Alfric swallowed hard. "I...I guess you are. Because friends take risks. They make sacrifices for each other. At least, that's what the shepherd said."

Jotham stared. "What shepherd?"

"The one I met in Dominus," Alfric answered. "He was kind and very wise, much wiser than I realized then. But per-haps you also met him."

Jotham frowned thoughtfully. "I met no shepherd, but I slept in a shepherd's cottage. Morning Star took me there. Per-haps it belonged to this same fellow. What else did he say?"

Alfric's face grew puzzled. "Something strange. He said he had given his life for his sheep. But he wasn't dead, so I'm not sure what he meant."

Suddenly, Jotham understood. His eyes shone with joy. "He was dead! But he lives again! I know him after all! I should have guessed! The shepherd is Morning Star himself!"

Alfric gaped, incredulous. "That can't be! Morning Star is a prince. Why would a prince be a shepherd?"

"Because he loves us!" Jotham's words tumbled from him. "That's why he died—to buy us back so we could be adopted. It's all in the Book. Oh Alfric, don't you see? He's both Prince and shepherd. He cares for all the King's children like a shepherd does his sheep."

Jotham stared intently at Alfric. "Just like he cared for your mother!"

Alfric looked as if he thought Jotham had completely lost his mind. "What are you saying?"

Jotham grasped Alfric's hands, willing him to believe. "Your mother was a child of the King. And your birthright's not burned. It's safe. It's all in the letter."

Alfric fought for breath. "What letter?"

Jotham fairly shouted the answer. "Your mother's letter! The Widow Nessa has it. She's bringing it with her. She thought it safer for us to leave separately. But she will be here soon. We must wait for her at the cabin. And while we do, we can read the Book together. You will read it now, won't you?"

Wordlessly, Alfric nodded yes.

CHAPTER 26

Love Fruit

⌐⟊⌐

GWYNETH'S EYES clung hungrily to the flickering candlelight bobbing like a lifeline in a sea of darkness. She must keep the widow in sight, but she dared not get too close. There must be distance enough between them that if she made some small misstep in this blanketing blackness, the midwife would not hear. Her one hope of finding Jotham and Alfric was to follow this woman. And so she crept onward, onward...

Crunch! Gwyneth froze at the sound. Now she heard more crunches, and a whinny. Gwyneth sank to the ground, scarcely daring to breathe. Behind her, low voices murmured. Saddles creaked. Brush crackled from the heavy step of horses' hooves.

This must be a search party, hunting for Alfric, Gwyneth groaned to herself. Dread seized her, lest they find her or the widow. For what seemed an eternity, she lay motionless. At last, the sounds receded. Cautiously, she raised her head... even as the glow of the soldiers' torches vanished into the night.

To her dismay, Gwyneth realized something else had vanished too. The widow's flickering candle was nowhere in sight. Perhaps she was hiding and would soon reappear. But as Gwyneth's eyes combed the darkness, no welcoming light emerged. The midwife was gone.

Still, Gwyneth did not lose all hope yet. She had learned tracking skills from her father. When day came, she might yet find the widow's trail. But she could do nothing till dawn. Gwyneth waited.

Behind her, Elymas waited, too.

ALFRIC AND Jotham sat hunched together over the Book. Outside, the first streaks of dawn spread across the sky. Absorbed in their reading, they never noticed. Nor did they hear the soft pad of approaching footsteps. The rap at the door caught them by surprise. Jotham jumped like a startled rabbit. Alfric toppled backwards in his chair, eyes bulging in panic.

"Alfric? Jotham?"

They grinned in relief. It was the widow's voice.

"I'm sorry I've taken so long," she told them as they ushered her inside. "There were soldiers about. I was forced to detour through the hidden caverns..."

"Did you bring the letter?"

"Yes, Alfric."

The widow opened her Book and drew a parchment from its pages. Blinking back a tear, she placed it in his trembling hands. Alfric stared in wonder at the flowing script. "Her writing, I have never seen her writing...," Alfric's voice choked. The aging ink blurred before his eyes. He swallowed hard, took a deep breath, and read in a quivering voice.

> My dearest child,
> If this letter has reached you, my strange foreboding came to pass. Life slipped from me even as your own began. Now these words I've penned must reach out to you across the years and speak for me. Yet there is so much they can-

not do, these pale shadows of the yearnings of my heart. Dry ink on cold parchment cannot hold you, stroke you, soothe your fevered brow. It cannot watch you grow, or share your joys, or wipe your tears. It cannot...

Alfric faltered. A lump rose in his throat. Wordlessly, the widow grasped his hand. Jotham squeezed his shoulder. Alfric read some lines in silence, then began aloud again.

Though my poor words cannot take the place of the mother I had longed to be, I dare hope they may guide you to a Father who will be all that, and more. He will meet your every need and fill the empty spaces in your heart with his inexpressible love. This great Father and King adopted me some months ago. Now my highest privilege and purpose is to serve him and his Son, Morning Star. It is my deepest desire that you, too, know them and serve them one day.

It is also my wish that you one day possess as your birthright lands granted to my family by the King in long ages past. But he has warned me that Prince Abaddon seeks to seize this birthright for himself. Should the deed fall into his hands, dire harm would result. So you cannot receive it until you become a child of the King. Until then, what pertains to your birthright will be held in trust for you by my dear friend Nessa.

May the day come swiftly when you serve the King and Morning Star. May their tender care make up the measure of what I could not give you. And may they keep and guide you always, my child.

All my love forever,
Your mother, Karissa

Alfric lifted burning eyes to the widow. "Why did you not tell me sooner?"

"I longed to, but I dared not," she sighed. "I feared you would think me a liar and the letter counterfeit. But now, at last, the day I've always hoped for has come!"

For an endless moment, no one spoke. Alfric's awed whisper broke the silence. "It's all true, isn't it? Morning Star is the shepherd. He ransomed us. He gave his life. He died, but lives again."

"Yes, Alfric," the widow said softly.

Jotham's voice rang with triumph. "Surely now you will be adopted!"

Alfric's face grew mournful. "It's too late!" His shoulders slumped. He spoke in a despairing tone. "After all I've done against him, the King would never want me."

"No, Alfric, you're wrong!" This cry burst from the depths of Jotham's being.

"How do you know that?" groaned Alfric.

Jotham thought of the love fruit he had eaten at the border bridge. The Prince's words rang in his heart. *"When the time is right, you must give some to Alfric."* Jotham reached in his pocket already knowing what he would find there. He pulled out a piece of blood-red fruit. "The King does want you!" he exclaimed. "And so does Morning Star. They sent you this."

Jotham held out the fruit. Alfric took it, staring at it uncertainly.

"Just taste it," urged Jotham.

Alfric bit deeply. His face filled with wonder. "Why, the flavor's exquisite! What is it?"

Jotham beamed. "This fruit is agape, a species of love. It's especially hardy. It cannot be destroyed."

"Nor can the King's love for you," the widow added. "You cannot earn it, nor can you lose it. There is no greater love."

"No greater love," Alfric whispered. Something stirred in him. A shadow crossed his face.

Jotham saw it. "What's wrong?"

"Gwyneth!" The shadow deepened. Alfric's face grew pained. "If I go to the King, I shall lose all hope of winning her."

The widow gazed at Alfric somberly. "Sometimes you must lose all to gain more."

"Besides, what chance have you with her now, after what has happened?" Jotham argued. "Prince Abaddon and her father count you as an enemy. Surely she will not abandon them for you. Give up this foolishness!"

Alfric slumped in a chair, staring at the letter, wrestling with his feelings. Jotham and the widow waited, their hearts pleading with the King on his behalf. At last Alfric leaped up, speaking in a firm voice. "You are right! I will go for adoption!"

Jotham thought he would explode with joy. He flung his arms around Alfric. "Now we will be more than friends! We will be brothers!" he exulted.

The widow embraced him. "Your mother's deepest longings have been fulfilled this day," she whispered.

Alfric squeezed her tightly, then drew back, glowing with anticipation. "And now, you must give me my birthright."

The widow was taken aback. "No, not yet! First you must be adopted. Then of course you shall have it," she replied.

Alfric recoiled, stung. "Why must I wait? Don't you trust me?" He searched her face. "I guess not!" His expression darkened. His voice grew bitter. "You don't believe in me, do you? Just like my father didn't. And the King won't, either. Why be adopted? It won't change a thing. It's useless!"

The widow's heart sank. It was Abaddon and his tricks she did not trust. But she could see that Alfric, long spurned by his father, would not understand this. Now it seemed her refusal might make him lose heart and turn back from adoption. She glanced at Jotham. Her fear was mirrored in his eyes.

The widow wavered. An inner voice nudged her to keep silent. For once, she did not listen. "What you ask for is not here, Alfric," she sighed. "It is hidden. I will tell you where to find it, but you must promise you will not retrieve it now. Go first to the King. It is the only safe course. Trust me in this!"

Alfric brightened. "I give you my word!"

The widow nodded. "Very well. Your mother placed what pertains to the birthright in a strongbox. She bade me bury it with her. It lies beneath her headstone."

Alfric hugged the widow once more. "Thank you! Thank you!" he cried. "Don't worry! I won't disappoint you!"

GWYNETH FOUGHT back a wave of disappointment. *Her tracks are here somewhere! They must be!* But though she had found the widow's trail at dawn, it had disappeared once more. *It's as if the earth opened and swallowed her up,* Gwyneth groaned.

She gazed around at the eastern foothills cloaked in bleak morning mist. Her mind felt clouded too, but she must think! Perhaps the clue was in her head and not beneath her feet. What might the widow's destination be? What was on this hillside except rocks and brush and trees?

As a child, Gwyneth had loved pouring over old maps with her father. Now she struggled to see those parchments in her mind. All at once, an image appeared . . . a marker, a tombstone. Jotham's words to Alfric in Dominus came to her, *"You have a place of refuge too, near your mother."*

"The old graveyard!" Gwyneth exclaimed aloud. "That's where the widow was going. Alfric's mother must be buried there. And the widow must know that. Jotham must have told her. Maybe he is there with Alfric, even now. And it can't be that far."

Gwyneth hurried on her way.

Elymas did not follow this time. He just watched, savoring the news. Indeed, he would have smiled if frogs could smile. *So Jotham is back! His Highness will be pleased. I must fetch him.*

⌒⫘⌒

"WE WILL WAIT here till dark," the widow said. "It is the safer course. Then we must fetch the provisions I left in the caverns. I brought them, hoping Alfric would decide to go for adoption. One of the cavern passageways leads part way to the western crossroads. With luck, by dawn we will be safely on the border road."

Jotham smiled wryly. "Never did I dream I would ever count that road a place of safety! Did you, Alfric? Alfric?"

"What? Sorry!"

Jotham saw his friend's mind had been far away. He placed a gentle hand on Alfric's shoulder. "Still thinking of Gwyneth?"

Alfric nodded.

"I've been thinking of her too." Jotham's voice was edged with sadness. "How I wish she could know the King. But I suppose it's hopeless."

The widow looked thoughtful. "With the King, all things are possible."

"Not that!" Alfric's tone was emphatic. "She is Bogdan's daughter."

"We do not always finish where we start," the widow murmured. "And she is a thoughtful girl."

Jotham's eyes grew wide. "You know her?"

The widow began to explain about Devlin and the birth of little Grace. Suddenly Jotham felt a disturbing sensation, a tingling of his skin. "Shhhh!"

The widow and Alfric started, staring at him in alarm.

Jotham mouthed his next words. "I feel we're being watched."

His eyes darted to the window. He thought he glimpsed a pair of bulging eyes. But if so, they were gone in an instant. He turned back to the others, mouthing again. "Someone may be out there, but I can't be certain."

Then before anyone could stop him, Alfric sprang to the door. He eased it open a sliver and peered through the crack. "Gwyneth!"

Alfric flung himself outside. "What are you doing here?"

But the voice that answered wasn't Gwyneth's. It was another voice, a gloating voice bursting with evil triumph. "Leading me to you!"

Jotham and the widow froze. The speaker was Prince Abaddon!

CHAPTER 27

Ragnar's Reward

❦

"S EIZE HIM, MEN! Check the cabin!"

Abaddon's words bellowed like a death knell in Jotham's ears. The door burst open. Soldiers stormed inside. Jotham tried to run but iron fingers gripped his flesh, pinning his arms behind him. He saw that the widow had also been taken captive. A soldier seized the Book she clutched and tried to wrest it from her. When she resisted, he raised his hand to strike her. Jotham's heart lurched. He cried out in horror. "Nooooo!"

Another soldier intervened. "She's just an old woman, Giles!" he exclaimed. "Let her be!"

Giles scowled. "Her kind deserves no mercy, Devlin." But he dropped his hand, contenting himself with yanking the widow out the door. Jotham felt a hard shove. "You, too. Move!" He was pushed after her.

Jotham's eyes now met Gwyneth's stunned, stricken stare. *She did not intend this*, he thought. He wrenched his gaze away, looking for Alfric. Jotham found him pinned in the grasp of a huge, hulking form. Shuddering, Jotham recognized the gaping sneer, the broken teeth bared like the fangs of a wild beast salivating over its prey. "Ragnar!"

Ragnar licked his lips. A leer of delight spread over his

craggy features. "So...we meet again."

"As do we, my boy." A black-robed figure swept before Jotham. "Bow!"

Jotham stood his ground.

Abaddon glared. "Make him!"

Searing pain surged through Jotham as the flat part of a sword blade crashed against his calves. Knees buckling, he fell forward.

"That's better!"

Abaddon turned his attention to Gwyneth. "I choose to think you meant no disloyalty by your actions, Gwyneth. Perchance you hoped you might yet convince your friends to mend their ways. But I fear it is too late to redeem them now. Why, this Alfric even leaped upon me and sought to kill me."

Alfric strained to pull free of Ragnar's grasp. "I did no such thing!" he shouted. "I sought only to keep you from burning my birthright. But you never even had it!"

A flicker of surprise crossed Abaddon's face. His eyes narrowed. "Who told you this?"

Jotham's stomach tightened in alarm. He glanced at the widow. Her eyes searched for Alfric, screaming a silent plea, *Say no more!*

Alfric did not see her warning look. His gaze was fixed on Abaddon. Impulsive as always in the heat of passion, he gave no thought to the consequences of his words. "My mother, in her letter," he blurted.

Abaddon's eyes gleamed. "What letter? Where is it? Give it to me!"

"I...I did not keep it," Alfric stammered, realizing his mistake too late.

Abaddon laughed mirthlessly. "I doubt that!" He motioned to the soldiers. "Search him! Search them all!"

The soldiers obeyed. Then they ransacked the cabin. All the while, Jotham pleaded with the King to keep the letter safe. The widow had slipped it back between the pages of her Book. If only they did not look there!

But at last a soldier seized the Book, ruffled through its pages, turned it upside down, and shook it roughly. Jotham waited in dread for the letter to drop out.

It didn't.

"Never mind the letter," Abaddon snapped, gazing full on Alfric. "Where is the birthright? Surely you must know!"

Alfric's eyes flashed. "I would die before I told you!"

Abaddon grew cunning. "Come, let us be reasonable. Perhaps I was too harsh with you after all. It is just that I know the King so much better than you do. You cannot imagine how dangerous it would have been to leave Jotham in his clutches."

Alfric glowered. "That doesn't explain why you lied about the birthright."

Abaddon answered confidentially. "The reasons are complicated. It was a matter of security. The land granted in the birthright is vital to the defense of my kingdom. But it is arid wasteland and has no worth to you. Relinquish the deed, and swear lifelong loyalty to me. In return, I shall grant you full pardon and your commission." Abaddon paused. "I shall even give you Gwyneth's hand in marriage."

Gwyneth's face flushed. She opened her mouth to speak, but Abaddon silenced her with a look. Without removing his gaze from her, he spoke again to Alfric. "Come, Alfric. Do as I ask, and Jotham shall be spared as well. I shall even release the widow if you wish it."

Gwyneth understood his meaning. If she complied with his wishes, she could buy her friends' freedom. She bit her lip and said nothing.

Alfric, too, kept silent. But a fierce battle raged deep inside him. Never had his desire for Gwyneth been more consuming. Everything paled before it, even his birthright and adoption by the King.

Jotham saw the danger. A frantic shout burst from his lips. "Don't do it... Ugh." A soldier's fist smashed into his stomach. Jotham doubled over, too winded to speak. But his heart could still cry out. *Oh, King, make Alfric see the truth,* he begged.

Alfric wavered, gripped by his passion for Gwyneth. He glanced guiltily at the Widow Nessa. She gazed back with a look of deep concern and utmost love. It made him think of the love fruit. In his memory, he tasted it once more.

Then something astonishing happened. Instead of the widow's face before him, Alfric saw the face of the shepherd. The shepherd's words sounded once more in his heart. *"I am a friend to my sheep. I have even laid down my life that they may live."*

Suddenly, Alfric knew that this shepherd's love and the love of his Father the King far surpassed any other love, even what he felt for Gwyneth. And he knew he must choose this love above all else.

Another image rose before Alfric—Abaddon's face contorted with cruelty as he set the phony birthright ablaze. Deep inside, he heard the shepherd's voice again. *"Our deeds reveal our character."*

A new thought struck Alfric. *If Abaddon has deceived me once, why would he not do so again? Once he has the birthright, why would he not simply break his promise?*

Abaddon frowned impatiently. "What is your decision, Alfric? I have made a generous offer."

Alfric's voice was firm. "I must refuse!"

Good for you, Alfric! Jotham cheered silently, his heart flooding with gladness.

"Woe to you!" shrieked Abaddon, erupting in fury. Grabbing Gwyneth, he drew his sword, placing it against her neck. "If you will not give your birthright for Gwyneth's hand, perhaps you will do so for her life!"

A gasp of horror rippled through the watching soldiers. The widow's limbs went numb. Gwyneth froze in shock. Alfric stared at Abaddon, then shouted out in disbelief. "Not even you would do such a thing!"

"Wouldn't I?" Abaddon moved as if to press the blade into Gwyneth's flesh.

"Stop! I'll tell you! It's buried in the graveyard underneath his mother's headstone. Her name is Karissa."

It was Jotham who had spoken.

The widow and Alfric gaped at Jotham, stunned. Abaddon beamed in triumph. "Well, well," he crowed, sheathing his sword. "I am glad there is still one among you with some sense! If you've told the truth, no harm shall come to Gwyneth. But if not..."

His words trailed off. At his order, a soldier seized a shovel lying near the cabin. "Take the prisoners to the graveyard," Abaddon barked.

In the flurry that followed, one soldier edged closer to Gwyneth. It was Devlin. He had watched all this with a growing sense of dread. Now he whispered the question uppermost in his mind. "You don't think the prince would really harm you?"

"I...I'm not sure."

Gwyneth's halting reply chilled Devlin's heart. He thought of the help she had been in the birthing of his daughter. How he loved little Grace! He would die to protect her. A sudden prompting, an almost audible voice, told him what he must do. He must find Gwyneth's father and warn him his child was in danger.

As the soldiers herded the prisoners toward the graveyard, Devlin hung back, managing to slip away unnoticed. Hurrying to where the horses were tethered, he swung astride his mount and urged it forward.

For some moments, Devlin rode blindly. Suddenly, he pulled up in panic. Where was he going? Where would Bogdan be? Would he be at home, or at the fortress, or still searching the countryside for Alfric? "I have no time for missteps! What am I to do?" Devlin groaned aloud.

The scene of another crisis flashed through Devlin's mind. Brie was writhing with birth pangs. The widow needed help. And she had cried out to this King of hers. Hesitantly, Devlin cried out in his heart. *Oh, King, if you will, help me now!*

A white dove swooped across Devlin's vision, hovering before him. The bird seemed to beckon him. Somehow, Devlin knew he must follow.

"FASTER! FASTER!" Abaddon's harsh voice cracked the stillness like a whip. Alfric forced his shovel into the hard ground. Sweat poured from his brow as he labored in the chest-deep hole. Dirt flew, spattering the uprooted headstone lying on the ground above. Jotham watched in mute misery.

"Faster!"

"I . . . I can't," gasped Alfric, swaying with fatigue.

Abaddon jerked a thumb toward Jotham. "His turn."

Jotham felt himself shoved roughly into the hole as Alfric was dragged out. He seized the shovel and dug in a frenzy of frustration. Though he sensed the widow and Alfric watching, he could not meet their gaze. He could only berate himself for what he had done. *Whatever possessed me to tell Abaddon where the birthright was buried?* he agonized. *He would have killed Gwyneth, I know it! Still, even that was not reason enough to betray the King. I have failed him, and Morning Star, and Alfric, too, and the Widow Nessa . . .*

Thunk! Jotham's shovel struck something harder than earth.

"At last!" Abaddon's voice hissed above him. "Quickly now!"

Writhing with guilt, Jotham scooped dirt aside. Moments more, and the strongbox lay exposed. Abaddon pounced down, grabbing it as soldiers yanked Jotham from the pit.

Abaddon crouched eagerly over the box. With a look of pure jubilation, he lifted the lid and withdrew two parchments. Jotham cringed, barely able to watch as Abaddon perused them. He stole a look at Alfric and the widow. Their features were portraits of misery. He glanced at Gwyneth, who was held by a soldier. Her face was relaxing in relief.

"What treachery is this?"

Jotham's eyes darted back to Abaddon. The prince's demeanor had changed. His face was dark with anger. He glared at Alfric and Jotham. "Where is the deed that goes with this map?"

Jotham's breath caught in his throat. Alfric stared in amazement. "Is it not there also?"

"You have it already!" snarled Abaddon.

"No!" gasped Alfric.

Abaddon shoved a parchment in Alfric's face. "Read aloud what is written here."

Reeling, Alfric obeyed, as Jotham listened openmouthed. "My child, when you have uncovered this box you will already possess the deed to the land described by the map inside..."

"Enough!" Abaddon jerked the parchment away, enraged. "If you and Jotham thought to trick me, your feeble efforts have failed. You have only one more chance. Hand over the birthright... or Gwyneth dies!"

A storm of emotions swept Jotham now—relief that his actions had not harmed the King after all; horror at Gwyneth's likely fate; pain for Alfric, whose birthright seemed irretrievably lost. Or was it? Did the widow know more than she had told?

Jotham's eyes found the midwife. The look on her face screamed the answer. She knew nothing!

Alfric, too, glanced desperately at the widow. He now believed Abaddon would indeed carry out his threat to Gwyneth. But he, too, saw from the widow's expression that she was as mystified as he.

Alfric turned back to Abaddon. He begged. "I do not know! I swear it! Please! You must believe me!"

Abaddon's eyes bored into Jotham's skull. "And you?"

Jotham stood numb with terror beneath that stare, dizzy with desperation, helpless, naked...

"Your helmet is salvation..."

Jotham's brain stopped spinning. "Oh King, save Gwyneth!" he cried.

"Mindless fool!"

Jotham felt his face explode in pain as Abaddon slapped him hard. Then the prince reached for his sword. Suddenly, he paused as if thinking better of his actions. Hope surged in Jotham. It was short-lived.

Abaddon gestured to one of the soldiers. "Did you pack rope on your horse, and a bow and quiver?"

The fellow nodded.

"Fetch them!"

Blanching with dread, the soldier obeyed. Abaddon ordered the prisoners dragged to a tree at the edge of the graveyard. "Tie Gwyneth to the trunk," he barked.

"Please, Sire!" Gwyneth's voice was brittle, like breaking glass. "Have I and my father not served you well?" she pleaded. "Have we not been loyal? Surely you would not do this! You could not..."

"I will do what I must!"

Abaddon took the bow and quiver and held them high. "An officer's commission to the man who will aim an arrow at Gwyneth's heart."

"No, don't! Please, spare me! I have done you no harm. I beg you."

The soldiers shrank back, shaking their heads—all but one. Ragnar stepped forward, reaching for the weapon, broken teeth grinning in gleeful triumph. "I will do it!"

"Heartless swine!" Alfric howled the words like a raging wind.

Jotham stared with loathing at Ragnar. All at once, he saw him with different eyes—the eyes of Morning Star. Those eyes peeled back the cruel, smirking grin to reveal what lay beneath. Jotham understood. His loathing ebbed away. "No, Alfric. Not a swine. A sheep. All alone and frightened. Flailing. Feeling small and helpless. Clinging to a lonely ledge. Fearing he will fall, he claws and scratches, wounding out of his own pain. Not a swine. Just a sheep. A lone, lost sheep."

"You're lost, not me!" Ragnar spat the words. Pawing for an arrow, he fitted it in place, aimed at Gwyneth, and pulled the bowstring taut.

Abaddon's eyes glinted with satisfaction. He turned again to Alfric and Jotham. "One last time. Where is the birthright?"

Jotham looked away, gazing in anguish at Gwyneth. Her eyes were fixed on the arrow, pools of disbelief swirling in a sea of bloodless flesh. The widow's gaze turned upward in mute entreaty to the King.

Alfric's eyes were riveted on Abaddon, willing the prince to believe the last desperate denial that ripped itself from his throat. "I told you . . . I do not know!"

Abaddon opened his mouth, but his words were drowned out in a sudden clatter of hoofbeats. All eyes turned toward the sound. Jotham seized his chance. Jerking free of his captor, he lunged at Ragnar, intending to either wrest the arrow from the bully or be shot in Gwyneth's stead.

Jotham heard a shout. He saw Ragnar stare in stunned confusion. All at once, the arrow flew. Jotham felt it brush his skin as it whizzed past, barely missing him. He spun, one thought in his mind, one cry on his lips, "Gwyneth!"

Jotham hurtled toward her, barely noticing the horse that thundered past him. Now he spied the arrow, lodged beside her in the tree. Its point had pierced the rope that bound her. Jotham yanked the severed cord loose, clutched Gwyneth's hand, and turned to flee.

Thwack! A cold, clammy form smacked Jotham's face. He grabbed for it, peeling it from his skin and hair. For an instant, he stared into the evil, bulging eyes of the giant frog. Then he hurled it against the tree trunk and ran, pulling Gwyneth with him.

Meanwhile, chaos reigned near the graveyard. It was Bogdan himself who had galloped past Jotham. He had seen Gwyneth's danger and had watched the arrow fly. Pausing only to make sure his daughter was safe, he had charged toward Ragnar, scattering soldiers in his wake. Alfric and the widow had broken free, even as Bogdan leaped down upon the bully, clutching him by the throat.

"I'll kill you!"

Ragnar babbled in terror. "Hand slipped...not my fault ...Abaddon...he ordered...aim arrow..."

Still gripping Ragnar, Bogdan spun to confront the prince, who had hurried toward them. "Why?"

"It was only a ploy, a bluff," Abaddon snapped.

"But..."

Abaddon saw something from the corner of his eye. "Not now. The traitors are getting away." He shouted past Bogdan to his men. "Quick! After them!"

FOR SOME MOMENTS, all Jotham knew was the jagged gasping of his breath, the pounding earth beneath his flying feet, and Gwyneth's icy hand in his. He fled blindly, the landscape passing in a blur. All at once, the silent stone faces of great boulders loomed before him. Glancing back and seeing no soldiers, he pulled Gwyneth after him into a small crevice hidden among the towering rocks.

Leaning against the stone, they stared at each other, winded, overcome by what had just happened. Gwyneth spoke first between gulping pants. "I ... I'll be ... all right. My father..."

"That was he?"

She nodded. Her face grew tender. "You saved me!"

Jotham blushed deep red. "It was the King!"

"Your King was no help at all!" she flared. "He sent you off with no proper armor, and no weapon either. A Book is no sword."

Jotham's eyes widened. "How do you know this? Unless... You went to Dominus!"

"Yes," she murmured. "To rescue you."

Now Jotham saw mirrored in Gwyneth's face all the feelings that welled up in his own breast. They drew closer as if pulled by a magnet. Their lips met. For an endless instant, they were lost in each other.

In that instant, someone else found them.

Alfric, glimpsing which way his friends had fled, had followed, hoping to overtake them. As he neared the boulders, a strange intuition gripped him. Quietly, he crept among the stones until he discovered the pair wrapped in a tight embrace. Alfric's observation only confirmed what, in truth, he had long suspected. Heavy-hearted, he turned aside to continue his flight.

Meanwhile, Gwyneth gently pushed Jotham away, reeling from the powerful wave of emotion that gripped her, yet knowing that his peril was dire. "You ... you'd better go," she stammered. But her eyes clung to him.

Jotham swallowed hard. "If we don't meet again ..."

"We must!" she cried. "I have your mother's quilt."

He brightened. "It's safe?"

Gwyneth smiled. "Yes. She does lovely work. I wish I could have known Justina."

Jotham gaped in surprise. "Who told you her name?"

Gwyneth's eyes twinkled impishly. "A laughing daisy." Her face grew somber. "But enough. Leave. Quickly!"

Jotham started to creep from between the rocks. Suddenly, he froze. Gwyneth, at his elbow, gasped. Bogdan blocked their way.

Jotham stared at Bogdan.

Bogdan stared back. Yet he saw not the boy before him, but another young man in a cabin long ago—the young man he had seized as a traitor.

Gwyneth peered at her father, seeing not her father, but the stern general who had once arrested his own best friend. Surely, he would do the same to Jotham!

He didn't. Instead, he stepped aside, nodding ever so slightly.

Jotham understood. He raced past Bogdan, vanishing from sight.

Bogdan gathered Gwyneth into his arms.

"How did you find me, Father?" she asked.

"I'd been hunting for Alfric all night," he told her. "Morning found me in the eastern foothills. Suddenly, a young soldier burst upon me. He was frantic and could barely speak. He mumbled something about the old graveyard and you being in danger. Then he fell in a swoon. I thought Alfric had taken you captive. I never dreamed..." Bogdan's voice trailed off.

Gwyneth raised her head and searched his face. "Did Abaddon mean to kill me, Father?"

Bogdan stroked her hair. "No, my child. It was only a ploy. Nonetheless, it went wrong. And Jotham risked his life to save you."

"Thank you, Father, for letting him go," Gwyneth murmured gratefully.

Bogdan's voice was somber. "I owed him a debt. Next time we meet, it will be different."

"But I don't see why..."

"He serves our enemy, and always will. I must do my duty."

Bogdan gazed at his daughter for a long moment. "Still, I shall not relish it. Had Jotham not chosen to follow the King, he might have suited you well. I sense in him an unusual promise of greatness. Only once before have I seen such potential in someone. Sadly, he turned traitor, too."

Bogdan took Gwyneth's hand and led her away. Her heart was leaping. Though her father held no hope for Jotham, she did not agree. Had Jotham not placed her life above the King's interests in the graveyard? That proved she had at least some power over him—maybe more than he knew. She might yet win him away from the King. And if so, her father's words held out hope for a future together. Gwyneth vowed she would not give up—not yet.

CHAPTER 28

A Hope and a Future

❦

"DID MY MOTHER ever come here?" Alfric asked the widow, lifting the lantern and playing its light on the giant crystals standing silent watch in the hidden chamber.

"No. The caverns weren't used in her day," the widow answered. "The map is from an earlier time."

"Thank goodness you showed it to me at your cottage!" exclaimed Jotham. "Otherwise, I never would have found this place."

"Well, I stumbled upon it without much trouble," observed Alfric ruefully.

The others laughed. They had reunited in the secret caverns. Now Alfric turned to the widow, puzzled. "Speaking of finding things, where is the letter?"

"Just where I put it, in my Book," she said with mischief in her voice.

"Then why didn't the soldiers discover it?" Jotham wondered. "Unless the King hid it from them."

"He did, indeed," she smiled.

Jotham picked up the volume, rifling through it. "But the

King wouldn't hide it from me, and I can't find it either."

The widow chuckled. "You won't. Not in there! That's your Book, Jotham. Just as the soldiers burst upon us, I slipped mine into a deep inner pocket of my coat."

"Oh!" Jotham felt rather foolish that he hadn't figured this out.

The widow withdrew her Book from her pocket, retrieved the letter, and handed it to Alfric. He fingered its folds, his eyes filling. "I'm so grateful this has been restored to me! It's all I have of my mother's now that the birthright is gone."

Jotham's face grew pained. "I'm so sorry...Aaaaah!" He jumped as something slapped against his cheek.

Alfric saw what it was and chuckled. "It's just a bat."

Jotham's face, taut with tension, relaxed.

The widow studied him. "What did you think it was?"

"A...a frog," he stammered.

"Like the one at the graveyard?" she asked grimly.

"You saw it too?"

She nodded, frowning. "Have you met such a creature before?"

"Only twice," said Jotham. "In Acrasia, in my room, just before I went to the border. And at Flotsam Manor on my Leaving Day. Yet since childhood I have often felt someone spying on me." He peered at her intently. "You once said the dark prince has watchers. Is this frog one of them?"

The widow looked grave. "Yes, I'm quite sure he is."

"But why would Abaddon have Jotham watched?" Alfric wondered.

"Doubtless for the same reason the prince sent you after him," she mused. "He must sense some potential, some talent he would use for his own purpose. He wants Jotham!"

"Everyone wants Jotham!" Alfric's tone was bitter now. "Abaddon. Gwyneth..." His voice choked off. He turned to Jotham, tortured. "I saw you kiss."

Jotham reddened. "I...I'm sorry. I never meant this to happen."

Alfric's features softened. "I believe you." His eyes searched Jotham's face. "Do you love her?"

"Yes," sighed Jotham. "Perhaps I always have. But I tried to deny it. I did not want to hurt you. And now, though I know she loves me too, I fear no more can come of it. She would only turn my heart from the King."

Jotham's gaze met the widow's. "You were right when you said we must lose all to gain more."

Alfric gripped Jotham's shoulder. "Will you come with me to the border?"

Jotham brightened. "Of course!"

The widow beamed. "We will all go."

AND SO THEY did. What struggles they encountered will not be mentioned here. But at last, they stood at the edge of the chasm, gazing into Dominus again.

"Prince Morning Star! My shepherd and Prince!" cried Alfric in a loud, joyous voice.

Then out from the shadows stepped Morning Star, his arms stretched wide. Alfric raced across the bridge to his welcoming embrace. "I have come to be adopted!" he exclaimed.

The Prince draped Alfric in his white robe. "I will take you to the King," he smiled. Then he turned to the widow and Jotham, who had joined them. "And you must come with us."

SO IT WAS that Alfric's friends knelt by his side in the throne room of the King as he, too, was given his gold ring of sonship. They listened as he, too, learned about the inheritance that would be his.

"And now, my child, at last you may receive what I have kept for you," the King told him.

Morning Star took a parchment from a golden box and handed it to Alfric.

Alfric stared at it. His heart almost stopped. He was holding the deed to his mother's land. "My birthright!" he gasped.

"Yes, Alfric," said the King. "Knowing the danger from Abaddon, I bade your mother leave it here with me."

Alfric hesitated. With a trembling hand, he offered the parchment back. "I cannot take this, Father. I do not deserve it. I cared for it too much. But I need no birthright now, except you and Morning Star. I love you most!"

"And that is why you may receive the deed as well," the King said softly. "It is a trust, a stewardship I have reserved for you. When you have been properly prepared, you will return to Withershins. In time, you will visit this land of your birthright. I have a mission for you there for which I have ordained you. It is part of my plan to restore the rightful rule of that kingdom to myself, and to Morning Star, one day."

"For which you have ordained me?" Alfric spoke the words in awe. How different was this Father from the one he'd always known. This Father valued him! That knowledge sang in his heart, drowning out his old worthless feelings in a rising wave of joy. His whole body tingled as if nerves long numb had suddenly awakened—as if something dead had now become alive. The King valued him! This truth flowed like a soothing balm into all his wounded, hurting places, squeezing out the pain in a healing flood of tears.

Jotham and the widow wrapped Alfric in a warm embrace, basking in the moment with him, sharing his rapture. Morning Star and the King looked on in silent blessing. At last, when Alfric had somewhat regained his composure, the King spoke once more.

"And now Jotham, is there something you have cared for too much?"

"Yes, Father. Gwyneth. Forgive me," Jotham choked. "I'm sure you don't want me to be your ambassador any longer. I have failed! I am not worthy!"

"None are worthy," Morning Star said gently. "All have failed, even the greatest. Even your father!"

For some moments, Jotham could not speak. At last, he found his voice. "My father was a child of the King?"

"Yes, Jotham."

"So that's why Abaddon called him a traitor! And why Mother said he was a good man!" Jotham quivered with excitement. "Please, Your Highness, will you tell me his name?"

"No, Jotham. It is not yet time," Morning Star replied. "But you have already been given a way to learn it when the hour is right."

"Why must I wait?" Jotham groaned in disappointment.

"The King's purposes, like fruit, must ripen in their proper season," the Prince explained. "And now you must return to Withershins to do his work once more."

Jotham's face grew pensive. "It is strange," he sighed. "In years past, I used to go alone and dream. I carved images in my mind, even as I did on wood. I carved the father I never had. I carved the family I longed for. I carved myself a kingdom filled with all my heart's desires.

"Yet no carving, no image, no dream ever touched what I have now. Never did I imagine *this* family, *this* Father. Never did I dream such a kingdom, such riches, such love would be mine. Gladly will I go and serve the King, hard though the road may be. It is my sacrifice of gratitude. Nor could it touch the sacrifice you made, my precious Prince."

Overwhelmed by emotion, Jotham wrapped his arms

around the Prince's feet. "Oh, bright Morning Star," he cried, "if only I could carve your glory for the world to see! Yet I cannot, any more than the widow could paint such wonder. Now at last I see why she called her portrait of you but a pale shadow. What canvas, what wood could hold such splendor? What tool could sing such praise?"

"You, Jotham! You are the canvas and the tool!" the King boomed in a mighty voice. "I am the artist. I will etch upon your heart, your mind, your soul, the image of my Son. In you I will display his glory and my own. And you will be our tool, our instrument, to carve our truth in others. Even as your father was."

Jotham knew no words that could express what he felt now. Yet how could he contain what shouted out from every fiber of his being? "Oh, thank you!" he cried. "Praise you, Father! Praise your Son! All hail the King and Morning Star!"

Alfric and the widow, their own hearts bursting, joined the chorus. Unseen others swelled the sound. Jotham felt engulfed, surrounded by it, swept up in its billowing crescendo. "Praise the King! Praise Morning Star! Oh, praise them! Praise them! Hallelujah!"

Epilogue

⟨※⟩

THE FIRE DIMS. The hour grows late. The tale is over...yet not over.

"What happened to Jotham next?" the listeners ask. "And to Alfric, and Gwyneth? Did Jotham learn his father's name? Please tell us!"

"Not now," smiles the white-haired storyteller, "though there is more to hear. Dark times came upon the People of the Book. Great were Jotham's deeds, and Alfric's, in those days. But they also faltered, heeding their own voices rather than the King's. Nor did Jotham's love for Gwyneth cease, much as he tried to cool his feelings for her. But how their lives intertwined and the parts that they all played in the great struggle for Withershins is a legend for another day.

"If it is a legend. Some say it is true, and we too can be adopted by the King—if we go to the border of our hearts and call the Prince's name. Morning Star. Or his other name —*Jesus.*"

A Word from Bill Bright

⟨ornament⟩

IN THE BEGINNING, there was God. And then there was a story...the story of how He created the heavens and the earth. We've been learning about God and His marvelous truths through stories ever since. I felt impressed that in today's entertainment-based culture such a canvas would be a compelling way of illustrating the life-changing truths of the gospel—how to know Christ and discover our new identity in Him.

Fictional works like *Pilgrim's Progress* and *The Chronicles of Narnia* have touched millions and inspired young and old alike with profound spiritual insights. I asked Marion Wells to co-author this novel with me and to create such a fictional story through which we could weave the transforming biblical concepts that I explain in greater depth in my book *Living Supernaturally in Christ*.

At first, all of us, like Jotham, are orphans—spiritual orphans. Like Jotham, we have an unfulfilled yearning in our hearts. Like Jotham, a mighty King calls to us. If we will only accept the gift and be cloaked in Morning Star's white robe, we too can become children of the King and receive the riches of the kingdom.

Yet like Jotham, we also have an enemy. Even after we're adopted, this dark prince seeks to deceive us. He doesn't want us to claim the birthright which is ours. He seeks to lure us into distrusting the King, and then tricks us into fleeing from forgiveness. He would have us ignore the blackened ring of the Spirit's displeasure. He would blind us to our inheritance and rob us of our spiritual riches. He would keep us from tasting peace, joy, and love—fruits that the King wants to give us. He would have us be flavorless salt, beaten and discouraged, living as the spiritual paupers we no longer are!

It needn't be so! If we only knew, a grand adventure awaits us! The King desires to etch on our hearts, our minds, our souls the image of His Son, Prince Morning Star. Together, they desire to display their glory in our lives, and make us their ambassadors to share their truth with others.

This novel was designed to be a companion piece to my recently released book, *Living Supernaturally in Christ*, which describes these foundational truths in great detail. If you would like to learn more about how you can become a child of the King, how you can be empowered by God's Holy Spirit, or how you can grow in understanding and live out the new identity you, as a believer, have in Christ, visit our website: **www.achildoftheking.org**.

Through the enabling of His Spirit, Christ worked through first-century believers to change the course of history. He wants to do the same in and through us today. It is my prayer that parents will learn these concepts and teach them to their children. Perhaps you will want to study them as a family and read *A Child of the King* together. God will illumine your minds and help you discover the beautiful biblical nuggets that are life-transforming.

Jesus promised, "I tell you the truth, anyone who has faith in me will do what I have been doing. He will do even greater things than these, because I am going to the Father ... You may ask me for anything in my name, and I will do it" (John 14:12,14, NIV). I entreat you to take Him at His Word and enjoy your new identity and the abundant life which He freely gives to all who love, trust, and obey Him.

In His unfathomable, unconditional love,
Bill Bright

Resources

Living Supernaturally in Christ

A refreshing cascade of hope, power and renewal, *Living Supernaturally in Christ* vividly illustrates the many benefits of knowing Jesus Christ personally. With rare clarity, it reveals how your relationship with Christ will help you live in harmony with God's plan. It will introduce you to scriptural passages and principles that convey the incomparable blessing we share in Christ, and help you open the door to victorious Christian living. 1-56399-145-4

The Supernatural You

Written in a convenient, take-along format, this booklet helps you discover and live according to your new, supernatural identity in Christ. The booklet outlines five essential steps to living supernaturally in Christ, made easily memorable by the acrostic CROSS. As you apply these biblical truths, you'll discover a life of incomparable power, liberating freedom, triumph over adversity, everlasting peace, and infinite joy. *The Supernatural You* is an ideal companion booklet to *Living Supernaturally in Christ* and *Why Do Christians Suffer?* ISBN 1-56399-147-0

Why Do Christians Suffer?

Why do Christians suffer? It's a valid question that many believers—even some nonbelievers—wrestle with from time to time. As a stand-alone booklet or a companion piece to Dr. Bright's book *Living Supernaturally in Christ*, this informative purse or pocket guide will direct you to the Bible's illuminating answers. By remembering the acrostic TRIUMPH, you can experience God's peace even in the midst of adversity, pain, and heartache. Ideal for personal reference or to share with friends in need. ISBN 1-56399-149-7

GOD: Discover His Character

In this thorough, easy-to-grasp book, Dr. Bright helps make God knowable as few books (save the Bible itself) have done. Based on more than five decades of intense, personal study, Dr. Bright's penetrating insights into God's character—and its significance to mankind—are certain to energize your walk with God. ISBN 1-56399-125-X

GOD: Discover His Character Video Series

Thirteen 30-minute video segments, complete in three volumes, will help you (and those to whom you minister) discover God's awesome character. All are presented with powerful teaching, dramatizations, and graphics to help adult and teenage audiences appreciate God as our Great Creator, our Perfect Judge, and our Gracious Savior. Your life, worship, and ministry will never be the same.

Vol. 1: Our Great Creator teaches you about God's attributes of ability—His power, knowledge, presence, and sovereignty. ISBN 1-56399-122-5

Vol. 2: Our Perfect Judge explores God's attributes of integrity—the fact that God is holy, truthful, righteous, and just. ISBN 1-56399-123-3

Vol. 3: Our Gracious Savior contains four compelling lessons about God's attributes of relationship—how God is loving, merciful, faithful, and never-changing. ISBN 1-56399-124-1

GOD: Knowing Him by His Names

El-Elyon, Adonai, Jehovah-Sabaoth. To most Christians, the Hebrew names of God are unknown and unpronounceable. But much can be gained from understanding the meaning and significance of the names by which the Israelites knew their Creator and Protector. In this compact overview of God's names, today's Christians will not only learn more about our heavenly Father, but also become more worshipful of His nature. The booklet includes 16 character-revealing names of God, and concludes with the "Names of Christ" and "Applying God's Names." ISBN 1-56399-140-3

GOD: Seeking Him Wholeheartedly

Based on the greatest commandment, recorded in Matthew 22:36,37 ("Love the Lord your God with all your heart…"), this booklet explains seven steps for seeking God with a whole heart. Bill Bright deals with the sincerity of our love for God, the priority of our relationship with Him, and the evidence of our wholehearted devotion—obedience. His insights enable any follower of Christ to grow closer to our heavenly Father and to enjoy the fullness of His blessings. ISBN 1-56399-141-1

GOD: 13 Steps to Discovering His Attributes

In this abbreviated guide to discovering God's attributes, Dr. Bill Bright shares the fruit of his lifelong study of God. These wonderful truths are certain to enrich your life and energize your walk with God. Keep this booklet handy in your pocket or purse to read during quiet moments, or to share with friends and loved ones. ISBN 1-56399-126-8

These and other fine products from *NewLife* Publications are available from your favorite bookseller or by calling (800) 235-7255 (within U.S.) or (407) 826-2145, or by visiting www.newlifepubs.com.